Swords & Heroes

Also Published by Tule Fog Press

Anthologies

Fistful of Hollers
Strange Worlds of Lunacy
Monster Fight at the O.K. Corral
While the Morning Stars Sing
Residential Aliens Volume 1

Collections

Pale Reflection: Tales of Dark Fantasy by Gustavo Bondoni
Fragments of a Greater Darkness by Michael T. Burke
Tule Fog Tales, Speculative Fiction Volume One
Tule Fog Tales, Speculative Fiction Volume Two

Individual Works

Razored Land: Crimson Sacrifice by Charles Gramlich
Abductions Trilogy by Perry and Konrath
The Sword of Otrim by Lyndon Perry
Christ of the Abyss by Joel V. Kela

Residential Aliens Magazine

Swords & Heroes

An Anthology of Sword and Sorcery

Edited by Lyndon Perry
Published by Tule Fog Press

Swords & Heroes ~ An Anthology of Sword and Sorcery
Lyndon Perry, Editor and Publisher
Vega Baja, Puerto Rico

This collection © 2023 by Tule Fog Press. All rights reserved. Individual stories in this collection are copyrighted by their authors. Cover art and interior illustrations are copyrighted by their creators. Published via Amazon ~ Hardcover ISBN: 9798392209958

Each story is a work of fiction. All characters and events portrayed in this anthology are the creation of their respective authors. They are fictitious; any resemblance to actual events, locales, or persons, living or dead, is entirely coincidental.

No part of this publication may be reproduced, stored in a retrieval system, or transmitted in any form or by any means without prior written permission from the publisher, except in brief quotations in printed or online reviews. Email TuleFogPress@gmail.com for information.

Dedication

To those in the midst of the most noble struggle, contending in fidelity and truth, seizing the eternal age to which you were summoned, unashamed of the worthy profession which you've declared before many witnesses.

Triumphant in Battle

Table of Contents

Introductory Matters
    Foreword ~ Jason M Waltz   1
    Preface ~ Lyndon Perry   5

Stories of Swords and Heroes
    Keeper of Souls by Charles Gramlich   9
    The Path One Doesn't Choose by Gustavo Bondoni   23
    Lord of the Blood by Michael T. Burke   37
    The Price of Rescue by Teel James Glenn   51
    The Vault of Bezalel by Tom Doolan   65
    On Neutral Ground by Nancy Hansen   79
    The Swordsman and the Sea Witch by Tim Hanlon   95
    The Necromancer and the Long-Dead King
        by Frank Sawielijew   107
    Lady in Stone by Cliff Hamrick   123
    O Sapphire, O Kambria by J. Thomas Howard   137
    Welgar the Cursed by David A. Riley   151
    Ride the Fire Steed
        A Crimson Warrior Tale by Adrian Cole   161

Concluding Matters
    Afterword & Acknowledgments   181
    Our *Swords & Heroes* Contributors   183
    Copyrights: Stories and Illustrations   187
    Bonus Feature: A Round Table Discussion   189
    Support Our Advertisers   202

Foreword

The Color and the Dash

This style of storytelling we consider 'Sword & Sorcery' requires but a particular attitude from its hero to genuinely earn its labeling, a certain mindset holding to only two things:

Foremost, an indomitable will with a passion to live. To *truly* live—not merely survive—at any and all costs even in the face of unbalanced or unnatural odds, no matter what. To ardently remain among the living until there is no more surviving to be had and Death finally wins.

Secondly, a nonchalant mercenary motivation. Such motivation must be non-'civilization' dictated, distinct and aloof from the manners and mores of 'accepted' society. Further, this motivation is tempered by a self-determined personal code of honor that often lends itself to doing the better even by others though that is not of primary concern.

This motivation—of beer, booty, *booty*, and battle—feeds the predominant passion to live but is not its only or even major fuel. No, that indomitable will is its own centrifugal force, its owner's nuclear reactor. One is either born with it or develops it during the aftermath of a traumatic experience. The motivations are the temporary rewards and respite the hero allows and accepts. Astute readers will notice that, while there does not seem to be hierarchy amongst beer-booty-*booty*, the thrill of battle, the lure of overcoming fear and outlasting death, rises supreme. As J.T. MacCurdy said in *The Structure of Morale* (1943), "…the conquering of fear produces exhilaration."

Or as Robert E. Howard shared through his most famous character when he let Conan voice his passion and motivation in answer to Bêlit's questioning:

> "I know not, nor do I care. Let me live deep while I live; let me know the rich juices of red meat and stinging wine on my palate, the hot embrace of white arms, the mad exultation of battle when the blue blades flame and crimson, and I am content. Let teachers and priests and philosophers brood over questions of reality and illusion. I know this: if life is illusion, then I am no less an illusion, and being thus, the illusion is real to me. I live, I burn with life, I love, I slay, and am content." ("Queen of the Black Coast")

And that's it. Put a protagonist with such an attitude into a story and you'll find a Sword & Sorcery (S&S) style tale.

Action, vitality, color—indeed! Thrilling, violent, weird—yes, please!

S&S stories burn with life, so naturally they explode with these and more. L. Sprague de Camp said S&S "combines the color and dash of the historical costume romance with the atavistic supernatural thrills of the weird;" and Howard Andrew Jones declared that S&S "moves at a headlong pace and overflows with action and thrilling adventure."

Let me live deep while I live. The conquering of fear produces exhilaration. I burn with life.

Swords, spells, sagas, separation, solitude, swashbuckling, the supernatural, secondary worlds…all are but accoutrements and do not make the whole. Dozens of strong stories delivering all of those rightly entertain yet cannot equally claim to belong among tales of S&S if their hero possesses neither of these two mindsets. Sans a passion for living life that bursts from the pages you have…well, *not* an S&S character. Remove the nonchalant from the mercenary and you will have the horrific grimdark; remove both the nonchalant and the mercenary and you'll have the Tolkienesque fantasy. Omit both components and thereby remove the attitude and frankly, my dear, I won't give a damn!

So just how did Bob Howard create such a style of storytelling that required naming fifty plus years back (over thirty after his death) and arguing about its composition ever since? The answer lies in his influences and motivations.

His influences include Bulfinch and the Bible. Edgars Poe and Burroughs. Homer and Haggard; Lamb and London. Alexandre, Rafael, Rudyard, and the 18th Baron of Dunsany. Mythologies of the Greeks and Celts, Norse sagas, swashbuckling adventure, gothic horror, historical fiction, the Arabian Nights, the Mythos of H.P. Lovecraft, the Wild American West of his recent and current history, theosophy and reincarnation, and two particular women, his mother Hester Jane Howard and his on-and-off-again gal Novalyne Price.

Without psychoanalyzing or projecting, his motivations are fairly identifiable. Prove he could not only survive but thrive through storytelling. Provide for and tend to his mother. Tell the stories he wanted to tell. To accomplish all three, Robert learned his markets, his skills, his competition, and his readers. Then he buckled down and wove it all into what we have and love and enjoy today: Sword & Sorcery. Except neither he nor anyone else needed a name for it then. Only when the decades had passed and the paying markets and the entertaining mores of society had changed did a cabal of writers determine they needed to differentiate and essentially pigeonhole what they were writing.

'Fantasy literature' as we know it today was just over a generation old when Robert began writing. Fantasy as we know it today is because Robert wrote.

Just as there were British fantasists who wrote before J.R.R. Tolkien there were American writers of the fantastic who predated Howard. Yet just as today, Tolkien is called the Father of High/Epic Fantasy, assuredly making him the Father of British-flavored Fantasy, Robert E. Howard is named the Father of Sword & Sorcery, a distinctly American-flavored fantasy that has reached far, far into the future. S&S influences much if not all modern American fantastical entertainment from literature to music to gaming to sports to movies. It is the rare avenue of popular diversion today that does not feature some aspect of S&S attitude.

Require proof? Brace yourself. Batman is a quintessential S&S character. Almost on par with the godfather Conan himself. Though Conan would have slaughtered Joker and the rest of the rogues gallery. Lou Anders, in his essay "Two of a Kind" (*Batman Unauthorized*, edited by Dennis O'Neil in 2008), shared this magnificent quote:

> "Legendary artist Dick Giordano once said of Batman, "The Batman does what he does for himself, for his needs. That society gains from his actions is incidental, an added value…but not the primary reason for his activities." ("Graphic Novel Reviews")."

No one doubts Batman's indomitable will or passion to live no matter what. *I burn with life.* Neither should one doubt his aloof and personal motivation. *The conquering of fear produces exhilaration. Batman does what he does for himself.*

S&S is exciting, violent, and personal. It requires an attitude of not merely surviving but of dominating living, all else be damned. S&S demands its hero continue living deep so long as fierce breath remains—until there are no more breaths to take! Unlike grimdark's existentialism and nihilism, the only -ism S&S promotes is *LIVE!*-ism. At its most basic this is similar to the survivalism mindset of keeping oneself alive through all adversities, though most likely it is a subset of absurdism's rebellion against meaninglessness. "I live, I burn with life, I love, I slay, and am content."—in other words, right here, right now (as Van Halen sang), is sufficient. "One must imagine Sisyphus happy," Albert Camus said.

So forge ahead, warrior, and enjoy the rich action and intense lives shared by these storytellers. Revel in the Sword & Sorcery attitude.

Live until you cannot.

Jason M Waltz
Boerne, Texas
February 2023

Preface

By Lyndon Perry

This is my tenth or twelfth anthology/collection I've edited and one of the most exciting, quite assuredly because of the quality of storytelling I get to feature in this project. It's an incredible kick to present such a strong selection of tales, especially in this fantastic genre.

One of the reasons I compile these volumes is because I get to meet so many wonderful writers and read such powerful stories…for free!

Okay, not exactly for free. I do have to select the stories and send out rejection emails to those authors I couldn't include here—which is one of the hardest things for me to do as an editor, actually. I also have to revise, format, secure illos, and in this case, organize a Kickstarter Campaign in order to bring this puppy to life. *Swords & Heroes* was a lot of hard work and definitely a labor of love.

Still, it was worth it because of, again, all the writers I get to interact with and all the fiction I get to experience during the process. The end result is just amazing. I am super proud to have each of these contributors grace the pages of this anthology. So thank you, writers, for being a part of *S&H*!

Let me share briefly how I select stories for any of my projects. As I read the subs (usually in the order they arrive), if I like it, I accept it. It's almost that easy. It's a matter of taste. I like traditional stories well told, usually featuring a noble hero. (Yes, yes. I understand. This genre is typically known for ambivalent heroes. Call me out, why don't you?) So I generally know after the first reading if I'll be including that particular tale in the ToC.

By the way, if someone is reading this and has had stories rejected by various editors, don't be discouraged. It pretty much all boils down to one's taste. Keep submitting fiction. One day you'll find an editor that gets you.

So if a story hits my fancy, I put it in my 'Accepted' folder. Those that are good but didn't stand up and slap me, I put in my 'Maybe' folder. Then, as the stories accumulate, I get a feel for how the whole collection is shaping up—the mood, the style, emerging tropes, types of characters, etc. This influences what story then moves from Maybe to Accepted. But sometimes it excludes a great story that I wanted to accept but just didn't fit the rest of the Table of Contents. (Sorry, Mike!)

I'm a pretty hands-on editor. I typically make a lot of revision requests and suggestions. So even if the story might need a bit of attention, if I like the direction it's going and the author's storytelling style, I'll work with the writer to help him or her craft a super solid tale. Those who've gone through this process with me usually tell me their story is better for it. Or, they withdraw their submission and tell me to take a flying leap. (grin)

Now that you know a little bit about what goes on behind the curtain, let's talk about the fiction. As you read the stories, you'll find quite a few buddy tales. I've a soft spot for traveling—and warring!—companions. Quite often, there's a quest involved but rest assured, I've attempted to select stories that reflect a variety of settings and ultimate endgames.

In Charles Gramlich's poignant opener, *Keeper of Souls*, for example, we have a unique take on the buddy tale trope, but one integral to the plot. Plus, there's a warrior on a battlefield, something isn't right, and the dead come back to fight. What's not to love? Evil wizardry, deception, and, ultimately, self-sacrifice. Wow! When I read this sub, I knew it was the perfect story to open this anthology.

When Gustavo Bondoni asked for my submission guidelines, I knew I was in for a treat. *The Path One Doesn't Choose* is like a side quest tale from his *The Song of Sangr* novel as it features a secondary character, Yella, who deserves a novel of her own. Fulfilling her duty, she's betrayed and finds herself in a strange land not of her choosing. How she gets home is the question of the day, but there are many dangers to face along the way.

Michael Burke's Ahanu Foxcloud in *Lord of the Blood* intrigued me. I remember reading an Ahanu story in *Whetstone*, so I went back and reread all of Michael's tales there. I enjoyed them and thought the character had a moral quality about him, but was definitely flawed and subject to his baser appetites. Pretty S&S. So rock on, I accepted this tale and even offered to publish a collection of Ahanu's stories: *Fragments of a Greater Darkness*.

The Price of Rescue by Teel James Glenn and *The Vault of Bezalel* by Tom Doolan are both high adventure buddy tales, no doubt. They're completely different, but I think of them as companion stories and so placed them together for your reading pleasure. I like the chemistry between each of the respective teams and definitely want to read more stories in both of their worlds. These authors were new to me, so I'm looking forward to finding more of their work once this project is complete.

The next three tales provided something fresh in my mind when I first read them. *On Neutral Ground* by Nancy Hansen taps a theme that hints at that sad and long-forgotten day when Old World Magic and the Creatures of Fae began to slip away. But not without a fight!

The Swordsman and the Sea Witch by Tim Hanlon is an intriguing pirate tale that features an obscene sea creature reminiscent of the classic pulp monsters of a bygone era. And *The Necromancer and the Long-Dead King* by Frank Sawielijew pairs an unlikely duo in a sorcerous encounter that offers thrills and adventure at every turn. I was unfamiliar with these authors and am glad each of them sent me a story to consider.

I'd run across a Jarek the Scholar tale by Cliff Hamrick when he posted a link in a Facebook group I'm in. Quite enjoyed it as our hero is a different kind of rogue than the typical *thew*-endowed barbarian. He's more of a, well, scholar. I can't remember who contacted who first, but I told Cliff I wanted a new Jarek story for this antho. He complied with the clever *Lady in Stone*.

Last year, I stumbled into the Whetstone Tavern, a Discord channel hosted by Jason Ray Carney who edits and publishes *Whetstone: Amateur Magazine of Pulp Sword and Sorcery*. (I'm Gareth, btw. Say hi and I'll buy you a mug of ale!) There I met J. Thomas Howard who's had two stories in *Whetstone* featuring a pterodactyl rider named Raul. In *O Sapphire, O Kambria*, our hero finds himself in a world off-kilter—and in the middle of a daring rescue. This 'buddy-by-circumstance' tale really resonated with me what with its themes of loyalty and sacrifice. I think you'll like it, too.

David A. Riley has published five volumes of *Swords & Sorceries: Tales of Heroic Fantasy* and I was humbled when he submitted *Welgar the Cursed* for consideration. Here we find Welgar, frustrated and discouraged, dealing with the fallout of his curse in typical barbarian fashion. A prequel story, *The Dark Priestdom*, tells how that curse came about and will appear in the next issue of *Savage Realms Monthly*. It's kinda cool to follow your favorite hero's adventures across various magazines, websites, anthos, and projects!

Speaking of prequels and sequels, our final entry is *Ride the Fire Steed* by Adrian Cole and features the enigmatic but oh-so-deadly Crimson Warrior, a relatively new character of Cole's. This standalone story continues the thrilling and sorcerous adventure begun in *The Burning Blade* which was first published in Issue 4 of *Sexy Fantastic* and reprinted in my newly relaunched *ResAliens Zine*, Issue 6. Of course, I am very excited to present to you this brand new story from Adrian who has been creating fantastic characters and amazing worlds for quite some time! Be sure to check out the map he provided that helps us imagine the world of the Crimson Warrior.

So that's it. Twelve fantastic tales ready for you to experience. Also, enjoy the illustrations (whose creators are credited in the back). Thank you for your interest and support of *Swords & Heroes*. – Lyndon Perry, Editor

"Bring the skulls!" Ishalla cried.

Keeper of Souls

By Charles Gramlich

– 1 –

Thudding hooves in the rain.

The whisper of black arrows, the shriek of horses and men.

Across the bloody field, the mailed riders charged in a flood of steel.

Valk the Gray-Eyed watched his last arrow carom off a knight's spaulder. He slung his bow over his shoulder and grabbed up the fifteen-foot lance of ash wood lying in the mud at his feet. It was big around as his arm and sharpened to a brutal point at the tip.

All around him, others did the same, preparing to meet the charge of the knights of Kuulumsraad. Some men babbled with fear; others cursed or prayed. But for now they all stood, facing the full weight of the cavalry rolling thunderously upon them.

Valk neither babbled nor cursed, though perhaps a silent prayer crossed his thoughts. His wet hands tightened on the lance. He planted the butt of it in the damp dirt and braced a booted foot against it. Rain dripped in his eyes; he blinked it away.

"If we must be here against good sense, then straighten your shoulders, brother!" Neana shouted from Valk's side.

The red-maned soldier did not respond. Her advice was neither needed nor appreciated. Arrows had taken down dozens among the advancing cavalry but the charge had not faltered. Now those enemies loomed huge before Valk's eyes—men on war horses of fifteen hands or greater. On their mounts, the knights rode faceless in steel helms, with armored fists bearing axes or great, glittering swords.

To Valk's left stood Utrik, a brawler and boaster around the evening fires. With a sudden wail of terror, Utrik dropped his lance and turned to run.

Valk had helped train these men. "Stand!" he bellowed.

Too late.

Other men heard Utrik's wail and their spines turned liquid. Too many of them broke and fled. Much of the rebel army had been farmers, or sheepherders, or wood cutters a bare week before. It was not nearly enough time to teach men war. Deadly gaps opened all along the defensive line of lances.

Valk was a professional soldier; he didn't flee, though he understood the battle was surely lost. He crouched behind his lance as the raging cavalry struck and sheared through the already broken defense of the rebels.

The tip of Valk's lance struck the horse directly in front of him high in the throat, above an armored chest. The animal screamed like a woman giving birth as the sharpened head of the spear tore through the horse's neck, splintering but twisting the animal's head to the side. The impact drove Valk and his weapon backward, his feet sliding in the mud as he strained against the lance.

Aboard the dying war-horse, the enemy knight was thrown forward but held like a burr to the saddle. The axe in his hand swung out to the side; in an instant it would swing forward and shear off Valk's head. Valk twisted the lance and exerted every ounce of his strength. The dying animal's iron-shod hooves slipped in the mud. It went down on its side, on top of its rider's leg. The knight cried out from beneath his helm.

The bulk of the enemy charge had surged past Valk now, close enough to feel the wind of their passage. Enemy knights hacked their blades into the backs of running men. Valk released the butt of the shattered lance and drew his sword. The knight he'd taken down struggled to pull his leg from beneath his mount. Valk leaped forward and thrust the tip of his blade into the throat between the man's gorget and the bottom of his helm. Dark scarlet rheum sprayed over gray steel. The man coughed and died.

Valk threw a wild glance around. The defensive line of which he'd been part was torn beyond all repair. Here and there, a few other soldiers still stood, their lances having tasted Kuulumsraadian lives. But they were too few and too scattered to form a fresh line.

"Run!" Neana shouted in Valk's ear. "Before the enemy returns for you!"

This time, Valk listened to his sister's advice. Without lances and any semblance of organization, it would mean death to stand toe to toe with mailed cavalry. The rocky field where they fought lay surrounded on all sides by summer woods. Valk launched himself in a dead run toward the nearest wall of the green-black forest.

Luck aided him. Most of the Kuulumsraadian knights pursued easier targets. As he entered the line of trees, Valk glanced over his shoulder. From a sky aswirl with rain and mist, a violet streak of lightning stabbed. It struck the knight that Valk had killed and broke into shimmering waves across the dead man's armor. The hackles rose along Valk's spine as the slaughtered knight twitched, then sat up. With preternatural strength, the dead man yanked his leg from beneath his fallen horse and rose to his feet. His vizor turned toward Valk; he lifted his axe to shake it in threat.

More streaks of violet light plunged from the sky, striking other dead knights of the Kuulumsraad. All of them rose, many with terrible wounds that did not bleed. In their eyes lived only hate.

"Run faster," Neana urged. "Much faster!"

– 2 –

While dead men stalked him, Valk floated in darkness, with only his face above water. The forest into which he'd fled lay tangled with vines and brambles. He'd struggled ahead, trying to move quietly while the sorcery-raised foes who followed hacked their way with swords and axes. Too, some intelligence guided those walking corpses, for they acted in concert to cut off every route of escape.

A stream promised Valk an easier path. He'd gone into the water, splashing down it to a small meadow and a pond dammed by beavers. Before his hunters sighted him, he dove below the surface to come up again beneath the dam. Luck had offered him a pocket of air underneath the piled logs. There was barely space for his mouth and nose but he could breathe. All he needed now was patience. To outwait his enemies.

Fresh air seeped to Valk through cracks in the dam. So, too, did sound. He heard the heavy tread of dead knights searching, voiceless as they stalked. His sister was not so silent.

"I told you we shouldn't have stayed in Kuulumsraad after the wizards' coup," Neana complained in his ear. "What matter to us if kings or sorcerers rule the peasants in this land. They are not our blood."

"Be quiet," Valk whispered back.

"We are mercenaries and these rebels don't even have gold. How have you been paid for training them? In fatty meat and half rotten potatoes? What foolishness!"

"Shut up!" Valk snapped, sending his sister into a pout.

But anger made him speak too loudly. The gray-eyed soldier froze as the bootsteps of one of the knights turned in his direction. He held his breath as the thing stomped onto the beaver dam. Fragments of decaying wood sifted down into Valk's face. He held his nose against a sneeze. For a moment, the stalking corpse paused just over head, but then passed on.

Valk sucked in a shallow breath of relief.

Neana's pout didn't last. "Lucky again!" she gloated. "But how long can such hold? I say we head south, away from Kuulumsraad and its troubles. This country will eat itself soon enough. No need for us to be consumed as well."

"The Fane of Ishkareth," Valk replied. "We'll go there."

"That will only take us deeper into enemy land."

"But it's a holy place. The Kuulumsraad sorcerers have no power there."

"Aye!" Neana blurted suddenly. "They won't be able to see to send their liches after us. A good thought for once, brother. And once they are blind to us, *then* we head south."

Valk said nothing. He had no intention of leaving Kuulumsraad yet but wasn't going to tell Neana and spend the rest of his time under the dam listening to her insults. He tried to relax as he waited for night to fall.

– 3 –

Between the descent of darkness and the rise of the ivory moon, Valk slipped free of his hiding hole and swam beneath the pond's surface to its bank. He inched out of the water, making no more sound than the black flies that bit at every inch of his exposed flesh. But his caution was unwarranted. No dead men waited for him. He slipped into the woods again and worked his way east.

"How far to the fane?" Neana demanded. "Do you even know where you are going?"

"I know," Valk whispered back. "Uphill for a bit, then down to the valley where the shrine lies. No later than mid of night before we reach it."

Neana harrumphed but said no more. For that, Valk was grateful. It gave him a chance to think about his real plans. Even if his side had won the battle, he would have gone to the shrine. He dared not tell the reason to Neana. She wouldn't understand and would make him suffer accordingly. But then, she wasn't in love.

– 4 –

The Fane of Ishkareth stood in a valley between two hills. There should have been the fires of a peasant army burning in that valley but Valk saw nothing as he stared down into the blackness. Shaking his head, he approached anyway.

The first sign that he was entering the area of the fane were the bones. These were the defleshed remains of animals and humans, hung here out of grief and love. They festooned the trees. With the skin gone, only thin wires held the bones together in the shapes of Ishkareth—diamonds and stars. Valk wove between them, careful to touch none less their rattling warn any potential enemies that he was coming.

As Kuulumsraad had prospered under a kind king, fewer and fewer supplicants had visited Ishkareth's shrine. Weeds had grown across the maze of pathways leading into the fane. Here and there, wires had broken on the holy shapes and bones had fallen. Yet, power still lived here. Valk felt it, and even Neana seemed to grow quiet with reverence as they approached the shrine's center and the point of reintegration.

Soon, Neana hissed to Valk that others *were* present. And not friendly. The gray-eyed warrior dropped into a crouch and inched forward. The moon was well up now, dripping a pale light into the open circle at the fane's heart. An eldritch glow flickered there, around the rough trunk of an ancient oak to which hundreds of human skulls had been affixed, many so long ago that they'd grown into the tree.

Valk glimpsed three men holding smoking torches around the oak. One was Utrik, he who'd first fled the recent battle and been the trigger for the collapse of the peasant army's defense. Valk did not know the other men but they, too, had fled that fight.

Utrik laughed as he used a dagger to pry skulls loose from the tree and let them fall to the dirt where they shattered. Already the ground lay painted white with shards.

"They're desecrating the shrine!" Neana whispered. "To destroy its power so the sorcerers can enter."

Even Valk felt the weakening of the fane's energy with each skull destroyed. "Time for a reckoning," he said, drawing his sword.

"Let me!" Neana snarled.

"No! Remain hidden for now."

Without waiting to hear Neana's response, the gray-eyed soldier stepped into the clearing. "Utrik! Hold!" he yelled.

The three deserters spun toward him. Utrik dropped the skull he held and drew his own blade. He snapped, "You! I thought surely the dead knights would have killed you."

Understanding burst into Valk's mind. "You serve them!" he growled. "The sorcerers. You abandoned the battle for their sake, to break our defense and then draw our remaining troops away from this shrine!"

Utrik smirked. "And it worked. The army encamped here believes there was a victory against the knights. They've left to finish off the enemy but they'll find a surprise waiting. Before long we'll see the total destruction of your fellow fools, the breaking of the rebellion."

"Too bad for you, I lived," Valk snapped. "And now I know your part. Soon all will know."

"Easily remedied," Utrik replied. He nodded at his companions, who stuck their torches in the mud to provide light and pulled their blades and shields. One shifted to the left and the other to the right so they could approach Valk from his flanks.

Valk did not wait for them. He charged. But not at Utrik, which would have brought him into the center of their closing circle. He attacked the man to the left, a heavy-set fellow with a thick black beard.

The bearded man cried out in surprise. He flung up his shield to block the expected blow from Valk, but the gray-eyed soldier turned his charge into a feet-first slide. His boots kicked up wet dirt as he slid beneath his foe's shield and blade and came back up onto his knees with his sword stabbing.

The sharp tip of Valk's weapon disemboweled his foe. The bearded man shrieked as he dropped his sword and grabbed for the intestines spilling from the awful wound. Valk plucked the man's shield from his grasp as he rose and hacked his blade through the neck, sending the head spinning away.

"Get him!" Utrik shouted to his remaining companion as he leaped to the attack.

The third man hesitated. Valk met Utrik near the center of the clearing, in flickering torchlight that set weapons and armor agleam. Their blades clanged. Valk bashed with his borrowed shield, knocking Utrik staggering back against the shrine's center oak. At almost the same instant, he twisted the sword hilt in his hand and flung the blade like a spear toward the third man. It was an action he'd often practiced but never used in battle.

Valk's last foe was young, barely out of youth. He stood frozen, with his shield and sword out of position. Valk's flung blade caught him in the throat and drove through, punching out the back of the neck in a spray of black droplets.

Utrik was not truly a coward. He regained his balance and flung himself upon Valk, hacking with his blade and shouting in glee at how his opponent had disarmed himself. Valk kept his borrowed shield up as Utrik rained blow after brutal blow onto the steel rim; the soldier was forced back but no strike could get past his defense.

Utrik kept up the attack, but he was a big man and not in the greatest condition for sustained effort. He began to tire. Valk was a professional, disciplined and fit. And he knew every trick of shield fighting.

As Utrik slowed, Valk went on the offensive, bashing suddenly and savagely with his shield—to the left, to the right, from the center. The iron boss on the shield's front hammered Utrik's sword aside. The next blow smashed the betrayer in the face, crushing lips and nose, shattering teeth.

Utrik cried out. Stunned, he fell to his knees, blood running from his mouth and nostrils. Looking up at Valk with disbelief, he tried to lift his sword. Valk spun off his right leg, bringing the shield around in a blur. The steel edge of the shield had been hacked nearly to shreds in Utrik's attack. Left jagged and sharp, it sliced across Utrik's throat like a serrated knife, opening the jugular to a flooding of gore.

Valk watched Utrik fall, then slung the shield over his shoulder by its straps and walked over to pull his sword free of the throat it had speared. Using the blade, he hacked through the younger man's neck, and then through Utrik's to separate heads from the bodies.

"If they rise now, they'll have a hard time finding me," he said to Neana.

"Well done, brother!" Neana replied. "But the battle may not be over."

"What do you mean?" Valk demanded.

"Riders are coming. Swiftly!"

– 5 –

Valk had entered the shrine through the woods from the west. A wide dirt road, partially overgrown, led in from the east. Along that road, fresh torches flared. Valk had time to hide, but not the inclination. And it was possible these were not foes. He reseated the battered shield on his left arm and lifted his sword. Both dripped with blood. A snarl curled his lips.

A dozen sweat-lathered horses galloped into the clearing around the ancient oak. They spread out. These were not the massive warhorses of the Kuulumsraad knights but sleek, well-bred stallions built for spirit and beauty. Ten of the horses bore soldiers; tough, lean men with dusky skins and spade-shaped beards. Their armor and weapons were of the finest quality, though gilded with gold. Valk knew them as Shadow-Guards, those who had provided personal protection for the king and his family before the coming of the usurpers—the sorcerers.

The eleventh rider appeared to be a monk. A simple gray robe girded his loins. Next to him rode a woman astride a golden mare. Valk knew her, with her red hair so much brighter than his own, and her green eyes that waxed cold or warm depending on her moods. He thrust his shield back over his shoulder and sheathed his sword, then went to one knee with bowed head.

"Milady Ishalla," he said.

"Sir Valk," Ishalla replied, though he had no claim on such a title of address. "Please rise."

Valk did as bidden but did not take his eyes from the woman, who wore a silver brocade vest over white shirt and black trousers. A sword hung at her hip, and not just for show. She was the chief priestess of Ishkareth in Kuulumsraad, a distant relative of the overthrown king, and Valk's secret lover.

"What happened here?" Ishalla asked. Her gaze took in the damaged shrine and the three headless bodies.

"They were desecrating the fane," Valk explained.

"And you stopped them?"

"Yes."

"Even though you are not a believer in Ishkareth?"

"There *are* things I believe in," Valk countered, though he did not elaborate.

Perhaps the faintest blush rouged Ishalla's cheeks, a blush to make devils yearn for innocence. She dismounted, though it disconcerted her closest guards, who flung themselves from their saddles to aid her. She shook away their attentions as she strode to Valk.

"If you are here at this time, then I take it the battle with the knights did not go well."

Valk shook his head. He pointed to the body of Utrik and almost spat on it before restraining himself. "That one," he said, "he and others deserted even as the knights' charge came. It opened our lines. Slaughter followed."

Ishalla winced.

"The sorcerers even raised the dead knights to continue fighting," Valk added. "I was lucky. The deserters *served* the sorcerers. At least these three did. When they fled, others followed. They earned their deaths."

Ishalla sighed. "I'm glad you survived, but am sorrowed that so many of ours did not." She turned to her guards. "Set up torches and a perimeter. Make sure we are not surprised here by more servants of the sorcerers." She looked toward the monk, who had not dismounted. "Quolish, prepare. We must restore the fane. I can feel it weakened."

"I as well, Ishalla," the monk intoned. "But I do not see how we can repair it without fresh skulls for the tree."

"We must find some way," Ishalla snapped. "Or soon the sorcerers will sense the weakening and come to finish the desecration."

Quolish merely nodded and dismounted. He stepped over to study the oak at close range. His hands explored the ancient, gnarled bark and the remaining embedded skulls.

Ishalla glanced back at Valk. She gestured toward the far side of the clearing, farthest from the shrine and the others. "I would speak to you alone, soldier," she said.

Valk nodded. He led the way to the forest's edge. His gray eyes met the green ones of Ishalla. Something passed between them. Ishalla lifted her hand as if to touch Valk's face, but then let it drop back to her side.

"I was expecting to join an army encamped near here," she finally said.

"So was I. But Utrik, the leader of those three I killed, he said the army was misled into believing we'd won a victory against the knights. They left to consolidate that victory, but it's a trap they'll be walking into."

Ishalla closed her eyes. "One of my people is with General Haman. I'll send him a warning and hope he gets it in time. And that Haman will listen."

Valk said nothing as he watched the trance enfold the priestess like a shroud. Her face softened; her body swayed. Her vulnerability called to him. As did the trust she showed by entering such a trance in front of him. He fought to keep his face impassive while all he wanted to do was embrace her. That he could not do, not in front of the others.

A few long moments passed; Ishalla's eyes snapped open. She took a deep breath that shuddered between her lips. "The message was received," she said. "Let's hope it makes a difference."

"And what now for us?" Valk asked.

Ishalla smiled at the soldier's double meaning. She chose to address only one of those, and not the one most important to Valk. "The fane is badly weakened by what was done to it. The sorcerers may be able to enter, and if they do our last rallying point will be destroyed. I must find a way to restore it. And quickly."

The soldier knew that Ishalla was *truly* the last rallying point of the rebellion, and if the sorcerers found the shrine they'd find her and kill her like they had everyone else who'd tried to resist them. He did not want to speak that thought, though. He said only: "To restore it, you need skulls?"

"Yes. Many skulls."

"What about the heads of the three men I killed?"

"No! They were not loved by anyone here. To use them would only corrupt the magic. But there may be a way for the tree itself to help." She turned to look toward the shrine, then glanced back at Valk. Again, her hand lifted as if to touch him, and again she thrust it back down to her side. "Would that we had a few moments alone," she whispered.

"But we don't," Valk replied. "Do now what you must."

The priestess nodded and turned away. Walking to the oak, aglow now in the light of flaming torches planted by her guards, she brushed her hands across it, particularly over the wounds left where embedded skulls had been torn out. Valk watched with curiosity as her hands began to glow. And then from the night all around arose a strange cacophony—the cawing of ravens, the howl of wolves, the scream of a panther.

– 6 –

The feral shriek of the forest night sent waves of gooseflesh rippling over Valk's body. He yanked his sword from its sheath and turned to face the dark woods. Ishalla's guards responded likewise, but Ishalla and Quolish remained focused on the tree, their hands weaving skeins of magical light over and around it.

Valk retreated to the center of the fane where the ten warriors of the Shadow-Guard joined him in a defensive circle around their priestess and priest. The calling of crows and other birds increased. The tops of the trees began to shake. From within the forest, the howls of wolves were joined by high pitched growls and cackles. Something roared, a bear or other large beast.

"Bows!" the commander of the Shadow-Guard bellowed.

His men sheathed their bladed weapons and drew black bows into their hands, nocking crimson arrows on golden strings. Valk stabbed his sword into the dirt between his feet and readied his own bow.

A wave of black shapes swirled from the treetops and came to land on the dirt of the clearing. Crows and ravens and grackles. Dozens of them. Their midnight plumage gleamed like spilled oil in the torchlight. Many carried things in their beaks. Valk at first thought the birds held white acorns, then realized what they truly were—the tiny skulls of mice and shrews and hummingbirds.

"What is happening?" the Shadow-Guard leader demanded.

"Perhaps a miracle," Valk replied.

"Yes," Neana whispered at his ear.

A dire wolf appeared at the edge of the forest. Then others. They, too, held skulls between their teeth. Big ones and small ones. And with a crash that reverberated across the clearing, a massive cave bear bulled its way from the trees. He dropped the thick skull of another bear to the ground and roared a challenge.

"Draw bows!" the guard leader ordered.

"No!" Ishalla shouted. "Do not shoot!"

Valk turned. The woman he loved gleamed with light. Her emerald eyes cut like torches as she looked toward the gathering crowd of beasts. "The tree has called them here," Ishalla continued. "Bring the skulls!"

The men of the guard hesitated. Valk stepped forward, stopping a few feet from the bear. He swallowed hard, then bent down and picked up the giant skull. The bear stood up on its hind feet but only swayed back and forth as Valk turned and carried his burden to Ishalla. The woman took it, straining with its weight as she lifted it high. It began to gleam. She pushed it against the tree and Valk gasped as the trunk of the big oak opened to accept the offering.

"More!" Ishalla called. "To both of us."

The guards slung their weapons, then stepped forward to gather up the skulls littering the ground, the tiny ones and the large. They brought them to the tree, handed them to Ishalla or Quolish, or piled them on the ground at their feet. The hands of the priest and priestess moved swiftly, placing skulls into the wounds left by the work of Utrik and his fellows. Exhilaration swept Valk. He felt it; the shrine's magic was healing.

From the opposite side of the clearing, from the darkest place along the road leading into the fane, a half dozen arrows flew. Some hit the tree. Two punched into Quolish's back and he cried out as he staggered forward. The light in his hands failed. He toppled.

"Kill them all!" a guttural voice shouted from the night.

– 7 –

Valk stared in horror as Quolish fell and died. From the road where the arrows had come, a burst of violet lightning leapt skyward. That column of fire birthed two dozen Kuulumsraadian knights—dead men mounted on dead horses whose eyes dripped black light. Behind the knights floated three figures limned in a sick purple glow. Two were men, one a woman. Though Valk had only seen them at a distance before, he knew them—the sorcerers of Kuulumsraad, those who had once served the king but who now sought to rule after murdering their liege.

Valk shouted to the Shadow-Guard, "Protect your priestess!"

Knowing that Ishalla was the last hope to unify Kuulumsraad and lead the people against the usurpers, Valk grabbed up his sword and charged the sorcerers. He knew he'd have to carve through the knights first. Perhaps an impossible task. Six knights carried bows; these rose in their stirrups and drew back on their strings as Valk came on the attack. Steel arrowheads glittered, all of them pointed at Valk's chest.

"No!" Neana shrieked.

From the leather pouch hanging always at Valk's left side, something like a tiny crystal moon emerged. It exploded, sending concussive waves of sound and energy forward into the faces of the knights. Even dead men screamed when those waves hit them. The arrows nocked on their strings disintegrated into ash. The bows caught fire.

Valk came in among his foes, his sword reaping. Heads rolled, limbs flew. Half the Shadow-Guard joined him; the others formed a shield around their priestess. Dead or not, the knights fell back under that onslaught.

Valk and the guards cut through. The sorcerers were not cowed. Their hands lifted. Glitters of lavender light bled from their fingers. A wall of gleaming blades appeared protectively in front of them. The crystal moon, which was the soul of Valk's sister, Neana, was smashed into the mud. Valk howled in rage. He hurled his sword like a spear toward the three sorcerers. It flashed into slag before it could reach them.

"To Ishalla," Neana whispered in her brother's ear. "Give me to Ishalla!"

For an instant, Valk hesitated. Then he spun toward the shrine; he had no choice.

"Ishalla!" Valk cried out. "Here!"

The woman Valk loved spared him a glance. Her green eyes bled with the pressure of resisting the sorcerers, but she saw him. Valk tore open the pouch at his side and pulled forth a gleaming skull. Human. But small. A child's. The gray-eyed warrior hurled the thing toward Ishalla. She caught it, and in the next instant triumph crossed her face as she plugged Neana's skull into a hole in the ancient oak of Ishkareth.

All three sorcerers shrieked as a massive spear of white light erupted from the rejuvenated shrine and struck them. Valk watched their forms waver. Fragments began to peel away from their bodies like decaying mummies shedding pieces of ancient linen.

The knights of Kuulumsraad tried to rally, to surround the sorcerers in a protective weave of dead flesh and steel. But now the beasts who'd carried skulls to the shrine attacked. The wolves and panthers and the bear, the crows and ravens. They raged upon their enemies, and the knights and sorcerers were torn asunder.

In the aftermath, Valk turned once again toward the shrine. The exhaustion of his past hours struck him. He swayed but forced enough strength into his limbs to stalk over to Ishalla. She leaned against the shrine, her hands on Neana's skull. The glow that suffused her shrank gradually back within her, leaving only the stains of bloody tears on her cheeks. Yet, she was lovely with her fiery hair and emerald eyes.

Her gaze met Valk's. She nodded toward the small skull of his sister, which still pulsed with light. "I didn't know," she said.

Valk nodded. "Neana," he said. "She was born with the magic. Even untrained, she was powerful. When she was ten she was murdered for it by evil men. I was sixteen. I killed them all. Then I buried her. All except for…." He indicated the skull. "She insisted I carry that with me. She's helped me many times. Though," he smiled, "she has not always been the easiest soul to deal with. And she talked a lot."

"But you love her."

"I do." He sighed. "I can't hear her now. Is she…gone on at last?"

Ishalla shook her head. "Not gone. Subsumed within the shrine. I'm afraid she won't be talking to you again, however. I'm sorry."

Valk nodded. "I miss her griping already."

Ishalla lifted her hand and brushed his cheek, not caring now who might see. If it were to recover, Kuulumsraad would have need of a new queen in coming days. And this queen needed a soldier.

Yella Faces the Unknown

The Path One Doesn't Choose

By Gustavo Bondoni

The room felt wrong.

Yella took three steps into the wizard's audience chamber and stopped. She studied the crowd in an attempt to decipher what had set off her sixth sense. She opened her mind, allowing the stray thoughts of the well-dressed courtiers to enter. They seemed innocuous enough—anticipation of the food to come, mostly.

Too much anticipation, she realized as she sifted through the scraps from the crowd.

...said he will serve both fowl and venison...

...haven't eaten in several...

...wine, he promised...

She pushed through the crowd towards the raised dais at the far end of the room where the figure of Abren sat in a colossal carved throne, a thing of grotesque skulls and dragons.

His eyes followed her as she approached.

...I don't want to go back to the slave pens tonight. Grun is waiting there, and he wants to...

The thought stopped her a handful of steps from the platform, and she looked around her for a slave. None of the people close to her were dressed in the grey rags of household chattel.

Then she noticed the brown stains on the front of the tunic of the man next to her. Bloodstains. Someone had been stabbed in those clothes. Probably the original owner. The thought struck her that the clothes around her were stolen. The courtiers were slaves.

Abren wanted to betray her! Yella pulled her rapier from the scabbard on her back and charged toward the steps, pushing several of the slaves out of her way.

The magician sighed and leveled his scepter.

"You bastard!" she shouted.

Light, backed by powerful magic, slammed into her. Then she fell into darkness.

~*~

I'm alive? Yella thought. *Why am I alive?*

She realized that she was lying face-down on a floor of dirt and loose gravel. Judging by the sharp pain, she must have fallen face-first and been dragged across rocks.

Yella pushed herself to her hands and knees with a groan. She opened her eyes to reveal darkness barely relieved by a soft greenish glow. Her rapier lay three paces away, so she crawled to it.

The weight of the sword in her hand gave her courage. With this blade, combined with her telepathic ability, she would give herself excellent odds against any swordsman: knowing what your enemy was thinking of doing tended to be an incredible advantage.

She stood and walked towards the emerald light, gravel crunching under her boots.

I've been sent to the eternal dark!

The thought came from her left, so she changed course and walked in that direction. Several steps later, she came upon a woman sitting on the floor, rocking back and forth, weeping.

"Be quiet," Yella said as she recognized her gown from the magician's throne room. "We don't know what else is here with us."

The woman looked around and peered at Yella. "Who are you?"

"Help!" another voice shouted through the darkness, a man's this time. "Someone help me!"

Yella sighed. *Did none of these people have any sense of self-preservation?*

Within minutes, a small group had coalesced around her: the distraught woman, a second female, and the man who'd been shouting. She suspected that they'd been standing in the effective radius of the spell that Abren had hit her with.

She also found parts of other people…the ones close enough to be affected but not quite close enough for the spell to enwrap their whole body. Those, she didn't mention to anyone. How would they react to knowing their lives were worth so little?

Besides, it was possible that the three slaves who'd been transported here with her were the lucky ones. The rest had been witnesses to what Abren had done, and Yella had friends who would seek to avenge her. Sangr, for example, would cut the magician into little pieces if he found out about Abren's treachery.

Yes. The ones with her were the lucky ones. They were likely the only people in that room other than Abren himself who were still alive now. And, depending on how far he'd sent them, they could quite possibly remain free when they made it back to civilization.

Provided they survived.

"All right," Yella whispered. "Follow me, and keep your mouths shut."

The slaves—for reading their thoughts, she knew that was what they were—came silently, submissively. Their minds were empty of everything but the thoughts of raw fear. Fear of the darkness, fear of death, fear of repercussions. She did her best to ignore them, cursing the gift that allowed her to hear people's inner conversations.

The greenish light emanated from some kind of rough growth on a solid rock wall.

Yella was disappointed; she'd hoped the illuminated area was an exit. As she pondered what to do next, she heard the tinkling of water and followed the sound until they reached a spring carved into the rock. A leaf floated past, which indicated they should walk upstream. Trees grew on the surface, not in caves.

The slaves knelt to drink.

Yella decided to wait a while to see if they survived before doing so herself. In the meantime, she brooded as they walked.

Abren had tricked her. He'd filled the room with expendable victims in order to keep her from hearing his thoughts. But when she caught on, the spell he'd hit her with—one which he must have prepared ahead of time—didn't kill her, it simply dropped her in some deserted cave. That meant he wanted her alive for some reason.

The stream meandered through the cave. They followed it for what seemed like hours, sometimes in pitch darkness, until the nature of the cavern changed and the rock, dust, and gravel gave way to packed earth.

Finally, the stream disappeared into a dark hole not quite big enough for one of them to squeeze through. Yella grunted with frustration, but a sudden gust of fresh, cold air gave her hope.

"Dig," she told her little group as she pulled at the hole. "It's just dirt."

It was hard, grimy work, made harder by roots and rocks, but they made steady progress and, in time, they stood on a grassy clearing beside a hill. The night air was cold—much too cold to be Tyrrha, the city where Abren's palace stood. This felt more like the far north. And yet, no snow covered the ground. Perhaps it was just an unseasonal chill.

"Which way should we go?" asked the woman she'd first found.

Yella tried to get a look at the woman's face, but the starlight made it impossible to make out her features. All she could see was a pale space in the darkness.

"Nowhere. We need to rest. We'll decide which way to go in the daylight."

They camped beside the stream. Yella covered herself with her cloak, grasped her rapier, and fell asleep almost instantly.

Two hours later, she felt someone sneaking up on her and, more importantly, heard the person's thoughts.

Bash her with this rock. I'll take her coat. And the sword. And her purse. She must have a purse. She has a sword. People with swords must have purses.

Yella struck out once, and the soft sigh and a body's immediate collapse told her she'd struck the thief dead, right in the heart.

Sensing no more treachery afoot, she closed her eyes again and slept on. Morning would be soon enough to discover which of her companions had made the misguided attempt to kill her.

~*~

She woke before dawn, as the sun's pink glow illuminated the far side of the hill. It wasn't the soft light that woke her, however, but the thoughts from her two remaining companions.

"So you didn't run," she said out loud.

"No. We…we don't know where to go," the man replied, which Yella found interesting. She'd suspected it would have been the make who would have tried to rob her in the night. She sat up and studied the half-frozen corpse.

It was the woman with the inscrutable visage, the one she'd found crying in the cave. Yella shrugged. She couldn't worry about every lost soul who made a bad decision. Not anymore, at least. Well, not until she made her way back to Tyrrha and put Abren's liver on a spike. And not until she felt Sangr's arms around her again. Once she made it back, she'd take on as many lost souls as her heart desired. But not now.

She kicked the body with her toe, conscious of the two slaves huddled together for warmth watching her. "Do either of you want to try kill me while I'm asleep?"

The pair shook their heads.

"Good. Now I have a question for you. You are slaves, correct?"

Nods.

"I imagine you've been branded?"

"Yes," the man said, bitterly.

"All right. Well, you're free now. The brand doesn't mean anything unless someone sees it. And since I can't see it from here, I assume no one else will stop you to look for it. So go."

"Where?" the man asked, distrust evident in his face and voice.

"I don't care. But I can't take care of you."

The surviving woman spoke for the first time since they'd emerged from the cavern. "Where are you going?"

"I'm going up this hill," Yella replied. "To see if I can spot a settlement beyond the trees. Then I'm going to walk into that town and ask questions."

"Alone?" the woman asked, eyes wide.

"I'll let you two come along that far, if you want. But you might be better off disappearing into these woods."

"We'll come with you," the man said.

The climb was easy enough. The hill was too rocky for much vegetation to hinder their way, and it was tall enough for them to see over the forest trees. She didn't spot a town, but saw that the ground descended to the south and the woods ended abruptly.

"We're going south," she declared.

A couple of hours later, they reached the end of the forest. She scanned the slate-grey sky and pointed to a pillar of smoke.

"People," the man said, nervously.

By midday, they'd reached a small cluster of buildings made of cut and planed wood. Yella breathed a sigh of relief when she spotted metal nails holding the planks together. This place looked like a farming and trading town, not a mining outpost. Metal would come from far away…and that meant that someone here could answer some of her questions.

The town seemed sleepy, even for a place as remote as this one seemed to be, so she headed for the tavern. It was easy to spot: the building with a sign on the side that showed a boar and a stag. That would be the name of the establishment. *The Boar and Stag*…or *The Stag and Boar*. It mattered not to her.

Words drifted out, but the place went silent when she entered. Chairs shuffled slightly away from her. She walked to the counter where a bearded man wearing a grey tunic eyed her fearfully.

"Do you have beer?" she asked.

He nodded and placed a tankard in front of her with trembling hands.

"Thank you. Now, I have a question: how far are we from Tyrrha?"

"Tyrrha?" the man asked.

"Yes. We're traveling to Tyrrha, and we'd like to know the best road to follow."

"You're not with the camp, then?" the man asked. His accent was thick with singsong tones. Yella, who had traveled from the Green Hell in the south to the Ice in the north had never heard the like. But this town was probably so far from everything that it made sense for its people to sound different.

"No. What camp?"

Immediately, the barman relaxed. The tension in his shoulders disappeared, and he smiled. In the tavern, chairs moved back and she heard some whispered words.

"Welcome to Hui," he said. "We don't get many travelers, and I can't say that I know where Tyrrha is. Would your friends like something to drink?"

"If they do, they can either negotiate it for themselves or drink from a stream," Yella said with a grin.

"Tyrrha is perhaps too far south. Could you show me the road to Krenn?"

The man shook his head. "I'm afraid I don't know of Krenn, either," he replied.

Yella wanted to take him by the neck and shake him. Krenn was the city that connected the North with the plains and the mountains. It was the crossroad of the continent. Everyone knew where Krenn was.

"Young lady," a new voice boomed. It was a confident voice, heavy with authority. She turned to see a robed man stand, thin and tall, with long blond hair. A woman dressed in what appeared to be layers of gauze clutched his arm. "We are not a well-traveled people. But to the south of us, you will find a camp of travelers. They lead a nomadic life, and my belief is that they pass near every city. They might be able to tell you what you need to know."

The man behind the counter paled. "Myurio, you would send them to the Wanderers?"

The long-haired man held the barkeeper's gaze. "It is for the best. We cannot help them, and they cannot help us."

The barman, chastised, turned away, and busied himself with something behind the counter. Yella could not see his face.

She turned to Myurio. "What's wrong with these Wanderers?" she asked quietly.

The long-haired man waved his hand. "Superstition and prejudice, I'm afraid. Our townspeople distrust anyone who isn't one of us. But we've dealt with the Wanderers for decades, and we have never suffered a theft or an attack. Not in my lifetime. They are camped an hour's walk due south."

The woman placed a hand on Yella's shoulder and smiled. "They will know things we don't. They visit every town we know and more that we have never even heard of. With winter approaching, they are the only travelers who come to us." The man nodded eagerly and Yella felt that here was the person who truly ran affairs in the village.

Yella also sensed the woman's words were the truth, but she couldn't actually hear her thoughts. Or those of anyone else in the room except the slaves she'd come in with. Which meant there was some kind of magic in the town, somewhere. Magic that could thwart a telepath.

Interesting.

"Very well."

~*~

The camp was unlike any Yella had ever seen. To start with, there were no horses. None. No pack animals of any sort, in fact, even though she counted twenty tents.

Worse, she still could not sense the thoughts of the people in the camp any more than she could sense the ones from the people in the town. She knew they were present, because she sensed a buzzing from the camp, like the noise of countless insects. At times, it felt like she could almost understand it but, just when meaning seemed to be in her grasp, it flitted away.

"I don't like this," the female slave said.

Yella shrugged. "Then leave. I'm not keeping you bound. I have no use for you, and you two would be better off running away and making a life somewhere else. I'm going back to Tyrrha, and someone there will recognize you. You'll be back in the slave pens hours after you return to the city."

Even under her riding cloak, Yella shivered, and her breath hung in the air before her. The slaves didn't seem to mind the chill, so perhaps they belonged here. Their white, pale skin seemed to indicate that. How they'd reached the slave pens of Tyrrha was anyone's guess.

Despite her advice, the two were right behind her when she approached the nearest tent.

"Stop!" A tall woman with red hair stepped out from beside a tent. She wore dark brown leather armor with a red pendant in the form of a heart over her chest. "You are early. Sundown is an hour away, still."

Yella's hand dropped to the hilt of her rapier. Something about the way the woman moved seemed unusual. Or perhaps it was simply that she spoke with a completely different intonation from the people back in the little town.

"I just need some information," Yella called back.

The woman studied the small group for a few moments and Yella's hair stood on end. The buzzing in her mind intensified. She grasped to sift meaning from it, but again failed.

"Did you come here of your own free will?" the woman asked.

Yella paused. "Of course," she said finally. "Do you think those peasants back there could force me to do anything I didn't want to?"

"Good. Then all is as it should be."

The tent to Yella's right shook and a man, dressed in the same leather as the red-haired woman, emerged. His face was pale, and his black hair pulled back in a long ponytail.

Again, she got the sense that there was something wrong with him. She stepped back.

He took another step towards her, and Yella realized what it was. Every time she let out a breath, it hung in front of her, the moisture forming a mist in the cold air. This man was either controlling his breathing amazingly well... or he wasn't breathing at all.

"Run!" Yella shouted, turning to go.

But the open field behind them suddenly held a half-dozen Wanderers—men and women, all tall, all pale, and all coming towards them. People whose minds she hadn't sensed.

Yella ignored her own advice and didn't make a break for it. Instead, she danced around, keeping out of reach of the man from the tent. She still wasn't certain what was happening—even though even though the situation certainly looked dire.

The slaves panicked. They tried to run through the six creatures that stood between them and the town.

For a moment it seemed that the man, outpacing the woman, would make it. The Wanderers trying to corral them looked sluggish, as if they'd been sleeping. One of them barely managed to get a hand on the slave's arm as he passed.

But it was enough. Either the slave was very weak, or the man who grabbed him was extremely strong, because, in an instant, the slave stopped and fell, his back hitting the frozen earth with a dull thud.

The male who'd captured him shrieked and flung himself on top of the former slave. A female beside him soon joined them.

Yella, still circling to keep the inhabitants of the camp at bay, couldn't see what they were doing to the male slave, but the female, watching with stunned shock, was swarmed by two of the creatures from the camp. Without bothering to send her to the ground, one of them bit into her neck and tore out a hunk of flesh. She went limp in his arms, but three more of the Wanderers rushed forward. They kept her upright as they fed.

"All right… so that's what's going on!" Yella muttered.

Acting on the premise that those she faced—whether monsters or revenants or some other devilish creation—were slow but extremely strong, she darted forward and, with a well-practiced blow, slashed the neck of the man before her. It wasn't a decapitating blow, but one judged to sever blood vessels and cut into the throat without getting embedded in the bone of the neck.

It was a killing blow. Or should have been.

Instead of falling to the ground, the man with the ponytail growled in fury—blood bubbling through the new hole in his neck as he did so—and rushed towards her.

Yella skipped aside and cursed. Even though she dodged her attacker, she felt she was moving too slowly if they all attacked together. She was used to knowing what her enemies did before they did it. Apparently, it meant that when she couldn't read their thoughts, she couldn't move fast enough to fight more than one or two simultaneously.

She looked around. Seven of the camp's inhabitants were heading her way, and she saw no clear path through them. She feinted one way and moved the other, gaining a few paces. All she needed was an opening wide enough to sprint through.

But the people hunting her were cunning. They couldn't quite keep up, but they seemed determined to keep the ring around her intact. As three or four tried to pen her in, others moved towards the spaces left unguarded.

The buzz got louder. Loud enough that, for a single moment, it interrupted her concentration on her pursuers and she noticed it was all coming from one place: the woman with red hair who stood aside, alone, in the afternoon shadows. She was the only member of the encampment not feeding or chasing Yella.

The pendant on her chest was glowing like a burning heart.

"Why does it always have to be magic?" Yella hissed as she avoided a grasping hand. "Why can't it be barbarians from the Endless Sea or something?"

She rolled between two women reaching out towards her and sprinted at the red-haired woman.

Her enemy saw her coming with her rapier out and didn't even flinch until the last moment. She ducked beneath the wildly swinging blade and backhanded Yella almost casually in the side.

Yella felt her bones creak as she rolled across the hard ground and slammed into a tent which, fortunately, collapsed and absorbed most of the energy from the fall.

For an instant she fought against pain which threatened to make her lose consciousness. Then, remembering the fate of the slaves, she forced herself to ignore the agony and jump back to her feet.

The nearest of the inhabitants strode towards her, mere paces away. They were in no hurry; she was surrounded, and her rapier had flown in a different direction.

Yella pulled a stiletto from the top of her boot. She was deadly with it, both in a brawl and in a knife throwing contest…but there were seven targets and she had only one knife. If she threw it into the eye of the one ahead, would the monster in human form fall over and leave a gap she could run through? Would it even feel the blade?

She didn't know. But she had to do something, or she would be nothing but a pile of bones, drained of blood and peeled of flesh, left for the scavengers that gnawed such things.

The creatures took another step.

A burst of anger coursed through her. Magic users had been her bane all her life, from the moment she was a child and had been cursed with telepathy. And now, this witch woman might be the end of her.

With a scream of fury, Yella threw the knife.

It struck true, and a keening scream pierced the air. When it ended, not one of the creatures around her was standing; and the buzzing was gone from her mind.

She picked up her rapier and checked the nearest body. The corpse smelled like a wet feral animal, rank but not rotten. Whatever had animated this monster hadn't killed the flesh. It had been alive before Yella pierced the pendant around the witch's neck.

Without bothering to check on the slaves, Yella walked over to the red-haired witch, expecting to find her inanimate like her followers.

Instead, she appeared to be illuminated by a ghostly green light that spread out from where she lay motionless on the ground.

Carefully avoiding the light, Yella leaned over and sliced through the thong that held the pendant on the corpse. She bent down and pulled the pendant away, threading the thick leather thong out from beneath the woman's head, careful to touch only the hilt of the dagger embedded deep inside it. The metal of the knife was warm to the touch.

Then she headed back to the village.

~*~

When Yella walked into the tavern, rapier in one hand and dagger in the other, the barkeep's eyes seemed to pop from his head.

The same group of people were still present. They were likely waiting to see if the sacrifice they'd sent the monsters had been found acceptable.

When he saw her, the man called Myurio seemed just as shocked as the server, but he recovered quickly. "Thank the Gods you've returned," he said with a forced smile. "Come Ulina, let us thank our savior. See how she has brought the heart of the Wanderers. See? There it is on her knife." He stood and the woman in gauze took his hand and they approached Yella.

Yella smiled in the friendliest manner she could and, when they were close enough, she buried the point of the rapier into the woman's belly, straight through the gauze. She yelped and fell as Yella pulled the blade out and swung it in a wide arc. Fueled by fury, she didn't bother to avoid the vertebra this time, and felt enormous satisfaction as the blade jarred as it hit bone.

But she'd hit the man hard enough that this one was a decapitating blow. Myurio's head fell from his shoulders and landed on the wooden floor with a wet thud.

The bearded man behind the counter trembled as she came towards him, but he didn't run. The rest of the people in the tavern remained very, very still.

"You are alive right now because you tried to stop that conniving bastard from sending us out. I suppose he was the local strongman, so you had to knuckle under, but you tried to resist. That means that you're at least halfway decent." She grunted. "Well, better than that carrion over there. So now we'll have a little talk."

"Wh…what do you want?" he asked.

"Beer, for starters," she said. "And you're paying for it this time."

"Y…Yes."

Yella put the dagger, still jammed in the pendant, now just a dark lifeless red stone, on the wood in front of him.

"I imagine they were extorting you? You sent them people—I would guess old people who volunteer—and they let you live?" she said.

The man nodded. "There was nothing we could do. They come every year, and every year we send one person. I've lost friends, neighbors…"

Yella bit her tongue. She had dealt with the problem in minutes…something they could have done if they hadn't been utter cowards. She spat. "Were you telling me the truth before, when you said you didn't know the cities I wanted?"

The man nodded. "The only city in this region is Üne…but we get very few travelers from there. It's supposed to be a fortnight's walk to the southeast."

Yella nodded. She'd never heard of the place. It was probably a market town in the hills somewhere. Still, someone there would know which way she had to go.

"Fair enough. Do you know of a man called Sangr?"

"The king?"

Yella laughed at the very thought. "No. The murderer and adventurer."

The tavern-keeper shook his head. "I haven't."

Yella sighed. "Then I guess I'll have to ask further south. Fill me a sack with the best provisions you have. Enough to last me two weeks. If I suspect you haven't given me the best you've got, I'll be back here to add another head to my tally. But at least you won't have to worry about that group over there. They fell to the ground as soon as the knife pierced that stone."

The man took some moments, but when he returned, the sack he gave her was heavy and smelled of fresh-cooked meat. "I think we all owe you our sincere thanks," he said in a voice loud enough for the others in the tavern to hear. He held Yella's gaze. "I sincerely wish you good luck."

"Thank you," Yella replied. She headed for the door, stepping over the squirming woman trying futilely to keep herself from bleeding out. It was no use: deep gut wounds took a while to kill, but they never failed.

"One moment," the tavern-keeper called out. "Aren't you going to take this with you?" He gestured at the knife and the magic stone on the bar.

"No. I'd rather leave it here. After all, if there are more Wanderers out there, they'll probably want it back, and I don't want them chasing me for it."

She left the tavern and walked into the night.

Behind her, silence reigned.

At the Mouth of Shezmu's Temple

Lord of the Blood

By Michael T. Burke

The grim stone edifice loomed before the horseman. A great bestial face, hewn from the rockface of the hill, gazed impassively back at him. Stones, like jagged teeth, jutted from the top of the cave mouth and thrust upward in the ground before it. It looked very much like a lion's snarl, the shadowed entrance suggesting the rider turn back.

A wide swath of dirt and scrabble spread out from the entrance like an earthen carpet; no vegetation grew within the space. No birdsong sounded in the air, no furtive scampering through the leaves. The eerie silence did not sit well with Ahanu Foxcloud.

Ahanu had ridden hard from Maniyat, knowing his time was limited. Now that he had arrived, he could not quiet the unease growing within his gut. Still, he had given his word.

He swung his right leg over the haunches of his borrowed black mare, dropping to the ground. Ahanu scanned the trees, his amber eyes piercing the deeper gloom for signs of movement. Stillness cloaked the glade like a shroud. He led his horse to an old tree, tying off the reins to a thick branch.

The mare huffed, pawing the dirt. Ahanu whispered soothingly, patting her snout. "Easy, girl. I don't want to be here either." He eyed the imposing structure before him. "But I must."

Ahanu glanced through the treetops, noting the sun's position. *Only a few hours remain to save Rahul.* He hefted his axe and striding into the sinister maw wondered again at the events that had brought him here.

~*~

Ahanu longed for the sight of another human; travelers through the Zimara Steppes had been few. It had been some time since he last spent so much time alone. He found he missed the camaraderie of his old life with the Mahkah. His years gone from the village, however, afforded him a perspective he would not have guessed as a youth. Such are the flights of the mind on long journeys.

It was on the eighth day out of his flight west from Kohan's capital city that Ahanu met the small merchant caravan. He had set his steed in the direction of the setting sun through the vast Steppes toward the country of Harijan.

The train of camels, horses, and wagons halted at the sight of Ahanu riding toward them. The caravan had traveled the length of eastern Harijan, hawking their wares through the many small towns that bordered the Steppes. Ahanu counted a dozen people, although he could not be sure if more rode inside the covered wagons. Only a handful carried swords.

"Ho, traveler! What brings you to us?" A swaggering, muscular youth approached, his dark eyes flashing. Ahanu recognized the arrogant blaze he saw there. He sat his steed, watching the boy's advance; his eyes flicked to the other merchants in line, but none made a move.

"Greetings," Ahanu waved. The boy's dialect was strange, although he understood enough of the base language from his travels. Ahanu hoped his reply intelligible. "I am late of Kohan and on my way west to Abhinav." He dismounted his horse, stretching his saddle-sore limbs. The youth stepped back, hand tightening on the hilt of his blade.

A middle-aged man in a colorful tunic waddled forward, coming to a stop beside the brash youth. "Forgive young Rahul, stranger," he huffed. The simple effort of walking seemed a burden for his lungs, and he wheezed every few words. "There have been several robberies along the border and my young friend is overly on his guard." He patted Rahul's shoulder. Color flushed the boy's face, and he opened his mouth to protest.

Ahanu inclined his head, the crest of his dark auburn hair waving in the slight warm breeze. "I understand. His caution is to be commended."

The man smiled, the folds of his cheeks swallowing the corners of his mouth. "I thought you might, traveling alone as you are. You do not have the look of a brigand but are definitely a man of action. You seem a simple wayfarer." He scratched his double chin, puzzled. "Although, I confess not to have encountered a people such as yours, with your copper skin and strange eyes."

"I don't imagine you have," Ahanu said. "My people—the Sekani—are far north and east of here. We are made up of many tribes and do not venture far from our lands. I wanted to see more of the world." Ahanu glanced pointedly at Rahul. "My eyes are uncommon even among the Sekani."

"You will have to tell me more of your people." The man inclined his head. "That is, if you would join us? We are but simple merchants trading in spices, clothing, and jewelry."

"I would, if you will have me for a time." Ahanu said. "If only to add a blade to your party should these robbers you mention come upon you."

The boy started. "We have plenty of swords, stranger!"

"Surely, an extra blade is no harm. I am glad to be of aid if needed." Ahanu's amber eyes gleamed. "I could do with some company on my journey to Abhinav."

"Wonderful! I am Oded," the portly merchant said. "I bid you welcome."

"You may call me Ahanu." He extended his hand.

~*~

Over the succeeding days, Ahanu did more than man the watch, endearing himself to his new companions by aiding the merchants as they unloaded wagons and set up their stalls in two border villages. Each day when the market opened, he watched the villagers and proceedings with keen wistfulness; much of the interactions put him in mind of home, when the Mahkah traded with neighboring tribes and villages. Ahanu did not expect such a sharp pang.

Aside from the odd food and colorful attire, there was little different between these people and his own. He drew the back of his hand across his brow. *It is certainly warmer here than home.*

Ahanu's own garb and amber eyes drew many curious stares. He answered pleasantly the questions posed to him, although he did not recall this much interest in how he looked elsewhere in his travels throughout the Symbrian continent. Granted, the bulk of his exploits thus far, had been in large cities like the Kohanian capital, Rostran, and Tovar Luz in Zurad, and his experience had been that many peoples crossed paths therein.

These errant musings dissipated, and Ahanu asked several questions of his own about the swarthy peoples' history and life on the Harijani border. He desired to know as much as he could. *The world is far larger than I imagined.*

The gaudily festooned ribbons of Oded's merchant stall waved in the slow breeze, and Ahanu picked his way through the milling throngs, stopping in front of the booth.

"Hai, Ahanu! How goes your day at market?" Oded's chubby fingers counted coins.

Ahanu chuckled. "Not as well as yours, it seems, my friend."

"Aye," Oded returned with a grin. "It bodes well for our return to Maniyat. We have been on the road too long. Many in our caravan yearn to return home to their families."

Ahanu frowned. "Oh?"

Oded pocketed his coins, pulling shut the curtains to his booth, signaling the end of his day, despite it barely being mid-afternoon. "Word has reached us that a band of thieves harassing our trade route are close. I am for another week on the trail before returning home to Maniyat, but I must abide by the decision of the majority. I do not wish to travel alone and am not quite the fighter I once was." His belly shook as he laughed at his own expense.

~*~

The sun struggled to stave off the encroaching dusk. The merchants pushed the caravan at a dogged pace—Maniyat was but a few hours away. Shadows lengthened across the hard-packed road. The green of the trees flanking the trail deepened to a sinister gloom.

Rahul, with a word to a fellow, broke his place in line, guiding his dappled mare abreast of the caravan. He observed the stranger Ahanu scanning the adjoining slopes and fell in beside him.

"What do you think? Will we make Maniyat before dark?" Rahul asked.

"I think not. If what Oded told me about the distance is true." Ahanu peered at the sky then the tree line. He shrugged, the wooden handle of the crossbow at his back rising over his shoulders like an alert sentry. "Darkness will be upon us in half an hour's time."

Rahul mirrored Ahanu's action, gazing at the sky. "Aye. Forgive me. That was a foolish question. I know we'll reach Maniyat after dark." He shifted awkwardly in his saddle. Crimson flushed his cheeks, and he considered spurring his mount into the surrounding woods.

Silence yawned between the two riders.

"Is there something you wish to say, Rahul?"

"Aye."

"Speak your mind."

Rahul had thought it so simple when he pictured this moment in his head, but his determination faltered in the face of it. Finally, he screwed up the courage to proceed.

"Tell me more of your travels. You must move from land to land, nothing holding you back. What adventure!" He stroked his horse's mane. "I fear that if I stay another season in boring Maniyat, I will go mad. Little occurs along the caravan route, and I desire excitement."

"This is not so terrible a life," Ahanu answered.

"What do you know of it? Have you lived this dull existence, whiling away your years in a dead-end village where nothing ever happens?"

"I have."

"And you left!" Rahul countered. "Thus, proving my point."

"My reasons for leaving my people were many. Even so, I still feel the pull of home. Be not so quick to dismiss where you come from. It is not all grand adventure out in the world. There is also death and sorrow."

"I wish to make my own determination," Rahul scoffed. "When you leave Maniyat, I would go with you to Abhinav. I was there once. I could be of help to you."

"I understand the desire to gain experience," Ahanu answered, wisps of his own youth drifting in his mind. "This might not be the best time for you to venture forth."

"I can handle whatever comes!" Rahul swelled his chest, patting the hilt of his sword. "I have talked to some of the old soldiers in Maniyat and along the merchant trail. I am more than adequate with a sword."

Ahanu frowned. "Have you stared into the eyes of a man that wants to kill you? 'More than adequate' with a blade means little if you have never actually fought for your life. There's a—"

They heard a scream, then shouts.

"Bandits!"

Brigands plunged from the darkened slopes flanking the dusty road, their booted feet pounding the earth, blades glittering in the dim light. Muffled twangs sounded in quick succession, followed by heavy thuds, dropping random merchants in the train. Panic and confusion seized the small caravan like a hawk descending upon its prey.

"Skan's balls!" Ahanu cursed, swiftly taking in the scene. He counted five assailants, three to the left across the merchant train and two rushing down on his side. A feathered shaft sprouted in the neck of his steed and Ahanu leaped clear as the horse fell. He tumbled loosely, letting the roll absorb the impact of the road. He saw Rahul's horse rear and the youth, taken by surprise, fall backward.

"Stay down!" Ahanu shouted to Rahul. He crouched, making himself as small a target as he could for the unseen archer. He whipped his head about, searching for better cover and a foe to strike. Cries of fear and pain rang out, mingling with the clash of steel and meaty thwacks. Ahanu unhitched the crossbow at his back, loading a bolt in seconds. His amber eyes narrowed as he searched the tree line for the sniper.

He detected nothing save the din of his recent acquaintances being slaughtered. Anger burned in Ahanu's chest. These people had graciously offered their hospitality to him; it was a rare gesture of kindness in his experience. Now they were being cut down by these dogs.

At the sound of a throaty yell, he turned to see a mustachioed brigand swing his blade at a heavyset cloth trader. Ahanu raised his weapon, sighted, and released; the bolt pierced the bandit's neck, lifting the robber off his feet to lie still a few feet from the stunned merchant.

Ahanu loaded another bolt from his quiver. The hidden archer was the biggest threat and could be drawing a bead on him this very moment. He pivoted at the sound of a high-pitched scream, seeing another brigand pull his blade from an old woman's torso. She wailed her death knell, blood running freely down her chest, then slumped in a heap. Ahanu snarled, loosing another shaft of death. Footsteps pounded behind him, and he whirled, knowing his shot true, and met his new assailant head-on.

The Sekani warrior moved like a striking cobra, ducking beneath the wide sweep of his foe's sword to ram the man in the throat with the butt of his crossbow. Ahanu dropped the weapon, drawing his dagger as the raider choked, and gutted him, ripping his blade upwards. Red warmth splashed his hand and forearm, and he kicked the man's body away.

Too late, Ahanu heard the soft whirr. Pain flared along his ribs and a scarlet ribbon opened across his skin. The arrow grazed his side and *thunked* into the wooden slats of a merchant cart. He watched the shaft quaver, knowing the sniper had targeted him.

Ahanu scooped up his crossbow on the run and dove behind the overturned cart. Safe for the moment, he inspected his wound with questing fingers. He winced but the flow of blood had already begun to slow. He loaded a bolt, risking a glance over the cart. The two remaining bandits had been dispatched, although not without cost. Several of his new friends lay wounded or dead. Rage smoldered in Ahanu's heart, and his eyes flashed like amber coals.

Only the archer remained.

Another shaft whistled dangerously close, and he dropped behind his makeshift cover.

"Ahanu, you're pinned down! I can distract him!" Rahul shouted.

"Quiet! Tell everyone to stay down!" Ahanu yelled. "I have this."

A loud wordless bellow split the momentary quiet. Ahanu peered once more from his shelter and saw a sword-wielding form madly rush the slope.

"Rahul! No!"

The youth did not stop.

Face split in a wicked grin, the sniper stepped from the tree line and loosed his arrow. The shaft struck Rahul full in the chest; the boy's body hung in space as if pinned to the air. Ahanu rose, sighted, and fired. The archer's smile exploded in a splash of red spray, and he collapsed even as Rahul tumbled down the hill, coming to rest in the dirt.

~*~

The old woman sighed, examining her patient with weary eyes. Rahul lay in sheets soaked with sweat. Eyes squeezed shut against some nightmare, pale from blood loss, he mumbled, spasms jerking his frame. Crimson seeped through the cloth of his dressed wounds.

After the attack, the survivors had pressed on to Maniyat, bearing their casualties. Some had perished from their wounds along the way. Only now had Ahanu learned that Rahul had survived the night.

"My son is alive. For now." The old woman looked grim. "Thank you for bringing him home. I am Sama."

Ahanu nodded, the dark auburn crest of his hair waving slightly. He had seen many wounds and knew the severity of Rahul's. "And for how much longer?"

Sama stroked Rahul's brow with a damp cloth. "Some poison from the shaft burns in him." She did not look up, keeping her attention on her son. "I am well versed in the healing arts, but in this instance, the oil that might save him is rare and I have none. Without it, Rahul will not live to see the morning."

Ahanu cursed himself, shame rising in him when he recalled diving for cover. All of this could have been avoided if only he had but kept his focus. Instead, he bantered with the boy, trying to impart his wisdom, as if he were a grizzled old soldier. If Rahul had not provided the distraction allowing him to kill the sniper, he may very well have been cut down, too. As it was, Rahul lay dying in his place. He owed the boy.

"What is it you need? I will procure it."

Sama ceased her ministrations, gazing into Ahanu's dark amber eyes. Ahanu faltered inwardly but held her stare. He felt a strange stirring echo, and not for the first time. Sama put him in mind of his own long-gone mother and the hushed whispers that surrounded her arcane knowledge.

"The oil is called cassia," Sama said, breaking the silence. "And there is but one place to retrieve it in time."

"Tell me where and I shall get it."

The old woman regarded Ahanu coolly. "It can be found within the Temple of Shezmu. An hour's ride northeast, where the forest meets the border of the Steppes, there is a cavern. You will know it by the lion's face that marks the entrance."

Oded lumbered into the tent, letting in the late morning sun, sputtering at what he had obviously overheard. "Are you mad, woman? That place is cursed!"

Sama looked askance at the trader. "Some say 'cursed', others say 'sacred'. All I know is what I need to save my son can be found there."

Ahanu noted the weariness and fear etched upon the old woman's face as her eyes shifted from Oded to himself. *Was she grasping at feeble hope sending him on a fool's mission? Had reason fled and a mother's love blinded her?* "What do I need to know?" he asked.

"Shezmu is 'Lord of the Blood'. He is a demon of the Underworld," Oded interjected. "He beheads all who enter unbidden. Only the Keepers of the Temple are allowed entry unharmed."

The stout trader placed a hand on Ahanu's shoulder. "Surely you don't intend to go, my friend? I know you are fond of young Rahul, but you will lose your life to the demon, then both you and he will be lost." Oded's eyes flicked to the boy on the bed, then to his mother. "I am sorry, Sama."

"Shezmu uses the blood of his sacrifices to create wine, perfume, and oils," Sama stated plainly. "The cassia oil is there, and with it, I can save him."

Ahanu made a sour face. "Sacrifices?"

"Yes," Oded said. "Every new moon. That night is not for another week. The Lord of the Blood will not look kindly upon an intrusion to his temple."

Ahanu regarded the boy on the cot, feeling the press of intervening summers. Rahul was about the same age as he was when he set forth from the Mahkah as a youth. *Was it truly so long ago?* "I need a horse."

"I have a steed, but I would need something in return," Oded rubbed his belly.

Annoyance flared across Ahanu's face, dissipating as swiftly as it swelled. *No time to haggle with this swindler* "We can settle terms upon my return."

"This is a hazardous quest you venture on, my dear fellow. What guarantee do I have of your return? I would be out a fine horse," Oded clucked. "I am, after all, a businessman."

Ahanu seethed, reaching into his purse. "Here." He dropped a fistful of coins into Oded's outstretched palm.

"Why, thank you, my friend." The plump merchant bowed.

Ahanu sighed. "Very well. I set out at once."

~*~

Torches burned in copper sconces along the cavern walls of Shezmu's Temple, and shadows fluttered in corners. The fires illuminated a wide room with smooth stone walls and floor. Three tunnel mouths gaped from the gloom at the rear of the chamber. A large table carved of black stone dominated the center of the space. Votives and offerings littered the floor surrounding the altar—crafted effigies, food. Coins twinkled in the torchlight. Ahanu circled the table, stepping with care. The stone he had mistaken for black was stained. From what dark substance he did not wish to guess.

A myriad of scents assailed his nostrils but underneath them all was the unmistakable stench of death. A clammy hand closed on his heart. Ahanu traced a finger along the blade of his axe recalling another cave many years ago and the terrible Owl Woman therein that turned out to be more than legend. That simple folktale cost him dear, and he still mourned that loss.

He turned from the mysterious altar, flickering light drawing his gaze to the walls. How had he missed these ancient carvings? *The firelight plays tricks with my eyes.*

Pictographs ran the length of the wall between each torch, meticulously set in three rows. Ahanu studied them but it was no language he knew. Several of the images repeated and he reasoned they told some lost tale. Their sheer age and import inspired in Ahanu an awed reverence. The most repeated image was of a giant with two arms and two legs, but with the head of a lion. Based on what Sama and Oded had said, this could only be Shezmu.

He heard the rasp of steel being drawn, and *felt* somehow that whomever, or whatever had drawn the blade, could have done so silently had they so wished. The sound was meant to instill fear.

Ahanu whirled, putting his back to the wall. A great dark form materialized from the gloom. Baleful eyes glowed green from beneath a shaggy mane and large sharp canines gleamed in the dancing firelight. His hand tightened around his axe. *That is no mask…*

A leonine head sat on a massive dark hewn body, hard and flinty like basalt. Ahanu did not miss the long wickedly curved blades in each giant fist.

"Shezmu." Gooseflesh sprouted on Ahanu's arms.

"On your knees, little human," the demon's voice rumbled.

Ahanu stepped back, superstitious dread chilling his heart. The fearful ways of his people were ingrained in him despite the passage of time and distance. His heel brushed the base of the cavern wall, and he felt the heat of the nearest torch on his shoulder. "Lord Shezmu, I wish to—"

"You trespass upon my temple and dare speak unbidden?" Shezmu snarled, sickle-knives flashing forward. The ring of steel on steel echoed in the cavern as Ahanu deflected the savage cuts with his axe blade. He marveled at his own calm in the face of such a monster, placing his trust in the preternatural senses he attributed to his long-gone mother, which had so often saved him in the past. He waited for the next series of strikes.

A curved blade licked forward like a serpent's tongue. Ahanu deflected the thrust, parrying the deadly sweep of the second sickle with a backhanded blow of his axe.

"Well met, little human." Shezmu did not press his attack, but instead regarded the man before him. Green glowed from deep-set eyes in his maned face.

A subtle sensation, like stepping slowly through gossamer curtains, rippled through Ahanu. The hairs on his neck stood on end.

"Curious. There's an air of the mystic about you, but you look to be a warrior." Shezmu inclined his head and lowered his scythes. "What do you seek here?"

Ahanu wondered at the strange rustling he had felt, and of the lion-being's assertion, but he put it to the back of his mind, sensing that further conflict might be avoided if he was clever enough to advantage himself of the opportunity. How best to acquire what he needed? Through truth or subterfuge? Ahanu thought truth to be the more prudent path and he stepped forward, axe still in hand. "Lord Shezmu, I would seek a boon from you."

"Show me the proper obeisance, mortal, and put up your weapon in my presence," Shezmu growled.

Ahanu's amber eyes narrowed. "I cannot do as you ask, Lord. I am, as you say, a warrior, and like yourself, must remain true to my nature." He tensed, trying to read Shezmu's inscrutable features.

The barest ripple of movement alerted Ahanu to dive forward. Shezmu's scythe flashed from the gloom in a wide arc. The whistle of sharp steel cleaving the air hissed in Ahanu's ears, as he rolled between the giant's legs. He slashed, his axe blade biting demon flesh.

Ahanu scrambled to his feet, poised to strike. He cried out as Shezmu's sickle-blade opened a gash across his chest in a vicious back slash. The warrior grimaced, gripping his axe with both hands. The demon was *fast*.

The expected follow-up attack did not come. Ahanu breathed heavily, each breath stinging his chest.

"I cannot remember when last a mortal struck and spilled my blood." Shezmu gazed at his calf. Thick dark fluid flowed from the wound, pooling on the cavern floor.

"Do we continue our battle, Shezmu? I will fight to the end, be it yours or mine."

"You are bold." Shezmu smiled, lowering his blades.

Ahanu adjusted his grip on his axe haft, but still held it before him, confused at the demon's reaction.

Shezmu appeared satisfied with the impasse. He simply stood, watching. "What is it you seek of me?"

Ahanu relaxed, although he remained wary. "Lord Shezmu, in addition to your terrible might, I know you to be a great maker of perfumes and oils. I seek cassia oil."

"To what end?"

"To aid in the healing of a young man to whom I owe my life. His time is short."

Ahanu stood before Shezmu's fiery gaze, waiting as the dark giant contemplated. "I will grant your favor, little human. You intrigue me." The green eyes did not blink.

"I thank you, Lord." The tension in Ahanu's limbs eased somewhat.

"It is not so simple as that, mortal. A price must be paid."

Ahanu cursed inwardly, knuckles whitening around his weapon. "What do you mean?"

"You must enter into a blood oath with me. I may have need of such a mortal as you in the future—one who is both warrior and mystic." Shezmu grinned and his fangs shined in the torchlight.

Ahanu stiffened at that. He did not wish to enter a pact with this demon but did not see any other alternative. He could fight but was not entirely certain he would survive a battle with Shezmu. Even if he did, where was the cassia oil? He might never find it in the vastness of this cavern. Ahanu could not see he had a choice without sacrificing Rahul's life.

"You say your time is short. What is it that holds you back? Perhaps I can spur your decision?" Shezmu's smile widened.

Ahanu glowered, irritated at the attempted manipulation.

"I might know something of your mother."

Ahanu jolted as if a torch flared in his belly. He'd lost his mother when he was but a child. He never knew his father. The pain of growing up without a sense of mooring, of certainty, informed much of his childhood. "Do not play games with me, demon!" he snarled.

"Nokomis. That is her name, is it not?"

Ahanu deflated, lowering his axe. That was indeed his mother's name.

"I can see that you believe me," Shezmu said. "I will tell you what I *might* know and give you the cassia oil, but you would need to do a task for me at a future date of my choosing. But I need your blood to seal this bargain."

"How would you know anything about my mother?" Ahanu asked.

"I knew her name, did I not?"

Ahanu could not argue that. If the chance existed this demon knew something of his mother, what choice did he have? He had longed for answers to her fate; the mystery clung to his youth like cobwebs in an elusive corner. And time was running out for Rahul. He could not foreswear the boy's mother.

He sighed. Everything was transactional. The bitter realization of this revelation burgeoned like a fungus sprouting through damp, dark earth. "Very well," Ahanu said, resigned to whatever fate Shezmu had in store.

Shezmu laughed, a sound like rocks scraping together. "So be it." He turned, flowing like a liquid shadow. "Follow me."

Ahanu took a deep breath, following the demon through one of the dark mouths at the rear of the cavern.

~*~

The late afternoon sun cast dappled shadows across the forest floor. The black mare still waited at the edge of the clearing, chewing the bark of the tree to which she was tied. She whinnied at the sight of Ahanu exiting the cave entrance.

"Hey girl," Ahanu stroked his horse's snout, relieved to see the beast. The Sekani valued horses and he took comfort in the familiar scent of an equine companion after his encounter in the cave behind him. He carefully wrapped the vial of cassia oil, packing it deep in his saddlebag. He turned to the monstrous mouth of the Temple of Shezmu, searching the gloomy entrance for answers, an escape, something.

Fool! How else would a demon that beheads its victims exact blood payment?

Ahanu shuddered, as he recalled the glittering sickle-blade and bitter taste of fear when that unholy steel flashed. The fresh wound on his neck throbbed. He reached a tentative finger to the sacrificial cut, thinking the bandage soaked through, only to find it dry.

Ahanu mounted the black mare stiffly. His chest wound ached beneath the bandage, and he did not relish the hard ride back to Sama's home. He sat for a moment, once again checking his dressings. He had definite reservations about the congress he had entered, but he owed his life to Rahul and would see that debt paid. No matter what.

"Skan's balls, what have I done?" Ahanu muttered.

The sun descended behind the trees and the warrior breathed deep, grateful that time enough remained to bring the cassia oil to Sama. He kicked the mare's flanks, setting off at a gallop to Maniyat.

Ahanu did not see the emerald eyes that watched him depart or the powerful silhouette which flowed from the jagged shadows of the cave's maw. Nor did he see the enigmatic gleam that flashed over Shezmu's leonine face, hitching his mouth upward in a sly grin.

The Lord of the Blood padded back into his temple as the echo of hooves faded into the dusk.

Rescued

The Price of Rescue

By Teel James Glenn

Ada of Umbria was already in a bad mood when she and Donal crested the hill and saw the ambush in progress. "This is just the thing to break the boredom," the dark haired warrior said as she drew her sword from her back sheath. She kicked her antlered mount forward and charged down the hill toward the battle below with an Umbrian highlander's war cry.

"Ada, no," Donal called after his companion of many months. "Why can't we ever simply avoid trouble just for once?" The sandy-haired bard made sure his mandolin was secure behind him on the saddle before he reluctantly followed his barbarian partner at a gallop.

Ada was dressed in leather trousers and doublet with no armor, but she took no mind, charging directly at the half dozen armed bandits on foot that surrounded the coach. The coach driver and two out-riding guards were already dead on the road from arrow wounds while a single warrior was engaged in blade play with two of the attackers.

Ada rode into the knot of bandits attempting to overwhelm them before they were aware they were under attack.

She wheeled her mount to slam it into two then leapt from the saddle with a savage cry.

"How are you doing, old man?" Ada called in Thorangian to the lone defender who fought with his back to the coach.

"Better now," he called back. He was an older man, a dark skinned Amarian with long silver locks and a full beard. His clothes were of the Thorangian noble class but the sword he wielded with skill marked him as an experienced warrior.

Ada fought two thugs who were armed with curved swords and whicker shields and wielded her straight Umbrian broadsword as swiftly as if it was a dagger. In her hand it moved like a thing alive, warding and slashing. It cut through the shield of the first man easily but stuck in the shield of the second.

Before Ada could free her sword from the second bandit the first dodged in at her back.

Abruptly, that attacker stiffened and fell forward with a dagger hilt protruding from the base of his skull.

"Stop dawdling, Ada," Donal called, hefting a second throwing knife.

"There's more."

Ada smashed a booted foot into her opponent's knee, which collapsed him with a scream of pain. She finished him with a quick throat cut.

The lone defender at the coach went down to a slash across his leg, and as he fell a second attacker lunged a pike through is body.

Ada charged at the two who stood over the defender, shouldering into one and whirling to hack through the neck of the second.

Another knife flew into the chest of the man Ada had toppled before he could regain his feet.

The two bandits that had been on the other side of the coach came at Donal now, one grabbing at his doublet to pull him of his mount.

"Ada!" he yelled. The fact that his right foot caught in the stirrup saved his life because his mount spooked and bolted forward to pull him out of the hands of the bandit before the second thug could strike at him.

The Umbrian woman was on the two attackers by now and hacked both men down before they could refocus their attention on her.

Donal's antlered, four-footed vorn had been trained to respond to the bard's whistled commands and stopped its flight when the bard found breath to whistle loudly. He extracted his foot from the stirrup and rolled to his feet ready to continue the fight, but it was over.

Ada ran back to the fallen defender of the coach who was propped against one of the wheels, blood streaming from his chest, his right leg almost severed.

"The child," the man gasped.

Donal raced up to beside the two, his eyes scanning all around for more danger.

"You alright, bard?" Ada asked the blond man. The two companions were a study in contrasts—she tall, dark, and muscular; he barely coming to her shoulder and with a small-boned build with thin arms and delicate long fingers that served his profession well.

"My shirt is filthy," Donal said. He wore the remnants of his performing finery, having had to leave his travel clothing behind them. "And I'm just a little bruised. This fellow has the worst of it, for certain."

Indeed, the defender was wheezing, his face already a deadly grey. His eyes were still bright and he focused them up on the handsome, square features of the Umbrian woman. "You must take the child to the Governor," he whispered.

"Easy, warrior," she said. Her own blue eyes assessed the wounds. She looked to her companion and shook her head.

"Reward," the dying man said, "Take...medallion...sacred mission to the Governor at Fort Stalik. They will try to stop you—these... are not alone."

The two companions looked at each other and then up at the coach where they noticed for the first time a single, small figure. Ada stood to look into the coach and was surprised by what she saw.

Inside the ornate coach with the government seal on the door was the tiny form of a young girl in crimson robes covered with symbols. Her hair was stark white and her skin a deep tint of red. The girl was staring ahead, her tiny hands folded on her lap.

When Ada put a hand on the door to the coach the girl turned her head and the Umbrian was startled to see that the child her eyes pale green. The preteen girl's soft features split into a shy smile.

"Tell the Governor that Racktar did his duty," the dying man whispered.

Ada looked down at the man and said, quietly, "I will."

The man had just enough strength to hold up a medallion on the chain around his neck. "Go to Gov—" Then he was dead.

"Who are you girl?" Ada asked. The child reacted to the coarse voice of the warrior woman with a little shudder then spoke, but in a strange language.

"What is she saying?" Ada asked Donal.

"I don't recognize it," the bard said. He was going through the dead man's belt pouch, removing some gold coins. He looked at the tall warrior woman. "It's not Thorangian or Cozen. I speak those fluently. Nor half a dozen other tongues I at least recognize."

He and Ada communicated in Umbrian, a Highlander dialect, though his was accented, hers native. They had none of the Lingua-rings that would have allowed them to understand the girl no matter her language. None of the dead men were wearing any of the crystal translators.

"Well, its not Belisian or Avonian," Ada said. She stayed with the girl, alert for more trouble, while the blond man went from corpse to corpse, first checking they were not just pretending to be dead then riffling their pouches.

"Business for bandits must be slow," he said while he rummaged. "They have less than we do."

"We'd have more and our Lingua-rings if we'd been able to spend any time at the inn," she snapped. He had killed the wardens of one religious site and defiled the sanctum of a second in Dariak so the two friends had to leave the city with speed, leaving behind money and most of their possessions.

Ada left the girl then went to the carriage vorn and set about unharnessing the antlered beasts.

"You know we couldn't risk it with both temples looking for our hides," Donal said. He brought their own vorns over to the coach and looked at the girl who was sitting quietly, seemingly untroubled by the violence that had swirled around her. "This girl looks like the Cozen nobility—the red skin and hair." He tried a few words in his native Cozen and in several other languages but the girl just looked quizically in his direction.

"You were able to take enough time to get your mandolin," Ada accused.

"My life blood, dear lady," the bard said. "I was in process of prying up the floorboards to get to our hoard when the temple warden entered the downstairs of the inn. I was lucky to make it out over the rooftops."

Ada fastened a makeshift bit in one of the carriage animals and looped ropes to the necks of the three other vorns. "Well, we are still better off than when we entered Dariak. We have a couple of more mounts to sell now, and we still have more money left in our pouches than we did then."

"Plus, my brand new mandolin," he added, "as well as the few coins from these tvek-spawns. And this gentleman's young charge." He gave a slight salute to the fallen Amarian.

"And the reward he promised." Ada said. She opened the door to the coach and reached up to put a surprisingly gentle hand on the smaller one of the girl.

"Reward?" he asked.

"The old man there said there would be a reward if we get the girl to the Governor at Fort Stalik. It's only a few leagues away, toward the mountains. We were going that way anyhow." The warrior woman did her best to sound comforting. "We'll get you where you're going, girl," she said. "I hope you understand."

The girl seemed to, letting Ada help her down from the coach and smiling. The Umbrian then lifted her up into the saddle of the vorn she had ridden and adjusted the stirrups for the girl.

"The fellow also said there would be more of these sort after the girl." Donal leaned down and took the medallion from around the neck of Racktar, tucking it in his waist sash.

"So," Ada said. She leapt up onto bare back of one of the coach vorns that had had its antlers clipped and took a long lead on the mount the girl was on. "I can use the exercise.'

"I know better than to argue with you, Umbrian."

Ada led off up the road with the girl following, the carriage vorns in a string, and the bard bringing up the rear.

Donal unlashed his mandolin. "You keep an eye out, barbarian, and I'll sing these fellows across. At least her guardian deserves a hymn."

"By Zondra," Ada agreed, "he went like a warrior. You do that."

The bard drew breath and began to sing:

> *Legions of clouds above our heads*
> *Armies of grass that cover the dead*
> *Always the warriors left on the field*
> *Always the ones who would not yield*
> *Paying the tariff for those who move on*
> *And so we remember with this little song*
> *We praise the payment and those who gave most*
> *The brave and the valiant of the warrior host*
> *Who consecrate here this place that we stand*
> *This home, this piece of our sacred land*
> *With the red of the wine cup we remember your blood*
> *And the love that flowed like the late spring flood*
> *So know that your sacrifice is n'r forgot*
> *That the blood that you shed on this awesome spot*
> *Is a hymn we will sing of for eons to come*
> *Till the voices to sing it have dwindled to none.*

When the song was done, Donal noticed that the young girl had tears in her eyes, a fact that he indicated to Ada when she looked back toward him.

"There are times I regret saving your hide, bard," the barbarian said, wiping tears from her own eyes, "but never when you sing."

~*~

The three moved down the road with no incident until the suns went down. They found a defensible camp in a cluster of large boulders near a small stream. They also created a small remuda for the mounts; but left their two beasts saddled, only loosening their girths, in the event of the need for a quick escape.

"We can risk a small, dry fire back by these rocks," Donal said. "I think we'll need the warmth tonight."

"One of us should keep watch," Ada said. She took saddle blankets and two cloaks and set them out as a makeshift bed up against the rock. The white haired girl stood quietly watching all the activity, her expression stoic.

When Ada had laid out the bedding she motioned the girl over. "Come, girl, sit. Have some food." She offered some meat jerky to the child who took it with a little dubious eye till the Umbrian took a bite.

After Ada's example, the girl tried some and obviously found it to her taste, quickly wolfed it down. She smiled and held out her hand for more. She chatted in her strange language giving it her approval.

"Well, she has a healthy enough appetite," Donal noted.

Once Donal had the fire going, he piled up rocks on the side away from the sleeping area then stepped away to look back at it.

"Not very visible," he said. "We should be good."

"What do you think her story is?" Ada asked.

The bard crouched by the two women and took a piece of the jerky to chew. He noted that the girl was watching him intently. "I don't know," he said. "Some nobleman's daughter? Maybe the Governor's. In any case, important enough for that Racktar to give his life for her."

Ada watched the girl while Donal spoke. "I think she understands us."

"She seemed to understand my song before."

"It was easy enough to figure out," Ada said.

"Why do you think they were after her?"

"For ransom? Revenge?" Ada asked.

"And you think we are clear of whoever is after her?"

"Those at the coach didn't have any mounts that I saw," she said. "But they didn't walk there—and I can't imagine they would leave their animals completely unattended."

"So if there was anyone else left with the animals they might ride for help."

"I think we should be safe till at least suns-up."

"Still," he said, "I'll watch till both moons fall."

"Then get me up," she said sternly.

He smiled and touched the barbarian's cheek with one of his long, delicate fingers. "Nestle down with her then, and I'll sing you both a lullaby. I'll then find a spot across the way to keep watch."

The Umbrian patted a spot in the little sleep nest she had made and the young girl joined her.

> *When winds of danger from across the sea*
> *Through portals dark and cold*
> *Come blowing hard with death and pain*
> *Our love will not grow old*
> *As suns that rise and moons that set*
> *Eternal is my heart*
> *So rest my constant warrior*
> *And dream of Umbrian hills*
> *Of cups of sack you've drunk deep*
> *And enemies you've killed*

His soothing voice calmed the Umbrian and the girl who snuggled next to the woman, hugging to Ada's back as they buried themselves under the cloaks and blankets. They were soon asleep.

Donal made his way across a small clearing to a space between two boulders that gave him a clear view of the road in both directions and some of the area around. There he hunkered down and idled away the night. After the two moons fell, he waited a while before deciding to wake his friend.

He walked slowly across the clearing, but before he'd come within sword length the Umbrian stirred and sat up.

"Heavy footed on purpose?" she whispered. Her eyes were heavy from sleep but she had a dagger clutched in her hand. The barbarian eased herself out from beside the sleeping girl who was snoring quietly. "Moons fall was a bit ago."

"I thought about letting you sleep the whole night through but my cowardice won over."

This made her laugh softly. "Your consistency is a reassurance in an ever changing world." She kissed him on the cheek and tossed him a blanket. "This will keep your soft Cozen body warm—this weather is quite mild for an Umbrian."

He took it from her though he did not believe her and settled down for a few hours rest.

~*~

The three travelers were up at first sun with Donal rekindling the fire to heat some water. His plan was to make a soup of the last of their food with some wild herbs that Ada had found. The young girl seemed unfazed by the night on the ground or the conditions. She sat quietly and sipped the soup with no complaint.

"This is the last food we have until we get to the fort, girl," Ada said to the child as they packed up to prepare to take to the road. The girl spoke again but it seemed more to pass the time then to inform since, without the wizard rings communications were mostly guesses.

The friends mounted their own beasts and the trio was moving down the road by the time the second, slower, sun topped the horizon. Donal took the lead this time, with the young girl behind and Ada leading the string of vorns in the rear.

The nature of the countryside changed from gently rolling hills to more rugged and rocky terrain. The road became a slash through high ridges and cliffs. Ada and Donal both sat straighter, hyper alert for danger—it was the perfect spot for an ambush.

The bard moved a little further ahead of the other two.

"This doesn't feel right," Ada called from the back. "We are too vulnerable on this road."

He looked back to answer just as a dark shape sprang from a ledge above and slammed into his vorn, knocking the animal off its feet.

"Donal!" Ada spurred her mount past the girl a moment after the bard's vorn fell on its side, bleating in terror.

The dark grey shape that tore at the fallen mount was the largest tvek the Umbrian had ever seen. The four footed, beaked reptile snarled as it ripped the side of the vorn, but Donal's leg was trapped beneath the mount.

The bard tried to pull himself away from the ravenous beast but the man-sized tvek's weight was on his left, exposed leg while his right leg was trapped beneath the fallen mount.

Ada rode past the girl but both vorns shied at the snarling reptile and the Umbrian was forced to spring from her mount, sword in hand to race toward the bard.

Donal cried out with pain and tried to fend off the tvek using one of his throwing daggers. The muscular reptile had ripped out enough of the vorn's insides that the mount was in its final death throws when it turned its attention to the struggling bard. It tore at his kicking left leg causing Donal to scream in pain.

Ada leapt onto the tvek hacking with her broadsword repeatedly into the thick juncture of the head and body. It roared in agony and turned on her, allowing Donal to drive a dagger into the eye of the monster.

The tvek snarled again and spasmed as the Umbrian drove her blade into its spine to sever it. Then it was dead.

Ada frantically grabbed the tvek and pulled it off the dead vorn. "Donal!" she yelled as she saw the blood streaming from the bard's leg where the beast had savaged him.

She jumped off the vorn and jammed her body against it to try and push it off him.

"I'm not doing well," he managed to gasp. He tried to help her by squirming but was weak from blood loss.

Ada roared defiance and put all her power into lifting the vorn, managing to shove it off the fallen man. Then she pulled off her belt to wrap it about the thigh of the bard.

"Don't you die on me you silly Cozenite," Ada scolded, tears streaming down her face. "I don't want to break in another lover—"

"I hope my mandolin isn't broken," he whispered weakly. His color drained and his eyes unfocused. "It was so nice—deep sound."

"Who cares about your damn plunker—" Ada sobbed. She looked around frantically but was at a loss for what to do. The blood flow had only slowed but not stopped and she had seen enough battle field wounds to know it was a fatal one. "Oh Zondra, help me."

Just then the young girl pushed past the Umbrian.

"Not now, girl can't you see he's—" Ada began but the girl looked up at the Umbrian with a calm, serious expression that quieted her.

The girl began to speak in a strange tongue and placed her hand on the bard's leg, his spurting blood bathing her forearms red.

Donal gasped and jerked at the touch of the tiny hands. A blue glow began to emanate from the girl's fingers and a chill spread from the site of the wound up his whole body.

Ada felt that chill and she involuntarily backed away from the girl.

"What wizardry is this?" the Umbrian murmured.

Donal moaned, his body twitching once, then he was still.

"What did you do to him, girl?" Ada said threateningly. The white haired child looked at her with a weary sigh and pointed to the leg. The blood had stopped flowing and as Ada watched the edges of the torn flesh began to knit back together.

The Umbrian leaned in to touch Donal's forehead and found it cool, then put a finger to his throat and found a steady pulse. When she turned back to the girl the child had lain down by the vorn and was deep asleep.

In a moment, Donal coughed and jerked and his eyes flew open. "Ada!" he gasped.

The barbarian wiped tears from her eyes and leaned over him to hug him to her.

"What happened," he asked when she released him. He reached down to feel his leg. "The wound—it's healed. Like it never happened."

Ada motioned to the sleeping girl. "She used 'craft."

"Now we know why those bandits wanted her."

Donal was too weak to move. "I'm really hungry," he said.

"No wonder," Ada said. "You've only had jerky for two days and lifting vorns is work."

"You're the one who lifted it."

"Don't argue with me," she said, "or I'll put it back." She took time to cut strips from the dead vorn and quickly built a fire to roast them. She left him to rest, which he did, closing his eyes.

While the food cooked and the other two slept Ada transferred the saddle to one of the coach vorns to be ready to leave.

In a short time the smell of the cooked meat seemed to revive the child who sat up and stretched like any casual sleeper. Donal opened his eyes soon after.

The three of them ate the gamey meat with more relish than the quality of it would normally allow. The young girl did not seem to mind the chewy food and smiled when she was done.

"We should rest longer, you are still not strong enough to ride," Ada said as the three of them remounted to continue their journey. She had resumed lead of the trio with added vigilance while an unsteady Donal swayed in the saddle.

"No," he insisted, "the more we linger the greater the danger. I will be able to handle this."

"We stop when you need it," the Umbrian said.

"I can take it if she can," Donal countered.

"This child seems unbothered by anything," Ada said. "She could almost be Umbrian by her demeanor," she added with a smile.

They came out of a rugged pass to a wide field and stopped. Across the flat space were three riders arrayed across the road. They had obviously been waiting for them.

"This is it," Ada said as Donal drew his mount up beside hers. "This is why they didn't attack sooner, they knew we'd have to come this way and must have found a way to get ahead of us…"

"The fort is just beyond that treeline—I can see the cook smoke,"

Donal said. "This will be their last chance." He checked his mandolin to be sure it was secure but noticed Ada rolling her eyes when he did so.

"No," she said in no uncertain terms. "Put the girl up with you, I'll take my vorn." She dismounted and held up her hands to the girl. "Come girl," she said, "I'll need the saddle to maneuver—and I want a real mount, not one of these carriage beasts."

The child seemed to understand what was going on and offered no resistance as she was carried and placed in front of the bard on his saddle. She spoke animatedly at the two friends but they ignored her.

"I promised to get her to the fort," Ada said. "If I can't—"

"I know," he said. "I will make sure you keep your promise, but I'd rather you did it yourself."

She hopped into the saddle of her own vorn and drew her sword. "So would I," she said. "I want to hear more of your songs, bard."

"I'll compose a ballad about this fight then," he said, "to sing to you when you're finished playing." This got a smile from her and she kicked her mount forward.

Donal held the girl tightly as they watched Ada charge across the field with a war cry, her sword whirling as if thirsty for enemy blood.

The three mounted men drew their own blades and the battle was engaged.

~*~

The warrior rode with sword in hand
The enemy was strong
But the Umbrian maid was fearless
So the battle was not long.

"In fact, it was barely long enough for me to compose this song," Donal said as they rode up to the gates of the palisaded Fort Stalik. Ada was still flushed with the excitement of the short combat, her skill on vornback and her sword having taken the first two out without difficulty. She'd fought the last on the ground and that too ended quickly.

The girl said nothing, her serene face stoic as they called to the captain of the guard who they were and their mission. Donal held up the medallion he'd taken from Racktar and they dismounted, leaving their beasts in a corral outside the fort. They were ushered into the private chambers of the province ruler, Governor Ettol.

The Governor was a former soldier and though in his fifties still had the bearing of a warrior, fierce and proud with a full black beard but not one scrap of hair on his head. "What's all this?" he said in a booming voice. He wore a Lingua-ring but spoke in Thorangian regardless. He moved to stand before the three visitors, looming over the young girl who stared back at him with unswerving eyes.

Donal handed him the medallion and explained all that had happened since the ambush.

The bald Governor listened with knitted brow and a grim expression. "Racktar was an old companion of the marches, he will be missed." He called out to the two guards in the room. "See to this child," he said. "Then we will celebrate that my old friend has once more done his duty to make us proud."

At a gesture, two uniformed guards stepped in and roughly grabbed the girl by her arms and bound her hands behind her.

"What is this?" Ada asked in confusion.

"This girl is the priestess-daughter of the leader of that rebellious scum from the Jorandor cult!" the Governor declared. "When we hang her head on a pike outside the walls they'll know we will not be disobeyed."

The child made only a slight whimpering sound as the two guards grabbed her but otherwise kept her gaze steadily locked with the Governor's.

Ada looked to Donal who nodded grimly, but with full understanding.

What happened next was between eye blinks. Ada drew her dagger and sliced through Ettol's throat before he could cry out. Donal drove both is knives into the two guards at the base of their skulls, dropping them instantly.

Ada cut the Lingua-ring off of the dead Governor's finger and donned it.

"We had no idea," the Umbrian said as she removed the bonds from the girl's wrists.

"I know," the child said. "The God Jorandor knows that we are imperfect beings."

"We did not mean to kill your people."

"Yes, you did," the girl said. "But not with malice, you thought your act was charity."

Donal took a Lingua-ring from one of the dead guards, making sure the door was barred from within. "We will have to slip out of here, get to the vorns and ride hard."

"I gave my word to Racktar to get you here," Ada said. "I now give you my oath I will return you to your people or die in the attempt."

"And will be blessed for it," the girl said. "You will also have my gratitude."

Donal searched the room and found a small stock of food that he bundled into a sack. He also found a door behind a wall hanging that lead to a tunnel descending via some steps. "This has to be his escape way," he said. "I know from experience that these nobles always leave themselves a back way out of trouble."

"It's our back way then as well," Ada said with renewed hope. "If we move fast we can steal our mounts from the corral outside the wall before they realize anything is amiss here." She took a torch from the wall and, after spilling some lamp oil on the wooden floor, set it alight. "This may keep them busy and give us time to escape."

"What is your name, girl?" Donal asked as they ducked through the entrance to the tunnel.

"I am Elondra, daughter of Vokus, Avatar of Jorandor."

"Well, Elondra," Donal said. "Welcome to the care of Donal and Ada once more. And don't worry, we've become experienced in this sort of thing."

"Running away from self-made disasters?" Ada mocked. "Yes we are getting quite used to it."

"No one I'd rather make disasters with, barbarian, than you," he said with a grin.

"By Zondra," she said. "I agree."

In the Vault of Bezalel

The Vault of Bezalel

By Tom Doolan

The raven-haired youth left the drinking haunt alone. His broad shoulders and deep, chain-encased chest made him blend somewhat with the rough-and-tumble mercenary crowd here, so he drew very little attention. Regardless, as he reached the edge of the building, he paused to ensure he was not being followed, then slipped into the darkness between buildings.

Liam was getting used to dark alleyways. It seemed endeavors such as this always brought him at some point to such a place. This particular night he had been handed a note by a barmaid, written in oddly familiar script.

Come to the alley behind this establishment to meet your royal destiny.

Cryptic though it was, Liam was more alarmed by the implication that someone knew who he really was.

When he had reached twenty seasons, his father, the barbarian king whose crown had come to him at the end of a bloody sword, had unexpectedly abdicated his throne to his eldest son. Liam had been trained well but knew little of honest conflict. Thus, his reign had been short-lived, as the wolves who ever lurked at the edges of his father's rule, came forth. Liam had escaped, with little desire to go back to boring court life now.

So here he was, skulking in a moonlit alleyway, seeking a stranger who seemed to know something of his past. This could either be dangerous or fortunate. Either way, Liam needed to know. And to deal with this one way or the other.

Whispered voices grabbed his attention, and he froze instantly. The alleyway became eerily silent, and for a moment, Liam questioned whether the voices had been a trick of his brain.

Sensing a presence, he decided to throw caution to the wind.

"Reveal yourself, and let us have our business done." His tone commanding.

Two figures leapt from the gloom, no battle cry on their lips, just grunts of effort as they sought to bring the former princeling down in a rush. Only his ingrained combat training at the hands of royal battle masters, along with a touch of his father's barbaric instincts, saved him from a short-lived career.

As a dagger sliced through the night air, Liam leaned away while bringing his right hand up to intercept. Though raised in royal comfort, Liam's muscles were as steeled as any man of northern blood, and the grip which took the assailing wrist was vice-like. He yanked the man off-balance as he turned to his left, bringing his first assailant in line with the second who was attacking from that direction. The shadowy figures grunted again, but in surprise as they became momentarily entangled.

Letting go, Liam skipped back, drawing his saber and dirk in one swift motion. Though his first attacker had fallen to his hands and knees in the exchange, the second managed to avoid most of the scuffle, and now leapt over his comrade. The long, curved blade of his Eastern sword thrust like a striking viper, and the princeling was hard-pressed to parry it. But parry he did, sending the blade just past his right shoulder. In riposte, he thrust his own dirk into the folds of the man's shadowy cloth raiment. To his credit, the assassin let out only a gasp between clenched teeth as the blade found flesh. Liam immediately followed with a slash of his saber. Like a reaper's scythe, the blade bit deep into the man's throat and neck, nearly taking his head off. The eyes behind the black scarf widened in shock, as his hand instinctively rose to his frothy throat. The would-be assailant collapsed in a silent scream, his lifeless hand dropping the sword with a clatter.

Liam was momentarily taken aback by his own work. He was still not as used to the grim task of life-taking as his father had often spoken of being. The hesitation nearly proved to be his undoing. The rustle of cloth in the dark brought the princeling around, and his instincts brought his saber up to block, as the first assailant bent his arm to the task. Blades clashed and all pretense at stealth was shattered.

The assailant was now maddened with fury, renewing his attack. Liam's initial shock was quickly replaced with the outcome of years of disciplined training, and each blow was met with a parry or block, as he rapidly gained the measure of his foe.

The man was not well-trained, his proficiency that of an armed brawler. These were not skilled assassins, but back-alley thugs seeking an easy mark. Liam's pride scoffed at such a thought, and he went on the offensive, riposting with furious attacks that soon had his foe reeling. Then, as he slapped his foe's blade wide with his saber, Liam's left-handed dirk thrust forward, and drove deep into the man's gut and upwards into his heart. With a cry, the ruffian went limp. Liam stood shakily, peering about for more danger.

"Well done." The voice was slithery and quiet, as if meant for Liam's ears alone. The prince whirled about to meet this new player, saber at the ready.

"No need for that." A slender shadow detached itself from a nearby wall, and a raised right hand was thrust, palm out, into the moonlight that illuminated the alley. The face behind the palm was narrow and set with sparkling blue eyes. His hair was long, pulled back into a neat tail that matched the ebony hue of his goatee.

Liam relaxed at the sight of a surprisingly familiar face.

"Gollof?" he blurted.

"You remember." The man smiled.

"Of course." Liam absently wiped his blades on the clothing of the two men he had fought, then sheathed them. "How could I forget the only childhood friend I had?"

"It touches me that you still think of me thus." He scratched at the beard on his chin. "Though we have both come far from those impish boys who ran through the royal halls playing at battle."

Liam smiled warmly, then paused. He looked down at the bodies of his assailants, then back to Gollof, his brow furrowing.

"Wait, you were there the whole time?" the prince inquired.

"Of course." Gollof smirked. "I needed to see if mighty Prince-of-old was still worth his steel." He absently smoothed his black leather jerkin as he appraised his new companion.

This statement took Liam aback as something in the words and tone spoke to him. He stepped a bit closer to the man who had once been a close friend.

"You sent these two, didn't you? And the note?"

Gollof's brows rose in surprise.

"You are as sharp as you ever w…"

His declaration was cut short by a meaty right fist that took him in the jaw, spinning him dazedly back into the shadows where he collapsed. Blinking away starbursts, Gollof stared up at his brawny companion in confusion.

"And now we know where we stand, old friend." Liam's disarming smirk shown in the moonlight behind his proffered hand. Gollof took the hand and was pulled to his feet. He looked into the prince's eyes and saw no malice behind the glint of understanding.

"Indeed, we do," the rogue stated, wincing as he rubbed his rapidly bruising jaw.

"So, tell me old friend," Liam embraced him around the shoulders as they walked casually from the alley, "what adventures are we off to now?"

"You ever hear of the ancient sorcerer, Bezalel?"

Liam thought for a moment. "The name does sound familiar…"

"Well, we're going find his crown and return it for a hefty reward to some fancy nobleman with more gold than brains."

"I'll try not to take that personally." Liam chuckled.

~*~

The torrent abated near midnight. The ragged pair had ridden for an entire day out of the city before the rains had begun. Another day under the deluge had them sodden and miserable. Yet they pressed on, Gollof assuring his taciturn companion that the minor augury he had paid the crone for had foreseen this. They need only ride until the rain stopped and then they would be at their destination.

Liam knew of these kinds of predictions. His father had employed a witch (reluctantly, by all accounts) for just such warnings and portents. King Boru had told his son that such things had saved his kingdom more than once. Liam's father had been a true man of the North, where magic was feared and often met with violence. So for him to trust in sorcery of any kind had lent credence to the claims.

The rain stopped with a jarring suddenness.

The pair had been following the remnants of an old road since late afternoon. Gollof had lit a hooded lamp after nightfall. That lamp was now dimming, its fuel near exhausted. This seemed to please the rogue as he grinned back at his companion.

"This is also a sign," he stated. "'When the blackest part of the night darkens more, you shall find the way,' the crone said. Our lantern grows dark, deepening the midnight further." Gollof dismounted. "Come, there will be a ruin nearby, long buried."

Foreboding trees surrounded the remnants of the road, barely visible in the dying light. In the gloom, the shadows beneath the trees were darker. Tying his horse to a low-hanging branch by feel alone, the prince slowly slid his saber free, and extended it out before him at eye-level as he moved forward. Suddenly the blade clinked softly against rock.

"Here," he stated, his voice uncomfortably loud in the night. Gollof, his lantern ominously dim, approached and stood next to his young friend.

The rock Liam had encountered was revealed to be a wall of ancient design. The cut and worked stones were half-buried in creeping vegetation. Following the wall to their left, they found an archway. Liam took the lantern, holding it forth with his left hand, his saber gripped firmly in his right, and stepped through.

His first step was met with wet leaves, but beyond that they were dry and crunched uncomfortably loud beneath his steps. Cringing slightly, he stopped and listened. There was no sound beyond what he'd made, not even the natural rustling of scurrying vermin he had expected. It was an unnatural quiet, and it set the hairs on his nape standing.

Liam let out the breath he hadn't realized he was holding and inspected his surroundings. Satisfied that there was no immediate danger, he turned back to Gollof, who had remained outside the archway.

"There is a roof here," the prince said, moving towards his companion. "We should make camp and dry our clothes. When the morning light comes, we will be able to see better."

Within a short period, the horses had been tied nearby and unsaddled. Their gear was brought into the alcove, and Liam cleared a space, revealing a stone floor beneath a heavy layer of leaves and detritus. Gathering what fuel he could find, he soon had a small fire going, bringing welcome light and warmth to their surroundings.

They were in a small antechamber, as the firelight revealed a closed door opposite the archway. The chamber was circular, the walls of the same worked stone as the outside.

Gollof's first instinct was to inspect the door. Satisfied that it would not open easily, he turned back to the fire where Liam was spreading his cloak to dry.

"As you say, when first light comes, we can better see what we have before us." He moved to spread his own cloak. "We should sleep well, but sleep light, my friend. I feel there is something beyond that portal that will demand our full attention."

"Indeed." Liam eyed the portal warily before bedding himself down.

As the pair supped on dried beef washed down with watered wine, a thought occurred to him. "How did you know I would be in that tavern?"

"I didn't." Gollof chuckled. "I went in there looking to find a simple mercenary to accompany me here. Imagine my surprise when I saw your face." He met Liam's gaze. "I never forgot the kindness you showed to a lowly soldier's son. Nor did I forget the strong sword arm our great king bred into his son." Gollof grinned. "It seemed the gods had favored me with a double fortune the night I saw you in that tavern."

"Clearly, they favored us both." Liam sighed. "I was at my wit's end for what to do with my life. What little fortune I had managed to smuggle out when I escaped the coup was fast depleting."

"Well, if rumors I have heard of the artifact we are after are even half-true, that shouldn't be a problem for the foreseeable future."

"Yes, you have been frugal with the details of our little quest. Do tell."

"Not much to tell, really." Gollof propped himself on an elbow. "There are plenty of legends about this 'Crown of Bezalel' that have been retold for decades. Though they often contradict one-another on certain points, the constants have always been the location and the description. After months of gathering clues, I finally landed upon the location." He looked over at Liam mischievously. "I just needed some muscly lunk to help with the heavy lifting."

The princeling laughed at that.

"Well, here I am, old friend."

~*~

Tendrils. Purple, misty tendrils reached for him, and Liam could do nothing. Paralyzed with fear, his body not his own, he stood alone in the black as those deathly wisps of smoke coalesced into the grasping tentacles of something from beyond sanity. He tried to look around, to see if there was any shred of hope, of solace, but his eyes were fixated forward.

The purple glow behind the tendrils sharpened as it grew in focus. As the tendrils wrapped their icy chill around him, Liam was only dimly aware of his body being wracked with the chill of the far reaches. For the glow had taken shape. A jewel, the size of his palm, was mounted in a golden crown, held in place by the teeth of a fierce beast. It was a magnificent and terrifying thing to behold.

All existence seemed to hold its breath as the crown filled his mind. The tendrils were now probing his being, and he felt them slither up his spine to wrap around his head. He had the sensation of wearing the crown that floated before him, and for a moment terrible power flooded his mind with ecstasy. But it was fleeting, for a dominating presence came over him like a dark shadow from beyond. He tried to scream at the hopelessness he suddenly felt…

Liam jerked upright, gasping for breath. The images of his dream were rapidly fading, leaving a void in his panicked mind. He cast about the chamber, seeking for the tendrils that had embraced him. Perhaps it was a trick of his mind, but he would have sworn he saw them retreat into the portal at the back of the room. Liam closed his eyes and opened them again. There was no sign of the tendrils.

In the light of dawn, the fire was nearly ash, with a few smoldering embers that leant no warmth to the morning chill.

Gollof lay still, his eyes wide and staring. For the briefest moment, Liam feared he was dead. But the thief blinked and let out a long breath.

"Purple tendrils?" Liam inquired.

"Yes," Gollof replied as he sat up, rubbing his eyes. "And a crown," he added, his voice quivering with avarice.

"Yes, I saw that too." Liam stood, stretching the kinks from his body. "Part of me wishes to turn back, for that crown was a dark thing."

"But another part of you is eager to find it." Gollof stood, a sly smile parting his lips. "Welcome to the life of a fortune-seeker, my friend."

~*~

Their gear repacked and their horses fed, the pair turned their attention fully to the door at the rear of the chamber. Gollof inspected it carefully.

"Well, first of all, this door was meant to keep something inside," he stated absently. "The lock is intricate, but clearly can only be manipulated from the outside." He pondered this for a few moments, then retrieved a leather case from his satchel. Liam noted the collection of tools and slender blades curiously.

Gollof selected a pair of implements and set to work on the lock. His movements were small and precise, and beyond Liam's understanding. Within a handful of steady breaths, there was a loud click, and the door shifted. As the seal broke, a hiss filled the surrounding air with the stench of the ancient. The rogue put away his tools in short order, then pressed his fingertips to the door and pushed. The door slid inward for a few fingerbreadths before becoming stuck.

"A little help, my muscular friend."

Liam lay his saber on the floor and placed his palms on the right side of the door, just as Gollof moved to his left and did likewise. The pair heaved slowly, and the door slid back with some resistance and came to a stop. The rogue placed his fingers to the left side and pushed. The door rolled to the right with surprising ease and very little sound. Liam retrieved his saber.

Beyond the portal was a short passage that opened into a wide, circular chamber. The walls and floor were of ebony stone. The enclosing wall was interrupted at regular intervals by five alcoves, each housing what appeared to be statues of some kind. The ceiling was high and domed, but otherwise featureless.

The light from outside didn't quite reach in here, and as their eyes adjusted, the pair realized that the chamber was lit by an unknown source. It was a bluish white glow, as if someone had captured the light of a full moon and spread it throughout the chamber like a tangible substance.

The statues within the alcoves were dressed in ancient robes. They stood ramrod straight, their hands folded across the pommels of large two-handed swords. Their heads were unadorned and appeared to be bare skulls, with leering sockets that seemed to follow the two intruders. The statue opposite the entrance was too shrouded to make out any details.

In the center of the room stood a short pedestal. While Liam's eyes lingered on the suspicious statues, Gollof's attention was fixated, and he cautiously began walking towards the pedestal. Liam heard a shuffling sound to his right, and he saw that one of the statues seemed to stir. He was about to shout a warning to his companion when he felt it.

For a moment, the princeling sensed the tendrils from his dream once more. But this time they were more subtle. And, to his shock, they came with a voice that slithered into his mind.

Claim it!

Liam's attention was suddenly drawn to the pedestal, the statue forgotten. His only thought was that Gollof was going to get the crown first. An urgent need to prevent that overwhelmed him. He moved toward his companion. But as he approached Gollof, saber raised for a deadly strike, the urge abated somewhat to a sibilant whisper, and he became aware of what he seemed to be intending. Liam lowered his sword in confusion.

"Gollof..." His companion stopped and turned to look at him, confusion crossing his features as well.

"I hear it, too," the rogue said. "Something is in here with us...speaking to us...urging..."

"That is not all." Liam raised his saber once more but turned to face a statue that was no longer just a statue. It was a robed skeleton, nearly a head taller than he, stepping forward. The whisper became more insistent, though the words were now incomprehensible. The desire to get to the pedestal, still several feet away, became stronger. Yet it conflicted with his fighting instinct. For a brief moment, he stood frozen. Casting his eyes about, Liam realized that the other skeletons were likewise approaching. All except the one opposite the door. The princeling noted in that moment that it was different from the rest. It bore no sword, and there seemed to be a faint, purplish glow in the eye sockets.

"Bezalel!" he hissed, the name suddenly bringing feelings of dread.

The revelation became irrelevant to the moment, as the first skeleton lifted its weapon to strike. Liam raised his saber on instinct, catching the heavier blade full on. The force of the blow staggered him, as he took a step back. Rolling his blade to his right, he reversed his parry into an upward stroke. The thing was certainly strong, but proved to be no match for Liam's speed, and the saber caught it under the exposed jawbone. The curved blade bit deeply, but the bone proved to be made of sturdier than normal stuff. Yet, there was enough of the mimicry of life in the thing that it staggered back, grasping where the throat would be. Liam quickly followed with a series of strokes to the head and neck of the creature. Though it managed to parry the first few, the final blow cunningly landed on the neck once more, and the weakened bone gave way with a snap, sending the skull tumbling. The body staggered a moment, then crumpled into a heap.

Though he felt the urge to sigh with relief, Liam spun to see the next two skeletons approaching, each intent on his companion, who was now on his knees fumbling with his satchel Liam briefly wondered what oddity he would bring forth to save them before leaping to engage the attackers.

"Aha!" exclaimed Gollof. Liam chanced a brief glance over his shoulder to see the rogue clutching an oddly shaped glass sculpture that glowed as if it held a lit candle inside. As Liam turned back just in time to catch another blow from a skeleton on his saber, he could hear his companion begin chanting. The well-learned princeling recognized it as a prayer to Balaise, a goddess known to many as the Weeping Maiden.

Now contending with three skeletons, two were intent on his destruction, while the third shuffled across the floor towards Gollof. Liam was fighting desperately, slashing at anything that came near him. One slice managed to slip past his defenses, and Liam was rewarded with a staggeringly sharp pain in his side. An instinctive kick to the ribcage of that skeleton sent it sprawling, giving the princeling a brief respite.

"Whatever you have in mind, do it now!" he growled over his shoulder, even as he ducked beneath another heavy sword stroke from the other skeleton.

Gollof paused in his chant.

"Prepare to move as quickly as possible!" He quickly resumed his chanting, parrying a blow from the third skeleton with his long dirk. Liam saw a glow begin brightening the room from behind him. Gollof's chanting reached a crescendo, then was punctuated by a shouted word in the ancient tongue.

"Cover your eyes and move!"

Liam dove to his left into a shoulder roll that took him several feet away. As he came to his feet, he instinctively took a glance back just in time to see the glass sculpture descending to the stone floor. He threw his arm up just as the object impacted, shielding his eyes from the bright flare that accompanied the shattering of broken glass. There was a rush of air and the sibilant voice of Bezalel, which had never ceased whispering in his mind, suddenly changed to a scream of anguish and rage.

As the flash faded, Liam chanced to lower his arm and saw the remains of the three skeletons littering the floor. He looked to Gollof.

"What was that?" Liam asked.

"A gift from a priestess who owed me a favor." He scratched his head absently as he surveyed the damage. "Though I daresay the scales have been tipped in her favor, and that I'm now in her debt once again." He chuckled.

Liam turned towards the pillar. What he saw made his breath catch for a moment.

The pillar was awash in the glow of a golden crown, the image of which had been burned into the minds of both men the night before. It hovered above the pillar, and a sudden desire seemed to wash over the men as they each moved towards it.

He will take it from you. The sorcerer's warning cut through his hypnotic avarice.

Liam glanced at Gollof. The man's eyes were fixated on the crown, his hand reaching forward absently. Liam felt a sharp anger well up. The crown should be his! And he, too, reached for the crown in earnest.

Anger and determination etched upon each of their faces. But this gave way to surprise and confusion when their hands passed through the crown with no resistance.

No, it will not be that easy. The voice took on a more sinister tone, and their attention was drawn to the remaining statue, which had somehow escaped the blast of holy fire. Upon the brow of that skull sat the very crown they both desired. The purplish eye-sockets flared in intensity.

Champion me, and you shall have the crown!

Liam turned to his companion, but where he should have seen an ally, he only saw a thief waiting to stab him in the back and take what was his.

Gollof lunged forward, daggers appearing in each hand as if by magic. One thrust at Liam's throat, and he lurched back, barely catching the blade on his saber, and turning it aside before it could do more harm than cut a thin line on his neck. He immediately countered with a thrust of his own dirk to Gollof's gut, but this, in turn, was also turned aside by the man's other blade.

What ensued was a dance familiar to both men. Sword strokes and dagger strikes were exchanged, the air ringing with the clash of steel on steel, and the grunts and breaths as each sought for an advantage. Blood was drawn from several strikes, though none as fatal as intended. All the while, the purple-eyed skeleton watched the battle play out with silent eagerness.

In Liam's mind burned a desire for the crown, certainly. But there was something else. Something of his father. With each dodged or parried stroke of his blades, a rage welled within him. This burning fed into his arms with renewed vigor. Soon, he was barely concerned with the crown, only the destruction of the man before him mattered. It was an unreasoning hatred that might have shocked the princeling, had he been in control of his faculties.

Beneath the unreasoning assault was the mind of a well-trained fighter, and the saber lanced out with precision. For all of his rage, the blows were calculated. As Liam's superior skill overcame Gollof's not insignificant defense, blood was drawn from nicks and cuts to the arms and legs of the rogue. Yet, something within the princeling staved off the mortal blow.

Flashes of a childhood spent in the royal palace. Running through the halls, stealing food from the kitchen, even teasing young girls. All things that men recall fondly of boyhood. And ever at his side in these visions was Gollof. With that realization, came a bit of clarity, and a strength of purpose he sorely needed at the moment.

"Liam!" Gollof cried, as he narrowly ducked a saber stroke. "We must stop!" Their fight had taken them across the room, and now the glowing eyes of the dead sorcerer were just beyond the rogue's shoulder, mere feet away.

As Liam pressed the attack, Gollof was forced to give ground, backpedaling. Liam saw the eyes of the thing just behind his companion and friend. Feinting low with his saber, he drew Gollof's defenses low, then reversed his stroke with the dagger, driving the pommel of the weapon into the thief's left temple. Gollof was dazed and driven to his left as Liam's rage-fueled saber stroke came up to impact the skull with the blazing eyes. Liam's consciousness was assaulted with a psychic barrage of anger, fear, and pain, as Bezalel shrieked and lashed out. Liam's mind reeled and his body followed as he staggered away from the thing that advanced on him stiffly, its bony claw outstretched.

The violet eyes flared with malevolence, and the pain in the princeling's head doubled him over. He sank to his knees. He could hear the thing's feet scraping along the stone as it approached. But, try as he might, he could only lift his saber defensively in front of him. A hideous laughter rang through his head.

You are beaten mortal. And your flesh will make my flesh whole again!

Just as the thing's boney fingers reached his forehead, Liam's mind was jerked free of the creature's influence. Opening his eyes, he saw Gollof had managed to crawl over the rubble, and with his remaining strength, grasped the creature's ankle and yank it back. It wasn't much, and would surely have doomed the thief to torment and death. But it was enough to distract the thing from its intended target.

Liam's mind was suddenly flooded with an innate rage that had been suppressed by the creature's onslaught, and with little thought he surged forward and slammed the handguard of his saber into the back of the skull. As the crack of bone echoed through the chamber, the creature attempted to turn back towards the princeling and renew its assault. But Liam did not let up and continued to pummel the skull with all of his remaining strength. The creature faltered, and though he could still feel its efforts to subdue him, Liam found his resolve up to the task of resistance, and he let loose with all of his fury on the bones of the walking dead before him.

Only after he could no longer feel anything foreign in his mind did Liam relent. He found that he had grasped the creature by the neck, and now that was all that was left. The rest of the skeleton had crumbled beneath the weight of his blows and lay in dormant pile of fragments at his feet.

As the fog lifted, Liam's eyes slowly moved to the crown on the floor before him. The rage on his face gave way to the avarice in his eyes, and he bent down to retrieve the object.

Liam focused on the golden thing in his hand. It was just as he had seen in his dream. In the center was a great, violet jewel pulsing with life.

Liam stared into that violet abyss and felt those tendrils once more. But whereas once they were enticing, they were now filled with righteous fury, and a dominating will.

Liam staggered back, realizing in a moment of clarity what had happened. And in that moment, a memory from his childhood was brought forth.

He recalled the description of King Boru tearing the crown from the brow of a defeated tyrant. That tyrant had been an evil, manipulative creature, and his death would prove to be a welcome respite to the land. Liam had always loved that image, for he had held his father to be a paragon of righteousness in his youth. And now here he stood, his pose very similar to the image in his mind's eye of his father's triumphant moment. The emotions of the memory struck the tendrils, and they seemed to recoil from his mind. At that moment Liam came fully to his senses. He realized that the jewel, and the soul trapped within, was trying to claim him. In his anger at this, his mind lashed out. The connection broke with a shriek that left the princeling breathless.

As the echoes of that psychic shriek died in his mind, Liam looked to his dazed companion. Gollof stared back at him with a mixture of suspicion and fear.

"Fear not, my friend." Liam heaved a weary sigh. "The danger of Bezalel has passed."

"For now." Gollof stood and brought forth from his satchel a sack of black silk and velvet, its edges sewn with strange runes in gold and crimson thread. As he approached Liam, the princeling turned his now clearing eyes towards him.

"The crown," whispered Gollof, "put it in the bag."

Liam flinched, a shadow of his previous emotions flaring for an instant. With a blink he dropped the crown into the proffered bag and Gollof cinched the drawstrings.

They both stared at the bag.

"Another gift from your priestess?" Liam asked, his voice ringing deafeningly.

Gollof simply grinned as he placed the bag gingerly into his miraculous satchel. The thief glanced around the room.

"Well, that's disappointing." He sighed.

"What is?"

"In my experience such crypts often hide treasures buried with the dead. But I see none of that here." He thought about that for a moment. "It's as if this room was nothing more than a... trap." He eyed the crumpled remains of Bezalel, then shrugged.

"No matter. The payment promised for the crown should be enough." As they turned to go, the rogue winced from what felt like a thousand cuts across his arms and body, as well as the painful welt at his temple. He looked at Liam with a renewed respect, and maybe a tinge of fear.

Liam caught the look and chuckled.

"I apologize, my friend. I was not fully myself." He smiled. "I resisted the urge to run you through as best I could."

Gollof laughed uneasily. "And I shall be forever grateful." His smile faded slightly. "And ever vigilant to stay on your good side."

"Come, my friend." Liam gestured towards the exit. "Let us return to the lands of the living, where you can visit an apothecary, and I can buy you a drink."

"That sounds like the best treasure I could hope for right now."

As the pair had turned their backs on the room, neither saw the eye sockets of the ruined skull flare to life…

On Neutral Ground

By Nancy Hansen

The battle on the wind-whipped plain had not gone well. The defenders had been outnumbered from the outset. Yet they fought on, for what was left of the Dalibor did not sell their lives easily. Nor would they submit their realm to an invading oppressor who had no right here in the lush lowlands.

In the end there were only a handful left standing, unhorsed and clutching weapons coated with gore, all of it the thin, ice blue blood of the Ivari; hulking, pale-skinned warriors from the lands of high altitude mountains and creeping glaciers. The enemy gave their ululating war cry and charged in from all sides, spiked clubs and blades of flashing crystal held high overhead. The small group of Dalibor still living, many of them hampered by wounds of their own—a few openly tottering—clustered around their bold leader, prepared to defend the warrior scion of their royal house to the bitter end.

"With me; to our death, if the gods will it so!" shouted the hoarse voice of the tall and broad shouldered armored figure in their midst, sword brandished high. At that rallying outcry and forward lunge, the remaining few Dalibor loyally stumbled onward toward their enemy one last time, weapons raised and grimaces on their faces, for each expected to meet a brutal end. Yet none wavered in their duty to liege and land.

Just as they closed in, Ivari spellcasters came forward from the four directions of the wind and created a ring of air resistance that could not be crossed by those not of their kind. The defenders hit it hard the first time and then fell against it repeatedly. Though they struggled with all their might they were always repelled; in the end unable to do more than scramble back and reform into a protective phalanx. Their leader abruptly pushed through those good men before stepping forward. Baffled yet angry, hatred and mistrust blazed sharply in the flashing hazel eyes that were the only thing that could be seen within the fully-visored helm.

"Are you Ivari such cowards that you fear to face a handful of injured soldiers?" came the taunting cry. "Is this the best you can do—kill us like cattle in a corral, now that we have nowhere to run, no way to reach you with our own weapons?"

On Neutral Ground

An Ivari warlord stepped close to the rippling waves of impenetrable air. He was similar in appearance to his brethren, draped in roughly sewn together furs; though he seemed older and more scarred than most. All the Ivari warriors were male, and this one was somewhat hunchbacked, with translucent skin the blue-white of glacial snow and long frosted hair with the crisp sheen of an ice bear pelt. He was taller than the Dalibor, heavier of bone and muscle, with a protruding brow, wide nose, and coarse features. Cold gray eyes the color of lead stared down the armored leader of the Dalibor, and with big forearms crossed on his broad chest he laughed, showing a mouthful of curving filed teeth turning dark on the ends.

"You amuse me human, because we could have killed you long before now," he said in a sepulchral voice that seemed to echo up out of a cavern. His accent was pronounced, but he spoke with intelligence and forethought. "Though your people fight well enough for the weaklings that you are, we have decimated your paltry army. Your ruler is no more than a crippled child surrounded by housecarls, so your citadel will not stand long. Bow to us here and acknowledge our overlordship, and no more of you need die; in fact, we'll spare your kindred when we take your realm for our own. Your men will make good thralls and the women servants and breeders."

"We'll all die fighting before we bend the knee to your kind," the Dalibor army leader snapped, and raised the sword again. "Come test us now if you think us weak, for had the battle been more even, we would have killed most of you."

The Ivari leader smiled briefly. "I respect your tenacity even as I smile at your foolish arrogance." He turned to his own men and swept a big six-fingered hand out toward the trapped Dalibor. "Take them prisoner, we will have sport with them tonight," he told his warriors in their own guttural tongue.

The circling air slowly closed in, squeezing bodies and robbing breath from lungs until it became impossible to remain conscious. One by one, the Dalibor warriors fell gasping until they blacked out, their leader the last to go down by virtue of the armor. When the wall of air lifted, all their weapons were confiscated; handled gingerly by enemies wearing thick hide mittens. Ivari soldiers came to bind them and carry them off, avoiding any contact with the mail hauberks the lowlanders wore. They dragged the unconscious leader away by ropes, for none would touch the gleaming steel armor suit.

~*~

When they came to their senses later, one or two at a time, most of the surviving Dalibor men were groggy and weakened by wounds. One of the injured had died and another was near death. That left among the living only five soldiers in one enclosure and their leader in another. The five were forced at weapon's point to remove their protective mail as well as those worn by the dead and dying, all of which were hauled off at the end of long poles. The Dalibor leader claimed to need assistance with removing the more complex armor, so was released still clad in plate. Prodded along by two Ivari soldiers holding long handled crystal tipped pikes, it was time to stand before their chieftain.

As far as could be told with these glacial beings, it was the same male Ivari that had addressed them when they had earlier been captured. Now he perched on a boulder spread with wolf skin furs, a circlet of beaten silver with crystal points gracing his broad forehead. The chieftain glared down with an implacable expression.

"Bow before me and pledge your obedience, and I will spare your life as well as that of your men," the Ivari insisted.

"I kneel to none but my own liege lord or our gods," the leader of the Dalibor snapped, back straight and malice in the returned glower.

"Then you are very foolish! I think perhaps we will play a game now." The Ivari leader motioned and one of the remaining Dalibor men was brought forward. He struggled in their grasp in just his padded undertunic, braes, and tights, not even allowed to keep his footwear. "You see this pitiful subordinate of yours? We will disembowel him slowly, right here and now, unless you submit to me. It will take a long time, with copious blood and much screaming, and it will be as painful as we can make it; especially when we burn his entrails while he still lives. One will die thus for every time you refuse me."

As the two Ivari warriors held the struggling man steady, another came forward with a curved and very sharp crystal knife and a clay fire pot. The Dalibor soldier spit curses at them and tried to squirm away but it was little use, for the Ivari were incredibly strong. He was too weakened from his wounds to resist as they cut most of his clothing free and hauled him off to be tied down to stakes driven into the center of the clearing.

"What is your answer now Dalibor? Will you surrender all to save his life?"

"Don't do it!" the man screamed but he was silenced when an Ivari kicked him in the face, breaking his jaw and shattering several teeth that he nearly choked on. Painfully he turned his head and gagged up blood and tooth fragments that dribbled from the corner of his mouth. The Dalibor leader's gauntleted hands balled into fists.

The other prisoners who were still conscious enough to have some fight left in them seconded his cry, but were silenced by blows from their captors.

"Well Dalibor, I am waiting," the Ivari chieftain snarled.

The leader gave one glance over at the trussed man, who now that he was helpless, his eyes had begun to show some fear. It would not be his death that he dreaded most, but the continual torture that made a man screech in agony and beg for mercy. He was a proud warrior who had a family back in the steppes, a wife and three children, but what would they be told of his final moments other than he howled for his mother like some swaddling whelp?

The crystal knife held by the Ivari executioner was just a few finger's width above his now bared abdomen. All the men who had died these last few days had others to mourn their loss as well, but those left behind would gain some comfort from the fact that their loved one had fought to the end. These mere handful were all that remained of what had been a proud and fierce legion. There had to be a way around this besides surrendering!

"Give us a moment to pray together," the leader insisted, hoping to stall for time. "Then you will have my answer."

"Only a moment," the Ivari leader growled.

Heads bowed and arms crossed over chests, while the men muttered the hero's appeal to the guardian spirits of the netherworld, the leader took that time to think. What little that was known about the Ivari, they were strictly an elder warrior race and they respected that sort of strength in enemies. Normally they would have simply killed the last of the Dalibor soldiers facing them, and displayed Dalibor heads on poles before they stormed their enemies' citadel. But for some reason these few Dalibor had been spared. So there had to be another motivation behind the Ivari warlord's demands for a surrender. Perhaps then, they could be bargained with...

The prayer ended when the leader waved to the men to stop.

"What is your answer?" the Ivari chieftain demanded.

"I have a counter proposal, Lord of the Horde," was the polite but firm address. "Like yours, my people are also a warrior race, and they would all rather die here than submit. So I cannot be any less brave than they are. You seem to desire a spectacle for your kindred, so I suggest this instead: on neutral ground, I will personally fight whatever champion you have to offer—his blade against mine. If your man wins, and I somehow survive, then I will kneel before you and concede. But if *I* win, my men go free, with safe passage back to our land. My life is forfeit either way, so you have little to lose."

The Ivari warlord seemed intrigued by the offer. He motioned one of his mages over and they exchanged a few words in their grunting, gruff speech before his cold gray eyes turned back to the armored Dalibor before him.

"So you will remain our prisoner, even if you win this contest?" he asked the Dalibor leader.

"I will." The answer came without hesitation.

"We might decide to torture you instead," was the callous reply.

"As you wish," came the retort with similar candor. "As long as you agree to let my men go free."

"My Lady Serilda, do not deal your life away like this!" the Dalibor men called out.

The Ivari chieftain laughed. "My Lady?" he challenged, his big, ugly head hanging down between his rounded shoulders as he glared at the Dalibor leader with a toothy smile. "That is a female's title, if I am not mistaken."

"Yes," the Dalibor leader admitted, and with head held high, Serilda yanked off her helm, wondering why they hadn't taken it or her armor from her before now. Her dusky black hair, cut short and barely touched with threads of silver, fell in waves around her grim face. A thin scar from an old battle ran across her right cheek from ear to chin, and her hazel eyes continued to glitter with hatred. "I am a woman, and cousin to our monarch, but I am also a warrior, and I fight for my land. I fear not to die, for my people are reborn, as yours are not."

The Ivari leader was visibly taken aback, but he recovered his composure quickly.

"A human female of middle years who leads an army, and she a relative of the young cripple who now sits your throne. This could prove...

interesting. So be it then, I accept your offer," he said in the Dalibor tongue, and then looked around the assembly of his own people. He continued in their rough language, "Secure all the other prisoners where they can watch their monarch's woman-kin fight for them and die. She is allowed one weapon, but I want that metal off her body, be sure she has assistance with removing that this time. Our finest warrior will face her, he has never been defeated in combat. She will not have a chance to strike him for I will see he is anointed by our shamans with protective runes and oils. Someone bring me a drink so I can toast her courage, for her life shall be swift ending."

~*~

The Ivari warrior chosen to face Serilda was paraded before his enthusiastic audience, and his people called out to him with fierce pride. Even at a distance, she could see that he was the biggest male of his hulking race. He wore no more than a loincloth of some thin and supple leather, showing off a tattooed body lightly scarred from previous battles. His long light gray and black striped hair was wrapped tightly into a topknot. He bore one of their great crystal swords, with its curving sweep and sharply pointed tip. It was primarily a one-handed slashing weapon, but deadly in its ability to slice through flesh and bone. This was not going to be easy—especially since the Ivari insisted she could wear no armor, as their champion would not have that advantage either.

Serilda knew her only chance was to stay out of reach of his blade, but to do that she had to be able to see well and move fast. So with the help of a reluctant Dalibor she willingly stripped off her armor, down to the tunic and tights she wore beneath, keeping the tall laced boots she preferred for riding. She cut a leather strip from her gear and tied it to cross her forehead and hang down in back so that her unruly hair stayed out of her eyes. She now had only to choose one weapon of her people from what the Ivari had taken from her and her men.

She realized she might be better off with a battle axe to deal with the tough skin and formidable bone of her adversary, but the only one they had was short hafted. If she had to come in that close for a wounding stroke, her taller opponent would have the advantage with his overhead swings and slashing blade. In the end Serilda took up again her own sword—the sword of her father, legion leader and brother of the old king—the sword that he had taken to battle for many a year. It was the same weapon that had laid atop his tomb in the necropolis; until the Ivari invasions of this past winter.

That was when she received leadership of the men who went out to cut off the enemy before they ravaged their way to the gates of the citadel. In her father's lifetime its blade had been bloodied often with that alien ichor that the Ivari warriors oozed as they died on its length.

Now the sword was hers to wield, and she too had killed her share of Ivari with it in battles over the intervening months. With that in mind she'd trust it once more, though this time it would not be brandished in downward sweeps from a gauntleted hand on the back of a galloping destrier with steel-shod hooves, but upward from the ground, two handed and swung far more often. She knew she had to wound this Ivari before she tired, for while they were slower than humans, they had much more stamina. Once she began to falter, their champion would crowd in to press his attack. Such was their way.

To concentrate on her own thoughts, Serilda sat apart from her men, sharpening both sides of her blade from tip down with a hone stone. Back and forth motions, slow strokes, alternating sides as she progressed, it became a soothing rhythm. Human skin was far easier to cut than the hide of the Ivari, which was thick enough to resist all but the keenest edges plied with great force. Sharpening was Serilda's favorite meditation, and it kept her blade in good condition as well. Only when the Ivari herald blew a blast from the crooked horn of a mountain ram, signaling that the time of the battle had come, did she lay her things aside, and taking up the sword by the hilt, followed a guard to where an arena had been chosen for them nearby.

It was within a ring of stones, upright monoliths left by the elder races who first came to the area. That made it neutral ground, for it belonged to those of the past. Around the stone circle the Ivari had set torches. They stood in groups to watch, drinking their foul smelling brew and gnawing on roast horseflesh that had once been fine Dalibor horses; butchered and cooked over open fires, many of them already bloated and stinking at the time.

Either their kind relished spoiled meat or they were starving, Serilda was thinking for some Ivari did appear haggard and thin. As she entered the ring of stones, a background buzzing began as soon as she passed between them, they must hold some sort of enchantment. Whether it was natural or created by the elders she did not know, but she had little chance to think on it. The time of reckoning was upon her, and these were the last few moments for sizing up the enemy combatant, and making a plan of attack and defense.

The Ivari warrior she was to face was already present within, his curving crystal sword in hand and his face a grim and darkened mask of war paint. He had splashes of it across his body, making him appear disjointed in the shadowy interior of the ring. He flexed his muscles and the painted areas rippled. That sort of swaggering didn't impress her, but she knew the fighting prowess of his kind and their excellence with their own weapons, and felt a moment of misgiving before she hardened her resolve. With the first stars peeking from the darkening sky and the rise of the maiden moon on the horizon, the fight to the death would soon begin within the enclosure of stones. This was no time or place for negative thoughts. She let the seasons of intense training and battle savvy take over, and smirked grimly back at him.

The Dalibor were no cowards, not even their women.

Serilda studied her opponent's size and stance as she stretched muscles cramped from hours of endless battle and then close confinement. He towered over her, though she was a tall woman of her race. He stood at least a head higher and was far broader, with heavily muscled arms and legs. He was built like the unforgiving mountains he hailed from, and without the hunchback of his warlord, he would move faster, though not with the speed she had. His gray and black streaked hair proclaimed that this was an Ivari still in his prime, so he would be far more powerful than many she had killed previously. Though his blade was shorter and curved, his long arms had better reach than hers, so it would be a more uneven battle than she had hoped for. Their warlord had chosen him well.

Announcements were made introducing the contenders and the terms of the ritual combat in first the coarse Ivari language and then in stilted, accented human speech. Serilda only half listened, her mind working over the puzzle of the Ivari's ongoing attempts to conquer humanity. It was also curious why they depended so much on hardened crystal in their weaponry, for even their clubs were studded with it. Perhaps the Ivari had not learned to work iron? That was odd because their mountain fastnesses should have plentiful ore. Their crystal certainly was a tough substance for all it resembled the expensive glass in the Dalibor temples and observatories. Nary had a weapon of their making shattered in use, and blades kept a keen edge without nicks or the need for constant sharpening. Their sword hilts were of bone wound with copper and leather for grips. No iron or steel anywhere.

Something was tickling her mind about that, for when she had been taken to choose a weapon of her own people, no Ivari would handle them. That might prove significant, but for the moment she had neither the time to puzzle it out, nor the energy to spare for any more such in-depth thoughts. At a second sounding of the horn, the moon was well up and the battle was about to begin.

~*~

Serilda and the Ivari champion started out by circling each other warily, he with a snarl on his face, showing the usual filed teeth. She ignored the crowd sounds around her and his posturing while she watched his gray eyes for him tipping his moves. One thing her father had taught her was that most enemies primarily focused their vision where their weapon was going. Sure enough, the initial big flurry of slashes and parries showed that adage to be true, for the Ivari clued her each time by first noting where her sword was and going for an unprotected spot on the opposite quarter.

She darted around him, mostly fending off his blows while trying to get in one of her own, figuring that with his slower speed, he'd not be able to turn as fast. While that proved true, he was supple and long enough of limb to be able to strike with just a twisting of his upper body while his sluggish footwork shuffled through its plodding movements. His curved blade was lighter and thinner than hers, making it less wind resistant as it whistled through the air in complex arcs that had her backpedaling and dodging constantly, unable to do more than parry. That she managed to get her blade up each time was a minor miracle in itself, and when the crystal hit the steel, her own sword clanged as if it had run into a stone wall. Such was the fury of the Ivari hack and slash method, and they seemed to rely on it almost exclusively. This one must have been a sword master's favorite, for he was damnably fast with his counters and effectively mixed up those sweeping overhead strokes with cunning side cuts and returns. Serilda was hard-pressed to get in any offensive maneuvers of her own.

His people hooted and pounded fists on rock-like thighs when he drew first blood, tagging her lightly across her off forearm as she retreated sideways, his blade skipping over her own as she pulled away. It left a searing line welling red, which ran down her wrist to her off hand backing her dominant one on the hilt of her weapon. Serilda pointedly ignored it, because to even glance away briefly would insure he'd take her head off her shoulders. The pain she could tolerate, for she'd been injured worse in previous battles, but the blood dripping down was making the hilt alternately slick and sticky. She adjusted her grip on the fly and came in sideways with an attempt to gash his thigh, but he was already there; his blade hooked hers and nearly ripped it from her hands as he yanked upward. She managed to free it and came back with another cut, but he met that one as well.

Serilda retreated again, never going straight backwards but angling behind him to keep the Ivari moving. The tighter the circle she made, the slower he was in getting his weapon where he needed it, and with a quick lunge, she missed a kidney thrust but jabbed the tip of her sword in one big rock-like buttock. It was more of an insult and inconvenience than a crippling hit, but it drew blood, blue and thin. Unfortunately it was not a very deep puncture, so the muscles driving his leg on that side would not be badly affected.

The Ivari flinched and then let out a howl of rage as he twisted to come around the opposite way with a level swing that nearly caught her unaware. Serilda barely managed to elude that, but momentarily lost her footing and went down on one knee. He was on her in seconds and she was unable to do more than stave off his furious sweeps from her awkward position. He shuffled around enough to gain a more advantageous angle and she took that moment to bound back to her feet, sword up and out in a guard as she did so. He came in over her blade using the curve of his own, barely missing her face when she leaned away, and stabbed her dominant hand's shoulder with the tip of his sword. She was retreating so he didn't hit the bone, but it burned like fire and blood ran down inside her tunic as her arm went somewhat numb.

Serilda edged around him again, her instincts fighting for her while her eyes watched for an opening. She was frustrated, because her arm had lost some feeling, slowing her response time. She couldn't seem to get her well-honed edges to do more than scratch his skin anyway, though that single thrust had pierced it well enough. Yet she had killed her share of Ivari on horseback, mostly with well swung slashing cuts to heads and necks. It must have been a combination of being somewhat above on a moving steed that had facilitated those kills, adding to the force. Here on the ground, she couldn't garner the same results. So if she was going to end this, it was going to be with a well-driven in thrust.

He must have thought she was more hurt than she appeared to be because he crowded her to try and get inside her guard. Her arms *were* tiring from the constant parrying and the dominant hand didn't have the feeling for the blade that she was used to, but Serilda hung on by pure stubbornness alone, for she refused to let this big pale skinned ogre of a male take her life so easily.

She had already noted he favored the leg on the side where she'd stuck him in the buttock—the only blow she'd landed so far, and that simply a poorly executed thrust. It hadn't been much of a hit, but maybe she had managed to cut something important after all. She maneuvered herself to come up behind him, but he was wary now, and kept his blade moving to fend her off. He appeared to be increasingly hampered by that one small jab which was looking like it had already begun to fester. She was heartened by that, and moved in close enough to take another swipe at his thigh on that side. She narrowly missed the cut when he moved the leg out of range in a sudden turn. She barely came up on the backswing in time to fend off a vicious slash to her own midsection. Her sword tip subsequently poked him in the underside of the upper arm. That too drew Ivari blood, and he snarled in rage and came straight at her.

This was what she had been hoping for! She met him with a flurry of long crossing strokes of her own, keeping him at bay as she lined up for another thrust. He could not get his curving blade back up and around fast enough to keep her off him so she managed to tag him in the chest, but it was not deep enough to do much more than ooze a bit. She had to fall back yet again and get the point up to protect herself. He missed with a wild swing, but instead of lining up the edge for the next slash and leaving himself open, he came around hard and bashed her in the side of her head with the flat of his blade.

It was like being hit by a brick.

The Ivari crowd was jumping up and down with a thunderous sound, hooting and smacking their fists together, hoping for the killing stroke. Her men were groaning or crying out in dismay, even though Serilda managed to drunkenly stagger out of range with her sword still in guard position. She shook her head and spit blood from biting down on her tongue, trying to focus on where her opponent was. There was the roaring of a winter windstorm in her ears and her vision was blurry; the world spun, and she was just barely hanging onto consciousness.

"Let me..." she said, steeling her resolve for one last action, while desperately shaking off the vertigo and the nausea, "show you Ivari...how hard it can be to defeat a Dalibor!" As her opponent shuffled toward her, his blade at the ready, she launched herself at him with a growl of defiance. As his blade came down and around to take her head off her shoulders, she suddenly lunged sideways past it instead. While he was bringing his weapon back around she charged into him on the off side and rammed her sword point into his gut, right below the rib cage. Her entire momentum was behind it, and the blade went deep but stuck there and would not pull free.

She was a dead woman without it, but Serilda didn't care. She hoped the blow had done enough damage to kill him as well; for with that knowledge she would die content. She was shocked when instead of yanking the blade free, the Ivari looked down at his pierced side with disbelief, then dropping his own blade collapsed in a heap. To the dismay of his people, he cried out something in their language as his eyes went from leaden gray through darker shades to plain black, before he twitched several times and lay still.

The Ivari were all strangely silent, and while her men were cheering Serilda waved at them to quiet down. This was no time to gloat, for they were still in mortal peril. She was injured, tired, weaponless, and ready to collapse herself as she staggered back to lean on the nearest of the enclosing stones. It barely registered in her weary mind that the monoliths no longer buzzed with otherworldly energy, but felt solid, as part of her own world.

"Congratulations, witch of the Dalibor, for you killed the only son of my loins with your tricks and cold iron!" said the hunchbacked warlord at last, and when she turned dizzily to face him, his own gray eyes were dimming in the flaring of their torches. "I'll not spawn another like him. He was the best chance we had to survive, the last hardy warrior of a long-lived clan of the Ice Fae. We gave him every advantage we had left; the choicest of our meager food, the finest training and weapons, and all the females he could breed, because he was to be our future chieftain and repopulate our land.

"Do you wonder why we came down from our mountain fastness then? I will tell you now, for we are a dying race without him. We sicken more every year up there, as your kind spreads through this world, killing its magic with your prolific breeding and ability to use iron, which is poison to all fae kind. To survive any longer, our only hope was to conquer you red bloods and make you work this land for us, for the mountains now hold so little game, we can scarcely feed ourselves. Our females are barren, our few infants born deformed or dead. We have no hope left."

Even though Serilda was swaying on her feet with a mixture of fatigue and relief, the anguish in his tone was sorely evident to her. She was all too aware of her own injuries and her vulnerability to the potential adversaries gathered around her. Yet she at least was still alive and it seemed the Ice Fae leader was as good as his word, so she was free to leave. She respected him for that; she raised her head and met his gaze.

"You could have come in peace, and simply asked for our help. We've made treaties before with enemies," Serilda pointed out.

He gave her a searching look, but said, "The Ivari do not beg. Do you not feel the difference? All magic is now gone. You have won this world and now begins a new era, so I suppose that earns you the right to live while we slowly die off. We will go back to our own land and fade away as all our otherkin have. Humans will rule here now, for even their females fight hard to survive."

And so it was that the Ivari gathered up their belongings and tramped off into the night, back to their icy fastness in the mountains to await the inevitable. The last of the age of magic and monsters would die out as humankind continued its ceaseless spread throughout the world. That night and into the next day the few Dalibor defenders left amongst the living knew only a sense of relief as they tramped off afoot or were dragged on litters, back across the ugly battlefield of bloating corpses with a myriad of scavengers picking at them, back over the cold plains beyond, back to Humanity, where there were warming fires, food, and welcoming embraces.

Another victory was celebrated as the dead were mourned and the wounded cared for.

~*~

Serilda, with her wounds tended and clean court clothing donned, took herself apart from the festivities and the mourners alike. She tossed on a cloak and wandered outside, gazing up at the mountains so far away.

She stood thinking of cold iron and the trickery of humans on what was no longer neutral ground, hoping that this very costly war with the Ivari would buy her people some peace for a while. She truly doubted that, for the Dalibor were also a dying warrior race, and surely there would be other conflicts ahead. Someday, perhaps, would come that peace, though not in her lifetime. Not while only she and her crippled cousin Matthis were the last of her lineage, and they being notably short on skilled warriors. One of them must produce an heir as well, or there would be other challengers to the throne down the road.

"We are not so different after all," she whispered to the mountains, then turned and went back inside to play her part in the charade that was called leadership.

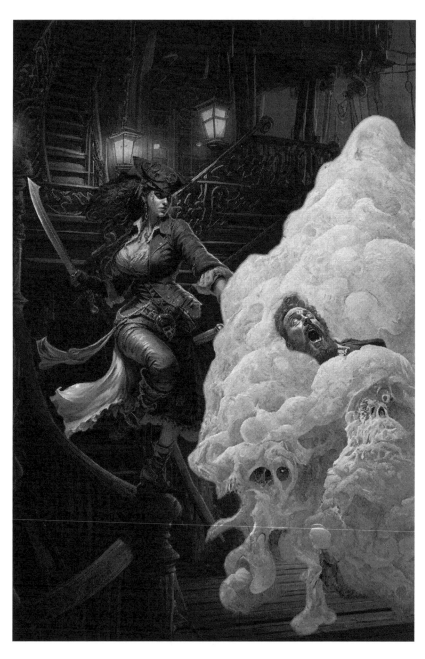

The Sea Witch Attacks

The Swordsman and the Sea Witch

By Tim Hanlon

Harkan the Swordsman regretted his choice of ship by the second day.

The Nabataean trader was trim and seaworthy and the weather accommodating, but the captain was mad. The man strutted across the deck on a search for the smallest breach to bring down inventive punishment on his crew. The sailors, for their part, watched him from the corners of their eyes and tried to vacate any space his rotund body inhabited. The First Mate, the mad captain's right-hand man and ally, was a gigantic Mubian ex-slaver who enjoyed inflicting the penalty as much as the captain enjoyed watching it carried out. By noon on day two, Harkan had seen two sailors summarily punished and he realised that it would be a long journey.

Things had not improved when he stationed himself outside the captain's cabin that same evening. Harkan could hear the man chanting and calling to spirits whose name the Nordman did not recognise. Still, the intention was clear enough, and when Harkan heard the crazy captain speaking in a language that seemed barely human, the big swordsman's hand went involuntarily to the grip of his ancestral blade.

The swordsman heard, also, sailors talk of missing comrades on their runs across the Soundless Sea. Experienced men disappearing unexpectedly. The crew would look quickly at the captain then shut their mouths when they noticed Harkan looming. The trader was known to be blessed by good weather, but it was not a happy ship.

Harkan, called Icebound for his northern heritage, stood at the top of the steps to the raised aft deck and watched. His time in the port city of Antioche had eaten into his store of coin quickly, and when Jameela had finally left him one rainy morning, the hulking Nordman knew that it was time to leave also. He had not had enough coin for the passage, so when the barrel-bellied trader captain offered him a berth in exchange for bodyguard duties, Harkan had accepted. To his regret.

The sun was directly overhead when the swordsman heard the lookout call. A sailor pointed behind the ship and Harkan turned to investigate. His eyes, unaccustomed to the distances at sea, could not mark anything unusual but the captain quickly joined him. The fat man raised his prized seeking-glass to his right eye and moved it slowly across the horizon.

"By the sea-god's left nut," the captain said.

"Trouble?"

The captain lowered the tube and looked at Harkan. "Pirates," he said. "You will be earning your coin soon, Nordman. I have a feeling that's the Sea Witch's ship in our wake."

"Who is the Sea Witch?" he asked to the captain's round face.

The man turned to look behind his ship again. "The most feared raider on the Soundless Sea. That is the Sea Witch. Some say she can turn the wind to always fill her sails. Of that we shall soon see."

Harkan had never heard of any Sea Witch but the look on the fat man's face was easy to read. The captain had a tic to the left side of his head and it began in earnest now. The round man turned to the belly of the ship and began to bellow orders. The crew, united under the threat, jumped to his commands. The fat man grabbed the rail of the stern-castle's ladder and descended without another word.

Harkan Icebound tested the soundness of his shield and was satisfied. Then he seated his throwing axe in his belt. He watched the crew scurrying to and fro and then sat upon a bench at the side of the stern-castle. The big Nordman took his sharpening stone from his belt and passed it across the edge of his ancestral blade, his face blank.

The fat captain climbed to the raised platform after some time; he carried a large brazier in his short arms. The man placed it near the rear of the command deck and struck it alight. When he seemed happy with the fire within, the captain closed the lid and secured it. He descended without acknowledging Harkan and began to bellow more orders.

A chase at sea was a strange thing. The following ship seemed barely to gain any ground and Harkan, in his ignorance of such things, imagined that they had escaped the pirates. Then the wind changed and the crew scurried to the lines, and the chasing vessel has suddenly much closer. *Perhaps this one called the Sea Witch does have the power to control the wind*, thought Harkan. He had seen stranger things already in his travels.

The down-trodden trader crew were still very good though—perhaps spurred on by the threat of death—and they had the ship's sails reset and the vessel slicing through the water quickly enough. Then Harkan the Swordsman heard a thunderous twang sound from the pirate vessel, like a giant crossbow had been loosed. He heard a thrumming overhead and turned at the yell of the rigging crew as the mast and central arm of the ship disintegrated into splinters. He watched what looked like a giant weighted chain spin off into the sea. The mast toppled slowly to starboard and the large sail caught the water and dragged the trader to a stop. Sailors jumped to clear the wreckage but there would be no headway after the damage sustained.

"Scorpion," observed the captain grimly without looking at Harkan. "I hope you know how to use that fancy sword, Nordman." He looked over the deck railing at the First Mate below. "Open the weapons chest. Ready those scurvy scum to fight."

Harkan stood, collected his iron helm, and placed it on his head. The Nordman had sold his ring-mail byrnie a while ago and sported now a simple boiled-leather cuirass. Still, with his helmet, body-armour and shield, and his indomitable northern strength, Harkan Icebound was a force with which to be reckoned. He drew his sword and stood at the head of the quarter-deck stairs and waited.

The pirate ship swung wide with the wind and Harkan watched its crew standing ready with hooks designed to lock the ships together in a deadly embrace. He saw, too, the pirate captain, a figure as slight as his own captain was round. The pirate captain pointed calmly, and the helmsman swung the ship's wheel. The pirate ship shuddered alongside the Nabataean trader and the battle was in motion.

The attackers swarmed. The ship's crew went to meet them and the two groups were locked together in mortal combat. Harkan knew there was no retreat here on the open sea. Victory, death, or enslavement were the only cards in his hand now. The Nordman watched the big First Mate swing an equally big axe and reap the swarming pirates, but then he had to focus on himself as the brigands began to climb the stern-castle ladder.

Harkan Icebound split the first attacker's head in twain as it cleared the last step, and blood and brain sprayed across the scrubbed deck. The second and third died too without raising their weapons, but more marauders were scaling the sides and Harkan had to give ground.

They were fierce fighters these sea dogs, but Harkan had slept with a sword in his crib as was the Nordman's custom and he did not countenance defeat. He cut and slashed and hammered with his shield and the pirates fell dead at his feet.

The crewmen of the ship battled on, but they were being overwhelmed, Harkan could see that, and so could the rotund trader captain. Harkan could hear the man cursing behind him, and he felt a sudden heat as the captain lifted the lid of the brazier. The Nordman heard a whump as something ignited and then a hum like a large bird had swooped above his head. The pirates before him paused in their attack, and Harkan glanced quickly behind.

The trader captain swung a sizable ball of something covered in burning pitch around his head on a long thin chain. The ball dropped globs of black goo onto the deck as it circled. Thankfully, they did not take and set the captain's own ship alight.

"You want my ship, Sea Witch?" yelled the fat man. "Well, it will cost you your own. By Poseitheon's balls it will!"

He swung the fiery ball of pitch around his head ever faster. Harkan Icebound stepped as close to the man as possible and said urgently, "Do not leave them no retreat, you fool." But the mad captain would not listen.

Harkan saw a slim, lithe woman swing onto the upper deck, a cross bow in her hands. She raised it at the captain and loosed it, but Harkan, on instinct, caught the bolt on his shield just as the fat man sent the ball of pitch sailing into the air.

The fiery ball soared across the gap and collided with the pirate ship's main sail. It left a burning trail as it rolled down the canvas and fell to the deck. Almost immediately flames spread to engulf the pirate ship. The slim captain, the Sea Witch certainly, turned to the belly of the ship and called, "Youssef, cut her loose before they both go up."

The fighting had stopped now. Harkan stood with his sword dripping blood onto the deck of the ship. Beside him the crazy captain stood at the brazier and Harkan could see his wild eyes. Burning pitch had fallen onto his head and fiery red welts dotted his skin, but the man still stood defiantly. The crazed captain rested his left hand on the brazier lid and Harkan could smell flesh burning.

"You are done for, Captain," said the Sea Witch. "Surrender."

The trader captain seemed not to hear the woman, though her voice was strong and clear. His eyes, a moment before wild as an unbroken colt, now looked vacantly at the wide sea. Harkan could hear him chanting frantically under his breath in that same strange language. The fat man stopped abruptly, and his eyes focused like a hunting hawk on the Sea Witch. He said in a voice high and fragile, "A curse upon you and all who sail with you, sea scum. You will not have my ship!"

Harkan saw the hand that rested on the brazier flex, and he knew what was coming. As the captain yelled, "I will burn it first," Harkan swivelled towards the fat man and the Nordman's blade was silver in the sun as it hacked into the captain's pudgy neck. The severed head flopped forward on a flap of skin and the man's body crumbled in on itself. The mad captain's scorched hand slid down the face of the blazing brazier, leaving a trail of cooked flesh as it went.

The Sea Witch stood with her crossbow dangling in her hand as she regarded Harkan. Her manner embodied complete control, one hip cocked as she rested her weight on one leg. Her face, smiling confidently, sported a horizontal depression as if her nose and cheeks had been broken and compressed under a violent blow.

She examined the fallen pirates that littered the wooden deck and the decapitated body of the crazed captain, and said cheerily, "Well, we could use a new man as our ranks have been thinned somewhat. And you seem to be bereft of an employer."

Harkan the Swordsman took seriously the giving of his word but the captain of the trader had violated the trust with his attempt to burn them all to the depths. He considered his actions to have been justified. He looked at the Sea Witch and the men clustered around her and then at the vast sea. "Why not," he said. "If I kill you all I'll have no chance of sailing this tub."

The woman laughed at this and said, "I am Tasmyra, sometime called the Sea Witch, although that does hurt a trifle. Men say I cast spells to turn the wind, but that is only because I am a better sailor than all of them. You may call me captain or boss."

Harkan slung his shield, bent down, and took a kerchief from the dead captain's pocket. He cleaned the blood from his blade and tossed the square of fabric overboard before sheathing his sword. "I am Harkan, called Icebound. I am an average sailor but will not begrudge you your skill, Captain. I will join you until I say otherwise, but I will not leave before or during battle. For those who play me fair, I see to the end."

"That sounds fair," said Tasmyra the Sea Witch. "Let us see what can be done about making some headway."

The survivors of the battle made their way to the main deck. There was but less than the fingers of two hands remaining, for the sea dogs had not expected the fighting skills of Harkan Icebound. This deck, too, was strewn with dead, particularly around the large Mubian First Mate and his weighty axe. The man had been mean of spirit but had fought until the end, his body marred by innumerable wounds. Two pirates grabbed the big man and tossed him over the side then dropped his axe onto a pile of weapons.

Harkan set to the task of clearing the deck while the Sea Witch and her helmsman discussed what to do with the damaged trader. It seemed that the strike from the chain-throwing catapult known as a *Scorpion* had been freakily accurate and wrought more damage than anyone had expected. The destroyed mast and sail had been cut away during the fighting and lost, and nothing remained on board that would be even a barely suitable replacement. There was only a small foresail that did not seem to Harkan capable of moving anything.

"So we are at the mercy of the vagaries of the sea," said Tasmyra, and her crew laughed ironically at what was a fact of their buccaneering life. "Pray for some wind, men, and we might be able to get this tub moving."

The Nordman found a place to sit and began to sharpen his weapons. Some of the crew glanced his way, but none were confident enough to test his skill again. The ship floated, marooned by a lack of wind, and as the sun went down a mist appeared to envelop the ship. The Sea Witch stood at the rail with her helmsman. Harkan Icebound crossed to the pair and waited until Tasmyra looked his way.

"Are you worried, Captain?"

The Sea Witch shrugged her shoulders. They were packed with hard muscle under her linen shirt for she was not a leader who shirked hard work. "The mist," she said. "To come with the evening like this. It is unnatural."

"Do you know this sea?"

"I know all the seas," the captain said. "And the ones I don't, Enzo does. This is just…strange."

She shrugged again and Enzo the Helmsman spat over the side. Harkan had nothing to add to the conversation, and he resumed his seat. One of the remaining crew who fancied himself a cook concocted a meal that was not the worst Harkan had ever eaten. A watch was set and eventually the sea dogs settled themselves down for the night.

Harkan awoke at the cry and splash, his sword immediately in hand as he rose to a crouch. The Nordman saw others standing or sitting up, but no immediate threat was obvious. The Sea Witch crossed to the port rail, her crossbow cradled in her arms. The mist had engulfed the ship, and visibility was not beyond the edges of the wooden deck. It lay low, too, so that people reclining were lost and those standing did not have any legs.

"Jakob!"

The pirates gathered their weapons. Harkan joined the Sea Witch to stare at the sea but nothing could be seen. "The lookout," she said. She turned to her remaining crew. "Jakob. Find him."

The sea dogs scurried away and called the lookout's name. Harkan examined where Jakob had been stationed. He crouched and rested his hand on the deck; it was wet and slimy to the touch. Harkan bent to the railing and found a piece of torn cloth, dark blue, wedged in a jagged splinter of the railing.

"Jakob's?"

"Yes," said Tasmyra. "He's too experienced to fall overboard in this sea. A survivor from the trader?"

Harkan looked at the mist-bound sea and shook his head. "We haven't gone far but that would be a lot of time to stay in the water."

"I agree."

Enzo the Helmsman joined them. "No sign of him," he said as he removed his cap and scratched his bald pate. "He jumped?"

The Sea Witch stood silently for a while. The sea lapped gently against the creaking ship, and the pirates returned to the upper deck. Their manner was subdued. "Set another watch," the captain said. "We will not find answers tonight. If ever."

~*~

The morning dawned clear of mist but the wind was still absent. The survivors languished in the heat of the fore noon and found cover as the sun rose. Harkan stripped to his breaches and found a nook under the quarter deck. They did not lack for food or drink, but the big swordsman wondered if the crew could actually die from inactivity. The mist returned as the sun fell. The crew settled but there was an unease among them; they tossed in their sleep and muttered into the silence.

Harkan heard bare feet padding towards him, and the Sea Witch settled at his side. She placed a torch and tinder box beside her and sat with her arms resting on her splayed knees.

"Sleep evades you?" asked Harkan.

"I have never seen the sea like this," Tasmyra said. "Not in these parts. It is…unsettling."

"The captain prayed to strange gods."

"His curse? It that what you mean?" she asked. "This is the work of vengeful spirits?"

"Perhaps," said Harkan the Swordsman. "The gods like to make life difficult for mortals. I cannot imagine that the fat bastard's are any different."

"There is something in what you say."

Harkan looked at the Sea Witch, the depression that marred her face pronounced in the low light. It was like a line of soot had been rubbed across her cheeks by a large thumb. At the front of the ship the lookout began singing quietly, and the captain turned to look.

"A memento from my time as a slave," said the Sea Witch as she scanned the vessel. "I left my master's head in much worse shape on the day I took to the sea."

The swordsman did not know how to respond to that, so he said nothing. He rested his sword across his lap and traced the design on the leatherwork of the scabbard. His father had embossed it himself, and the intricate swirls always reminded Harkan of his home.

The singing stopped abruptly. Tasmyra sprang to her feet and struck a spark against the torch. Harkan was beside her, and his sword grew red as the torch flamed. The Sea Witch strode towards the prow, and her voice rang out, "To arms. To arms."

The burning torch threw a circle of light that swept across the deck as Tasmyra hurried forward. She called the lookout's name, but there was no reply. Then, as the furthest circle of light touched the front, Harkan and the Sea Witch could see why.

The sailor was caught in a high mound of what looked like half-rendered fat, with only his legs protruding. These kicked vigorously as muffled screams squeezed through the diminishing opening. The sailor's torso could be seen as if through thick glass, his flesh melting from his bones and disappearing into the waxy mass.

"By the Red God!" exclaimed Harkan.

They were transfixed as the creature began to slide to the railing, the lookout still trapped within its maw. It was a faceless thing, a limbless thing, a thing that should not be able to consume a grown man in such a manner, and it stopped the two in their tracks. Then Harkan Icebound drew his throwing axe from his belt and sent the sharp steel head spinning at the monstrosity. The axe smacked into the transparent glob and with a wet tear it spun out the other side and was lost into the misty sea.

"Deeyako!" cried a sailor who had dashed forward.

The Sea Witch tried to stop him, but the pirate could see nothing but his friend in peril. The fellow had a curved dagger in hand, and he plunged it into the blob. The dagger and hand—and then the pirate's arm—

disappeared into the shapeless creature, and the man began to scream. His cries were not muffled like his friend's, and they were terrible.

The Nordman grabbed the sailor's other arm, and he pulled the fellow away. The man fell back and blood sprayed from his flayed shoulder. Tasmyra caught him as he fell, but where the sea dog's wound touched her bare arm her skin began to blister. She rolled the dying man onto the deck.

The remaining buccaneers, now two less, stood together behind their leader, and they watched the glutinous mass slither over the port railing, the lookout's feet the only thing visible. A loose splash sounded as it dropped below the surface, and the sea was quiet again.

~*~

There were six of them left on board the becalmed trader. They sent the mutilated pirate overboard with a few words, then there was naught to do as the day progressed but prepare as best they could for the night ahead. The buccaneers distributed the remaining weapons to all points of the vessel, but their shoulders were slumped with resignation.

Harkan sat with his whetstone and slid it against the edges of his war sword. The sound was sharp within the creak of the wallowing ship, and the sea dogs shot looks his way. When he was done, Harkan tucked the stone away and glanced up. The Nordman was preparing for battle, and the pirates could not hold his gaze for long. Harkan took the tinder box from the Sea Witch and climbed to the stern-castle. He set the pitch in the brazier alight and closed the lid.

"Are you going to burn this ship, too, Harkan Icebound?" she asked. "You seemed to disagree when the captain tried the same."

"This enemy is different," Harkan said. "And I will only do so on your command. We retreat here, Captain. Can you swim?"

"No. So, yes, you will not fire this tub until I say so. Although from what I saw, I do not think it will matter once we go into the water."

Harkan could not argue with that so he dropped to the main deck and sat and watched the sun descend and mist rise. Lamps were struck and the vessel was well illuminated, although the heavy mist still obscured vision. The men roamed the deck in pairs, and the Sea Witch joined Harkan in the lee of the cabin wall. She held her crossbow in her hands and a short, curved sword hung at her hip.

"What is that creature?" asked Harkan.

Tasmyra rubbed a thumb along the depression in her cheek. "Sailors have told tales of such things perhaps. Formless things that can take on any shape. A fish. Or perchance a beautiful woman. And of sailors disappearing, that is always part of it."

"And of how to kill these beasts?"

"No," said Tasmyra. "That never seems to be part of the tales."

The Swordsman laughed but it was more a guard dog's growl. "A Nordman does not fear death," he said, "but I will sit better in the Red God's hall if I take one of these things with me."

The Sea Witch said, "I will sit better if—" and then the screaming started.

It came from forward, and the two rushed there. The scene was identical to the night before, a pirate caught in the formless rubbery leviathan, but also now one lay on the deck, a lower leg gone. This was where the screaming came from as the man writhed back and forth, clutching at the blood-spewing limb. An imbedded naval pike slowly slid down the side of the monster and came to rest on the wood of the deck.

Tasmyra loosed her crossbow, but the bolt streaked through the mass and thunked into the wood of the ship bow. She grabbed the injured man and dragged him away, the sea dog leaving a trail of gore in his wake. Harkan stepped into the fray. The monster rippled like a breeze playing across water, and a tendril of waxy flesh leapt towards the Nordman. The big man stepped aside nimbly, and his sword smote the translucent tentacle where it tumbled to the deck with a wet slap. Harkan moved forward, but the sundered piece of the demon twisted towards him and the Nordman jumped away.

A pirate ran forward with the dead Mubian's giant axe raised, and the pale severed appendage launched itself from the deck, enveloping the man's face like a saturated piece of cloth. The pirate flew backwards, and his hands clutched at the thing covering his face. Wherever he touched, his skin began to melt.

Enzo and another buccaneer advanced then, and they both rammed sharp-headed pikes into the monster. It evinced no reaction; it had neither face nor throat with which to cry out, even if it felt pain. It slid quickly across the deck and the two men recoiled sharply, but a tendril flicked out and caught Enzo around the ankle.

The helmsman shrieked with pain. The Sea Witch chopped at the tentacle with her short sword. The edge parted the pale limb, but the severed piece sprang at Tasmyra's face. Harkan batted it aside with his shield face, and the rubbery flesh flew over the side of the ship.

The creature from the deep slid forward swiftly. The Sea Witch had her helmsman by the arm but the monster was quicker, and Enzo's lower body disappeared under the pulsing mass. His scream could have split an armoured breastplate. Tasmyra had to let her friend go as the beast surged forward. They had travelled vast seas together, her and the helmsman, but there was not a thing she could do for him.

The humans retreated down the ship before the relentless, formless beast. The first severed limb that devoured the sea dog's face suddenly sprang at the last pirate. He raised his arms to protect himself, but it was a flimsy defence as the amorphous killer wrapped around his skin. The pirate stumbled, overcome with pain, and the original monster split suddenly into two and engulfed the wailing pirate.

Only Harkan and Tasmyra remained; the riven monsters continued to stalk them. They left trails of pink slime and blood-tinged paths. The swordsman and the Sea Witch retreated up the ladder to the stern-castle where the two would make their stand against the monsters that could not be stopped.

Harkan Icebound went to the burning brazier and exposed the fiery pitch. The Sea Witch looked at him, her face dotted with small burns from the poisonous flesh of the beast. The Nordman's face was as hard as the prow of the ship, and the fire cut hard lines at his cheeks and brow.

"There must be another way," she said.

The Nordman stepped back a pace from the heat. "Then come up with it quickly, Captain," he said.

The two new beasts appeared, flowing over the railing to plop wetly onto the raised decking. Within each, fragments of the lost sea dogs could be seen. Tasmyra gasped as the face of her friend, Enzo, appeared pressed against the outer surface of the beast. His face was distended in a soundless howl that spoke of the pain the man had suffered.

The last survivors stood in a circle of heat from the brazier. The thing came forward, but it seemed to hesitate at the border of light. Harkan, desperate but determined, plunged his sword into the heart of the burning black pitch, ready to lever the mass onto the deck.

"Not yet," Tasmyra said.

At her voice a tendril shot out. She dodged aside and cut it from the air. It dropped to the deck. Another tendril came from the other side, and Harkan, on instinct, drew his sword from the brazier to smite the tentacle. The pitch clung to his sword blade. It was an arc of fire as it struck the lunging, translucent limb.

The tendril dropped to the deck and did not move. Instead, it shrivelled, collapsing into itself to resemble a bizarre dried fruit. Harkan crossed quickly, and his ancestral blade sliced through the blob the Sea Witch had recently severed. It shrivelled and collapsed also.

"Your sword," said Harkan.

Tasmyra jumped to the brazier, and she covered her own wide blade in fire. The two flaming swords turned the stern-castle red like a floating underworld. "For Enzo," she yelled as she brandished the fiery blade.

Harkan attacked the monster to their right and the Sea Witch was hard on his heels. It was not a time for finesse. Icebound swung his sword in quick strokes, carving pieces from the translucent beast. Tasmyra plied her short blade and sliced from the air any attacking tendrils and, in this way, kept Harkan safe. The two went forward and slashed and hacked and, finally, the thing to their right was no more. They stood within a circle of the desiccated remains of the formless, relentless sea beast.

The Nordman and the pirate captain, their skin scalded and hair smoking, turned on the remaining creature. Harkan raised his burning sword high, throwing strange, unsettling shadows across the ship. The beast did not come forward now but remained motionless, the face of Enzo the Helmsman still pressed against its side.

Tasmyra launched herself at the monster with a cry, her fire sword drawn back to strike. She was quick and focused but the sea thing, the formless slaughterer, was just as swift. It flowed over the stern-castle rail like a silent wave crashing and disappeared from view. The Sea Witch jumped after it and, this time, Harkan was in her wake.

By the time the two had regained their feet on the main deck, the leviathan was gone.

~*~

Harkan Icebound and Tasmyra the Sea Witch kept the brazier of pitch burning throughout the night, but the shapeless thing did not return. The mist cleared as the night progressed, and in the morning a wind sprang up and filled the small sail. They were still at the mercy of the deep, unforgiving sea, but the two survivors did not complain. Whatever lay ahead was preferable to the nameless horror they had hopefully left behind.

The Necromancer and the Long-Dead King

By Frank Sawielijew

Her hand clasped tightly over the deep gash in her shoulder, Ella stepped into the burial chamber. After countless riddles, mazes, and a deadly trap whose razor-sharp blades made her pay the toll of entry in blood, she crossed the final threshold towards the treasure she sought. The path had been littered with corpses. Many attempted the pyramid's beckoning challenge; few survived.

The burial chamber smelled of dust and old parchment. In small niches within the walls rested arcane tomes holding knowledge long lost to the libraries of man. Precious artifacts of glittering gold and jewels littered the intricate mosaic floor like discarded baubles. Lifelike statues and abstract sculptures alike guarded the corners of the octagonal room, the last surviving works of artists whose cultures had been swallowed by the sands of time.

None of it was of interest to Ella. She hadn't come for knowledge or riches, but a much greater treasure.

Revenge.

The long-dead king sat on his throne, skeletal arms resting on faded red velvet. His body was well-preserved for its age; scents of fragrant embalming fluid lingered on his skin. His desiccated flesh was dark and leathery. Shriveled lips pulled up to reveal the rictus grin of death, framed by wispy hairs white as the snow that covered Ella's home far, far to the north. His empty eye sockets were black abysses that seemed to stare back at her.

Rumor had it the ancient king was still alive, soul bound to his withered body by sinister sorceries. He amused himself by watching poor fools waste their lives in the pursuit of his riches.

Ella extended a probing finger to prod the unmoving corpse. As soon as her touch grazed his leathery skin, the king's hand went up and locked its bony fingers around her wrist. Brittle as his ancient limbs appeared, his grip was hard as iron.

His eyeless face regarded her with curiosity. It had long lost its ability to show expression, but Ella imagined to perceive a spark of amusement within the depths of his empty sockets.

She Seeks an Audience with the King

Her appearance must have struck him as unusual; her long auburn hair that tumbled to her waist in gentle waves and the fair complexion of her skin clearly marked her as a foreigner to these sun-kissed lands. Her thin blouse, colored light blue like the cloudless sky of morning – its fabric stained red where blood seeped from her wound – and artfully frayed tassel skirt the color of blooming lilacs were ill-fitting for a hazard-wrought expedition. The short leather boots and long cotton stockings that covered her feet were practical enough, but much too warm for this climate. She looked nothing like the adventurers that usually invaded his tomb.

She was no adventurer. She was the daughter of a northern merchant, lost and alone in a land of cowards, seeking help in the last possible place she could think of.

"What have you come for, mortal?" A cloud of dust emerged from the king's throat. He spoke Qarnahu, a language extinct for centuries; Ella had learned to read it from her father's books, but never heard it spoken. "Knowledge? Wealth? Power? – No. Something different it must be. You walked past all the riches a man could want and came to me. I should flay you for the intrusion, but you intrigue me. Like a blooming flower growing amid a field of jagged thorns, unfit for an accursed place like this. What do you seek from me?"

Ella looked into the king's eyeless sockets, wondering how much humanity was left in him. "Your help."

The silence of the grave settled over them. Neither she nor the king moved a muscle as she awaited his response.

After an all too long moment, his gravelly voice spoke up again. "You brave all the dangers of my tomb and approach me, Kaal-Hatharet the Cruel, Destroyer of a Thousand Cities, Scourge of the Four Corners of the Earth… to ask my help? Pray tell, young thing of vigorous life, what matter compels you to seek aid from a withered corpse?"

"My father was killed by a necromancer. I seek revenge, but cannot do it alone. I am a simple merchant's daughter. I barely know how to wield a sword, and sorcery is entirely out of my grasp. Therefore, I need help."

"And of all those you could ask, you chose a long-dead king asleep in his tomb. Wherefore?"

"No one dares oppose the necromancer. I sought help from sultans, knights, adventurers; all refused. I offered gold to mercenaries; they rejected. People are terrified of him." Ella stared into the king's empty sockets again. Where did his soul reside, she wondered? Within his dried-up heart, a mummified lump within his chest? "I thought you would not be afraid, so I came – and now I ask: will you help me avenge my father's death?"

Another moment of silence stretched long into discomfort. Sitting still, the undead king appeared like a regular corpse. Unmoving, unliving.

Ella flinched when the king rose from his throne, her wrist still enclosed within the ice-cold grip of his bony fingers. His bones creaked, the sound of limbs that had not moved in centuries. He walked towards a rack of weapons stacked against the wall, swords and spears and clubs that hummed and whistled as if singing to each other, and dragged her along. His gait was plodding and arrhythmic.

He picked a heavy mace of bronze from the rack of singing weapons and pushed it into Ella's hand. It was much lighter than it appeared. Its flanged head was of oblong shape, and sounds like a wind chime stirred by a gentle breeze emerged from holes drilled between the flanges. Like the head, its shaft was made of bronze, but hollow inside. Ella felt it softly vibrating under her palm.

"A fool once attempted to slay me with this," rattled the king's dusty voice. "It works well against the dead."

Ella looked up into his empty sockets. Even though she was no small woman, he towered two heads above her. "That is all?"

His bony hand rose up and pointed to the opposite wall. It was hung with shields large and small which hid the lavish mural that adorned it. "A shield to defend yourself. Choose which suits you best."

Instead of walking to the shield-hung wall, she stood and held his gaze. "A mace and shield – and that is all?"

Was it a twitch of amusement that came across his lips? No – a trick of the dim magical light that drew dancing, writhing shadows upon his withered skin, and nothing more. He stared at her for a long time, the depths of his eyeless pits yawning like a great abyss. No movement crossed his expressionless face.

But Ella was ready to stare him down. She hadn't come to be sent away with trinkets. She had come for an ally brave enough to face the necromancer alongside her.

"Stand not still as a statue, young thing of living flesh," the undead king said after what felt like hours. "Take up the arms I grant you, dress yourself for battle. I would not march at the side of one unarmed."

Ella's eyes lit up with hope. "So you will march with me?"

"When your revenge is complete, I shall have you flayed for thinking I would not. That necromancer plagues lands rightfully mine to terrorize. I shall delight in his destruction."

"Thank you, Kaal-Hatharet." She showed the long-dead king a smile, warm and genuine. "Dead you may be, yet the only man in these lands with a beating heart in his chest."

~*~

The toppled cart remained undisturbed, its load of exotic wares spread over the ground like a looters' buffet. The inviting prize remained here for weeks, but none had come to claim it. Only a swarm of flies hovered above broken jars of dried meats and fruits. The stench of rot crawled into Ella's nose; she grimaced.

"We were headed west, towards the sea. From there we aimed to book passage on a ship. As you can see, we were carrying goods from Tujjul and Tizarra – they would have fetched a good price in the north."

Kaal-Hatharet's eyeless sockets scanned the horizon. What he saw displeased him greatly. Where thousands of years ago a prosperous realm grew under his cruel but competent reign, now only rot and decay remained. Even the grass was brown and brittle, the trees withered and dying, and no birdsong carried on the wind.

"Here is where the necromancer slew your father," he stated.

"He approached us with an entourage of dead men." Ella's voice trembled. The recollection made her heart ache. "A man with unruly hair, a long black beard, and wild eyes that shimmered like gemstones in his haggard face. My father asked him what he wanted, but the man's reply did not come in a human tongue. I learned many languages during our travels, but I never heard its like before. The dead men leapt at our cart and wrestled with our horses. My father pulled out his wheel lock and fired…but the bullet did nothing. It struck a dead man in the chest and he did not even shudder at the impact. They tore out the throats of our horses and turned their attention to us. My father drew his sword, a good blade forged by the greatest blacksmith of Utrovik, our home…"

Visions of the haunting scene returned to her mind's eye. Five half-rotten corpses, their limbs still moving as if they lived, yet jerky and awkward in their motions. Five dead men who received her father's strikes as if they were nothing. And all she could do was watch as the dead men wrestled him down, unperturbed by his attacks.

"My father told me to run. I picked up his pistol and made to reload, but he looked me in the eyes and told me to…" Ella closed her eyes and took a deep, sobbing breath. "I fled like a coward and left him to die."

"There is no cowardice in sensible retreat." Kaal-Hatharet placed a bony hand on her shoulder. Its cold touch offered little comfort. "You risked your life to seek alliance with a long-dead tyrant. Such boldness is rarely found among the living. Had I sensed cowardice within your heart, I would not have chosen to aid you."

But why did you? Ella wanted to ask but didn't. The ancient king had his own reasons. As long as he helped her slay the necromancer, she cared little for what they were.

She pointed at a distant spire toward the horizon. "The necromancer's tower lies over there. I wish to raze it to the ground."

"So do I."

Without another wasted word, the unlikely duo marched onward. Their boots kicked up the dust of a dead land drained of all life. Kaal-Hatharet had cloaked himself with a long brown robe to conceal his nature from curious onlookers, but he needn't have bothered – no people dwelt in this accursed place; at least none living.

Far away as it yet was, his looming spire made Ella's skin crawl. Whichever eldritch sorceries he commanded did not belong in this world.

~*~

The tower drove its spire into the clouds like a screw. Its shape was a twisted spiral with angular oriels jutting out in all directions like unsightly warts that grew along the twisted façade in irregular patterns. No sane architect could have conceived of such a construction.

Ella's right hand was wrapped tightly around her mace; her left gripped a round wooden shield enchanted to repel arrows before they struck. It offered her a feeling of safety, even though she knew the necromancer would not assail her with mundane projectiles. His was a sinister art. No matter what cruelties Kaal-Hatharet had committed in life, they could not compare to the necromancer's violations of nature.

The undead king's touch tore her away from her thoughts. "Above," he warned.

Ella looked up. A swarm of featherless birds descended upon her, their naked wings restored to flight by membranes of cloth. They had long needle-like beaks and their skin was pale as bone. Ella struck them with her shield, and they were propelled away as if shot from a cannon. But more came, their hoarse squawks a cacophony that tore through the silent skies.

Ella struck at them with shield and mace, but some of the nimble creatures made it past her awkward swings. Their pointed beaks tore through her left sleeve and dug into the freshly bandaged wound she had sustained in Kaal-Hatharet's tomb. They drank her blood like hummingbirds sucking up nectar. Rivulets of red began to run underneath their pale skin, living blood coursing through their dead bodies once more.

Kaal-Hatharet snatched one of the beasts and softly chanted, *"Be still."*

The sorcerous life left the little creature's bones. Now truly dead, it dropped to the ground like a rock. One by one he snatched them up as they attempted to plunge their beaks into Ella's wound. One by one he released their tiny souls from the necromancer's service.

Ella went to her knees and slowed her hurried breathing. The experience of combat was taxing on her untrained body. Her lithe arms and legs were made for dancing, not fighting.

She touched the seeping wound at her shoulder and asked, "Can you seal my wound with your spells? The blood attracts his creatures."

"I cannot, for my magic is not of the healing kind." Something akin to a sigh escaped the undead king's throat. It was like the howl of the desert wind scouring the dunes. "Mastery over death precludes power over life."

Ella tore a few strips of cloth off her long tassel skirt and tied them around her wound. A certain melancholy flowed through Kaal-Hatharet's raspy voice. She started to wonder what it was like. "Do you have any regrets, ancient king?"

"Your boldness is admirable. In life, I would have executed one who asked me such." He raised a bony finger and pointed ahead. An eerie glow emanated from the tall peak of the necromancer's tower. "Yet for all the vile deeds I committed, never have I felt in my soul such foulness as emanates from this wizard's spire. Hurry, young woman of flesh. He prepares something unspeakable."

Ella nodded and marched grimly ahead. Kaal-Hatharet's urgency made her skin crawl. If even an undead sorcerer-king could be worried by the necromancer's conjurings, she did not wish to imagine the depths of their depravity.

Another flock of undead birds circled overhead but dared not descend. The bodies of their fallen comrades served as a warning. But Ella knew they were not the only beasts under the necromancer's command. Her heart pounded heavily and beads of sweat drenched the thin cloth of her shirt. She could not perceive the aura of vile magic like Kaal-Hatharet did, yet still she felt the wrongness of this place.

Whatever was happening in the tower the strange glow shining from its topmost windows only made it worse.

As they came closer to the stronghold, a cacophony of forlorn voices filled the air. They moaned and cried and screamed, but Ella couldn't ascertain their point of origin. Only when she approached the deep moat surrounding the tower did she realize that it was filled not with water but corpses. Their writhing limbs rippled like waves, half-rotten fingers reaching out only to sink down again.

The sight was enough to freeze Ella in place. Nothing had prepared her for this horror.

Kaal-Hatharet's hand touched her shoulder. It was as cold and dead as the hands that writhed in the pit. "Ahead, young woman. Fear not that which he has made. End him, and the necromancer's mark on the world will fade like mine did with the centuries."

Ella gripped her mace tightly. The long-dead king was right. She placed a foot on the wooden bridge that led across the moat and tested its strength.

It held her weight.

She crossed the bridge with confident steps, but once she reached its center, a plank broke beneath her feet and she slipped through the hole. The moans of the dead below grew louder, and the resentful hands of those condemned to rot in the moat reached for the living being above, eager to drag her down so she might share their pitiful fate.

Jagged splinters of the broken planks dug into the fabric of her clothes and scratched against her skin. Her elbows pushed against the planks to keep her from sliding all the way through. Her upper half stuck now, her legs dangling without purchase, she tried to pull herself up and out of the hole. Her attempts only weakened the brittle wood that held her. Kaal-Hatharet reached out to help her, but then the undead birds swooped down and rammed into him. A whole flock barreled into his chest and he fell into the pit. Ella watched him sink into the sea of corpses and cried out his name. "Kaal-Hatharet! No!"

But the necromancer's beasts left her little time to mourn. Corpses clad in rust-eaten armor emerged from the tower's entrance. They wielded broken swords that had long lost their sharpness, approaching Ella with slow, lumbering steps. When the first was within reach, she struck out with her mace. The flanged head connected with his legs, and the chimes that sang through its holes became louder. They resonated with his bones and made them vibrate with a lovely melody. Shuddering and shaking, quivering with song, the dead man's bones shattered into pieces. Ella grabbed her discarded shield and raised it over her face to protect herself from the flying shards.

But her movements made her slip down even further. The sea of limbs rose and fell in mighty waves as they attempted to grab her. Bony fingers scratched against her boots. The many hands fought amongst each other over the privilege of dragging her down. Some almost closed around her feet, only to be pulled away by jealous rivals.

The undead warriors above continued to march onto the bridge, swinging their rusted weapons against Ella with stiff, clumsy arms. She reflected their strikes with her shield and shattered their bones with her mace, but by doing so sank down another few inches into the hole whose jagged edges scraped painfully against her skin.

The ravenous hands below assaulted her dangling legs. They pulled off her boots, leaving her feet vulnerable. They tore into the fabric of her stockings, shredding it to ribbons with their sharp nails. They scratched against her skin, a hundred writhing fingers that felt like spiders crawling across her soles.

All of a sudden, their movement ceased. The dead men's hands retracted, sinking to the bottom of the sea of corpses. Kaal-Hatharet emerged from the depths, his desiccated limbs trembling with exertion. He chanted words of magic, far older than the ancient language he spoke to Ella, yet it didn't have the same inhuman sound as the chants she'd heard spew forth from the necromancer's mouth.

The undead king rose into the air until he hovered above the bridge. His hands ceaselessly weaved arcane patterns while his voice repeated the same incantation again and again. When he set down on the bridge behind her, Ella could feel the exhaustion radiating from his withered body; she would not have thought that fatigue could afflict the undead.

His bony fingers closed around her arms and lifted her up. Dead and cold as they were, they felt alive and warm compared to the hateful hands that had molested her feet. With his help, she pulled herself out of the hole and got back to her feet.

With Kaal-Hatharet close behind her, Ella marched forward, swinging her mace at the undead soldiers that kept pouring onto the bridge. She was careful to test the planks below her feet before resting her entire weight on them. The cheerful sound of wind chimes rang through the air as her mace made skeleton after skeleton splinter with melodious song.

Soon, the dead stopped coming. When she stepped off the bridge and felt solid ground under her feet again, Ella allowed her tired body to collapse. Every muscle ached. She had to inspect her feet for damage, as she could barely feel her wounds over the throb of exhaustion. Fortunately, the dead men's hands had only torn her stockings, not her skin.

Kaal-Hatharet sat down beside her. The same exhaustion Ella felt emanated from him, but it did not come from his body. "I am an old and tired soul. Grand feats of magic take a toll on the tenuous grip I have on this world."

"Then let us both take a moment to recuperate." Ella closed her eyes and took a deep breath. The stench of rot almost made her gag. It was a smell of death so very different from the dry and dusty scent of old embalmment she had encountered in Kaal-Hatharet's tomb.

The undead king rose from the ground, his ancient skin creaking like folded leather. "There is no time. His ritual is coming to a close. And I feel a familiar aura from his tower. I felt shreds of it linger near the wreckage of your cart. It is similar in texture to your own."

Ella's eyes opened in surprise. They shimmered with the moistness of soon-coming tears. "Father?"

Kaal-Hatharet offered a hand to help her up. "Let us ascend. It is a long way up."

~*~

With trembling legs, Ella took the last step of the spiral staircase that led to the tower's peak. Despite the warmth of these lands, the stone felt cold underneath her bare feet, colder even than the snow that often covered her homeland. It was as if this tower sucked the warmth out of everything it touched.

Although the ascent left her exhausted, she did not rest before swinging her mace against the sigil-inscribed door before her. The sliver of hope that her father might still be alive filled her with inner strength.

The door cracked and broke off its hinges. It fell inward, opening the way into the necromancer's ritual chamber. It was a large circular room with tall stained glass windows at the far side, depicting violent sacrificial rites. The intricate mosaic floor presented similar scenes underfoot, with glittering red gemstones forming rivers of blood that rushed from tormented bodies. Reality reflected the grotesque illustrations: the necromancer stood before a pool of blood, six victims tied to green marble pillars around it. They bled from countless gashes in their arms and legs, adding their lifeblood to the pool.

Ella's father was one of them.

"Father!" she shouted. His strength was quickly fading, but a smile crossed his lips when he beheld his daughter.

The necromancer turned to face her, his eyes bulging with madness. A sinister laugh passed his lips, seeping with malice. "The lost quarry has returned! Alas, too late to join your father in the ritual. But you shall have the place of honor in the next."

Ella charged at the dark wizard with a scream on her lips, her legs pushing forward with the last of her strength. The necromancer's hands performed uncanny motions as he muttered incantations in an inhuman tongue. From his palm a pitch black spike emerged, flying towards Ella at incredible speed. She raised her shield to deflect the projectile, but it punched right through the enchanted wood and pierced her hand. The force of the impact threw her back and the arcane missile pinned her against the wall.

The necromancer turned towards Kaal-Hatharet. The undead king raised his hands to prepare a spell of his own. "Many atrocities did I commit in life," he said, "yet never have I seen life be drained so callously. When I killed men, I did so for the benefit for my kingdom. But you—"

The necromancer drew a crude symbol into the air and uttered a word of command. Kaal-Hatharet lost control over his body. His arms, raised to weave patterns of magic, slumped to his side and his legs gave out from under him.

"I do not know your language, ancient one," said the necromancer, "nor do I feel the need to do so. While the body your soul clings to is subject to age and decay, I have discovered true immortality. Our world is filled with abundant life – and it is all mine to absorb! Behold as I rejuvenate myself once more…"

The necromancer rubbed his hands over a crystal orb mounted on a plinth before the pool. It glowed with sickly yellow light the hue of festering pus. He threw off his robe and bathed in the sickly glow. His body became visibly younger as the blood in the pool rolled like a stormy sea, waves rocking back and forth.

Kaal-Hatharet had exerted himself overly much when he escaped from the moat; it left him too weak to break the necromancer's grip on his body. But if the necromancer's mental focus were interrupted for a mere moment, the undead sorcerer-king could free himself from his arcane shackles.

Ella struggled against the black shard in her palm. She attempted to pry it off with her right hand, but it was stuck fast. Then she perceived Kaal-Hatharet's voice, silent as a gentle breeze blowing dust off an ancient tomb.

"Your shield," he whispered, struggling to form the words. "Throw."

She glanced at the shield that had fallen to the floor when the spike hit her. It was too far away to reach with her free hand. She stepped forward and stretched out her leg, reaching for it with her foot. A sharp pain stabbed into her left hand as it pulled against the thick spike embedded in its palm. She stretched her leg as far as it went, strained every muscle – and managed to touch the shield's rim with her toes. She scrunched her toes against it and pulled it towards her.

With heavy breaths, she picked it up and launched it at the necromancer. The wizard stumbled and groaned when it connected with his head.

It broke his concentration long enough for Kaal-Hatharet to regain control of his body. The undead king rushed forward as fast as his withered legs allowed and barreled into the dazed necromancer. The necromancer fell into the pool of blood. Realizing the mechanism of the ritual, Kaal-Hatharet drew a dagger from his belt. It was an ornate thing of gold and jewels, more symbol of his long-forgotten kingship than weapon, but sharp enough to cut.

A furious wail emerged from the necromancer's throat as the golden blade carved shallow cuts into his skin. His blood mixed with that in the pool, and finding himself on the opposite end of the ritual, his life force was drained into the spell. He closed a hand around Kaal-Hatharet's wrist and wrestled for control of the dagger.

But the ritual's progress was still in motion. The necromancer's body slowly lost its youthfulness. Deep wrinkles appeared on his brow and his wild black beard gained strands of gray. Standing where the necromancer stood before, Kaal-Hatharet experienced the opposite. The life-force collected in the pool entered his body and returned life to his mummified flesh. His leathery skin became supple and smooth, his wispy white hair grew thick and dark. Even the withered husks of his eyeballs, nested like shriveled raisins in the back of his sockets, returned into flesh.

The necromancer shrieked with rage. "Away, thief! Away! The force of life is mine to take, mine alone! I will not share it – never!" He let go of the ancient king's wrist and turned toward the pillars at the back of the pool.

Pointing his hand at a naked woman whose skin was pale from loss of blood, he shouted a magic word.

The ropes binding her to the pillar loosened and she dropped into the pool. Staring ahead with vacant eyes, she approached Kaal-Hatharet and threw herself at the rejuvenated king. The necromancer pointed his finger at the man hanging on the pillar next to hers and shouted again. He, too, dropped from his pillar and fell upon Kaal-Hatharet.

Ella observed the spectacle with growing panic. The necromancer was turning his dying victims into mindless slaves, their bodies mere tools to overwhelm her companion. She pulled at the spike pinning her to the wall with all her strength, but it didn't budge.

Another woman dropped from her pillar and joined the assault on Kaal-Hatharet; after her, another man. Only one remained before the necromancer reached her father, who was tied to the leftmost pillar.

Ella grit her teeth and braced her feet against the wall. She realized she couldn't pry the arcane missile loose – so she tore her hand away instead. An intense pain shot through her body as the wound in her palm was ripped wide open; but her willpower prevailed against its blinding throb. She grasped her dropped mace and ran, bare feet slapping against the glittering mosaic floor.

The necromancer turned to face her, his no-longer youthful eyes gleaming with rage. His fingers danced like skittering mice and his arms performed a throwing motion. Ella was launched into the air and hit the ground. The impact thrust the air from her lungs.

She had landed next to Kaal-Hatharet, and one of the almost-dead men turned his attention to her. She smashed her mace against his thigh before he could wrestle her down. His body vibrated with melodious tunes as the bones inside him shattered. He dropped to the floor, flopping around like a fish on land.

Ella got to her feet and turned to the necromancer. He pointed his finger at her father. The vile spell was almost upon his lips.

She was too late.

"Shatter his orb!" shouted Kaal-Hatharet. The four almost-dead had him pinned down to the floor; he could barely move.

The magic orb glowed brightly, bathing the room in noxious yellow. Ella wrapped the fingers of her mangled left hand around her mace and swung it overhead in a two-handed strike. She poured every last shred of her strength into it. The singing mace whistled as it descended on the crystal ball.

It shattered into a thousand pieces. The chiming melody of her mace echoed through the chamber like the symphony of a hundred wind chimes caught in a mighty storm. It was enough to drown out the necromancer's agonized scream. The euphonious chimes set the windows to vibrate until they broke, erasing the hideous scenes they displayed just like they thwarted the necromancer's own ritual.

The necromancer's body decayed rapidly. Within seconds he became an old man, then a corpse more withered than Kaal-Hatharet had been, until he finally crumbled to ash. A blinding flash of light appeared, and when Ella could see again, the blood in the pool was gone.

The mace dropped from her weary hands. It rang like a bell when it hit the floor. She approached her father, still tied to the pillar, still alive. She took him down and laid him on the ground. His breath was weak, his chest barely moved.

"Ella." A warm smile was on his lips. "I'm proud of you, my daughter."

"Father!" She looked over to the undead sorcerer-king – if undead he still was – with a pleading look in her eyes. "He's dying."

Kaal-Hatharet pushed away the corpses he was buried underneath and got to his feet. He looked like a young man, no more than thirty years of age. His face, now able to express emotion once more, showed sorrow. "I cannot help, for my magic is not of the healing kind."

Tears flowed freely from Ella's eyes and fell onto her father's pale skin. She whispered words of love into his ears as he expelled his last breath.

Kaal-Hatharet turned away, allowing her to grieve alone.

After a long moment, he heard her bare feet slap against the floor and turned around. Her father cradled in her arms, she held out her mangled left hand. A large hole gaped in her palm, the flesh around it torn and frayed.

With a nod, he tore a long strip of cloth off her skirt and bandaged her wound. She could not do it herself.

She had to carry her father.

~*~

They barely recognized the surrounding lands when they left the necromancer's tower. Trees bloomed with fresh green leaves and colorful petals. Lush grass caressed Ella's toes underfoot as she wandered through the meadows. All the life the necromancer had sucked from the land had returned.

Ella buried her father underneath an apricot tree. He had always loved the sweet orange fruit. She told Kaal-Hatharet how they buried the dead in her home; he helped her build a cairn over the grave, as was custom in the north.

The sun had almost crossed beyond the horizon when they were done. The warm red light of evening kissed the flourishing landscape with its vibrant glow.

Ella beheld her companion with curiosity. His withered flesh had returned to the fullness of life. A thick brown beard framed his regal face, and his skin was tan as if kissed by the sun, even though he had spent thousands of years entombed.

"What is it like?" she asked.

Kaal-Hatharet raised his hands to his eyes and stared at the unfamiliar appendages. It had been so long since he lived that his living body now felt strange.

"Earlier, you asked if I had any regrets." He hesitated for a moment. The memories of his misdeeds were a burden he had carried for countless years. "In life, I had many. In death, fewer."

He looked out toward the horizon and took a deep breath, enjoying the feeling of air coursing through his lungs. "In this new life, I hope, none."

Ella stood only at the beginning of life, but she understood. She stared wistfully at her father's grave. Had she only been a little faster to the necromancer's tower…

Yet it was no use to dwell on past mistakes. With every moment, life began anew.

Ella got to her feet and marched toward the sunset. She heard Kaal-Hatharet's footsteps following behind her. Where she was going, she did not know; of her old life, too little remained to be recovered.

Of her companion's, even less.

Perhaps they could find a new path to walk together.

A Lady in Stone

Lady in Stone

By Cliff Hamrick

A scream jolted Jarek awake.

He almost fell out of his chair as he dozed at the rough-hewn table in his rented room. He had been studying a few manuscripts, trying to piece together a translation of a clay tablet he bought off a jeweler with more silver than sense. The work was so tedious that he fell asleep.

His small lantern hadn't burned out yet so he could immediately take in his surroundings. The small room was empty except for the table, chair, and small bed with a flea-ridden mattress. When he saw nothing was amiss, he wondered if he had dreamed of the scream. Then it came again.

"Help me!"

A woman's voice cracked with desperation as she cried from the street just outside his shuttered window. More out of curiosity than concern, Jarek went and threw open the wooden shutters of his first-floor window. In the east, he could see the growing light of dawn.

A woman with long hair and a dark dress knelt in the cobblestone street. A large lump lay in front of her. But in the dim light, Jarek couldn't make out what it was. He held his lantern out of the window, which helped him see the bright yellow cloth that covered up whatever she was crying over. Seeing his light, the woman looked up at him.

"Please, sir," she said, "you have to help me. Help Melina."

The woman was young and pretty. She wore a dark green dress that threatened to reveal her large breasts. Her long hair was red, marking her as Thandalussian, and not a native to the mining town of Vardosa at the foothills of the Dupar Mountains. Jarek figured she was probably one of the many prostitutes that serviced the people who had grown wealthy from the silver mines.

He glanced up and down the street and noticed a few lights appearing in the shuttered windows of the stone houses that lined the cobblestone street.

"What happened?" he asked. "Who is Melina?"

The woman placed her hands on the yellow cloth of the immobile lump in front of her.

"This is Melina," she said before starting to sob again.

Something seemed wrong about the thing that lay in front of her, but he wanted to know what it was. Having fallen asleep in his cotton clothes, he only needed to slip on his leather boots to get dressed. Carrying his lantern, he climbed out of the window and onto the side of the street.

The wrongness of the scene only grew as he approached the kneeling woman and the unmoving lump that lay in the middle of the cobblestone street. The woman didn't look up at him as he knelt next to her and held the lantern over the lump.

It was a stone statue of a woman.

Over the years, he had seen many statues in granite and marble, and many different styles. But the likeness of the woman's face was so perfect, he knew that it was no statue created through the natural talents of a skilled artist. No ordinary statue would have forced Jarek's blood to run cold.

Melina, or her stone likeness, lay on her left side. Her hands clutched at her belly and her face was twisted in pain with her mouth wide open as if trying to scream. Everything was stone. Her hair, her skin, even her toenails. Everything but what wasn't a part of her.

The bright yellow dress clung to her stone shoulders and covered her body just as she had put it on. Her feet were bare and a pair of soft leather sandals lay next to her. Even the yellow ribbon which would have held back a wild mane of curly hair was still made of silk though the hair was now a gray stone. Even her gold earrings pierced through petrified earlobes.

Jarek felt his heart race and breath quicken as his mind tried to comprehend what his eyes were seeing. He had never even heard of anything like this before. It was a moment before he realized the red-headed woman's pleading eyes were watching him.

"Please," she said, "help her."

Jarek opened his mouth to speak, but before a word could come out, a crowd started to form. Several people stood around them holding lanterns and candles which only further illuminated the impossibility that lay in front of him.

"What's going on?" asked a tall, balding man.

"What's all this noise about?" a middle-aged woman asked.

A few people in the growing crowd made superstitious signs against evil once they saw the statue on the cobblestones. Jarek grabbed the girl's arm to get her attention back on him.

"What's your name?" he asked.

"D-Demetra."

"She's a Thandalussian," said the balding man.

"And you can tell he's a Northman by his yellow hair," said another man. "What kind of witchery are these foreigners bringing here?"

"We need to go," Jarek said as he pulled Demetra to her feet.

Holding her arm, he led her away from the shouting crowd. They may have been angry and were looking for someone to blame, but their fear prevented them from following the pair as they disappeared into the dark streets.

"What about Melina?" Demetra asked.

"I don't know if she can be helped," Jarek said. "But tell me what happened."

Demetra glanced back at the lanterns of the crowd before Jarek pulled her into a side street.

"We were walking home," she said.

"Home? From where?"

"A party. We were at Orso's house."

"Orso?"

"Yes, Orso Girald."

Jarek immediately recognized name.

He said, "You were at a private party with the man who owns one of the largest silver mines in Vardosa?"

She shrugged and nodded as if nothing was surprising about this. Jarek glanced at her again and wondered how expensive she must be for a man of Orso's wealth.

He led her down another side street and asked, "What happened right before she...?" he didn't know how to describe what happened to Melina.

"We were walking in the street. It was still dark so we stayed in the middle where the stones are smoother. We were just talking about what a jerk Orso is when Melina doubled over like she was hurt. I laughed because I thought she was just fooling around."

Demetra sniffed at the memory and rubbed her eyes dry before continuing.

"But then she looked up at me and screamed. At least she tried to. Her voice was just a thin whistle before she...she turned gray."

Jarek wondered if that was the sound of a human throat turning to stone.

"What happened next?" he asked.

"She just fell over. She sounded...awful." Demetra paused as she remembered. "I didn't know what to do so I cried for help."

Jarek led her through a couple more side streets until they arrived at his rented room. Once inside, he gave her a cup of tepid tea from a pot that had already gone cold while he gathered his investigative tools into his leather shoulder bag.

She looked over at Jarek. "Why don't you carry a weapon?"

"Everything I need is in here," he replied while hefting his shoulder bag.

"I mean a real weapon."

Jarek sighed as this conversation was old to him.

"A sword is only as useful as the skill of the one who yields it," he explained.

"So you don't know how to fight?"

"I was trained, but it was never my strong suit. Swinging a sword at a practice dummy all day wasn't where my interests lay. So I only practiced enough to get my father off of my back."

He glanced over at her and noticed she didn't seem convinced.

"If I carried a sword," he continued, "then I might as well carry a shield. And what good is a shield if you're not wearing armor? Pretty soon, I'd be burdened with a bunch of dead weight that wouldn't help me with what I really do."

"What's that?" she asked.

"Solve mysteries and make money."

She looked over the teacup as she sipped. Her eyes lingered on his plain cotton clothes and dusty leather boots.

"You should carry a sword."

Rather than argue, he took her tea cup and urged her out the door to lead him through the streets towards Orso's house and away from the growing crowd surrounding the lady made of stone in the middle of the street.

The sun peeked over the roofs of the two-story houses that filled the Trade District where Orso's house sat. The district was where deals were made and coins were exchanged for ore, slaves, and services. The perfect place for a couple of pretty, young prostitutes to do business.

Orso's house wasn't as large or as opulent as Jarek expected. It had three stories, making it taller than most of the buildings in the district. But its overall size was still restricted by the mountainous area. Palatial mansions simply weren't possible in a mining town like Vardosa.

Along the way, Jarek tried to think of a convincing lie to get him past the guards at Orso's gate. He needn't have bothered as there were no guards and the gate was unlocked. He walked into the small courtyard with Demetra clutching at his arm.

She whispered, "Where are the guards?"

He whispered back, "Were there guards last night?"

She nodded. Jarek wondered why they would have left their post, but thought they might be inside the house.

She whispered again, "I don't think we should go in."

"We need to find out what happened to Melina or it might happen to someone else. This is the last place she was before...whatever happened to her."

Demetra didn't seem certain, but she also didn't argue. Jarek stepped up to the front door and knocked. The unlocked door creaked open from the force of his knock. Demetra looked up at him and shook her head, but Jarek gently pushed open the door the rest of the way.

As he stood in the doorway and listened, he knew something was wrong. No sounds came from inside the house, not even the regular creaks and groans of floorboards as someone moved around.

In the growing light, Jarek could see the sitting room with comfortable couches and luxurious pillows. A large stone fireplace dominated one wall, but the fire had burned down to smoldering ashes. Polished brass ornaments and silver mirrors glinted in the morning sunlight.

He decided to try his luck and called out, "Hello?" When no one responded, he paused before calling out again, "Orso?"

Silence.

He looked down at Demetra who looked back at him with worried eyes. She grasped his hand as he stepped inside the deathly quiet house. The *creak* of a floorboard under her sandaled foot made him freeze. She looked up at him and mouthed the word 'sorry.' But the jarring sound didn't bring any curious occupants of the house.

"I don't think anyone is home," Jarek said.

"Someone is always home," Demetra said.

"How do you know that?"

"I've been here a few times with Melina. Orso rarely leaves. And there's Celina their cook and servant. Oh, and Prisco."

"Who is Prisco?" Jarek asked, getting a little annoyed that he wasn't given all of this information earlier.

"Prisco is Orso's friend," Demetra replied, clueless of Jarek's annoyance. "Melina and I always assumed he was rather funny."

"Funny?"

"You know," she said with a shrug. "Doesn't like girls."

"Ah," Jarek said as he led her towards the narrow staircase.

"Where are we going?"

"I assume Orso's bedroom is upstairs."

"Yes, but why are you going there?"

"I assume he's still in bed. Maybe he's sick."

"Hung over, more like it."

Jarek wasn't certain what Orso's state would be when they found him. He just hoped that the man hadn't turned to stone.

He led Demetra up the stairs and down a short hallway. Three closed doors greeted them, but she pointed out the door to Orso's bedroom. Jarek walked closer and pressed her ear against the wooden door, hoping to hear signs of life coming from the other side. Silence. Jarek knocked softly and listened again. When he heard nothing he knocked a little louder.

"Orso?" Jarek asked.

When there was no reply, he quietly opened the door. Morning sunlight streamed in through an open window. Orso's massive bed filled most of the space, and Jarek knew that the wealthy mine owner could easily fit two or three girls there.

A lump lay under a heavy blanket and silk sheets.

Afraid of what he would find there, Jarek stayed in the doorway and knocked loud enough on the wall to wake up whoever might be sleeping. When the lump didn't stir, he took a step closer, making certain to scrape his boot heel on the wooden floor. Still nothing. He looked down at Demetra who was just as puzzled as him. Jarek took a deep breath and walked right up to the bed and pulled back the covers.

A silk bundle had replaced Orso's body.

There were no seams or cuts in the fabric. His body had transformed into silk just as Melina's had turned to stone. Jarek saw the outline of a nose, the roundness of a head, and folds at the creases of the arms and elbows. Orso had turned into a silk doll that no seamstress could ever replicate.

"What happened to him?" Demetra asked.

"I have no idea," he muttered.

Jarek was getting frustrated with a problem he couldn't understand, much less solve. He flipped the covers back over Orso's silken body and turned to walk past Demetra. He knocked on the door across the hall before looking back at her.

"This is Prisco's room, yes?" he asked. She nodded in reply.

This time Jarek didn't wait. After he knocked once, he threw open the door with no idea what he might find on the other side. A shirtless man sat in a chair in front of a writing desk. His body had turned into wood. Just like Melina, he was the perfect sculpture of a human figure. Too perfect to have ever been formed with a mallet and chisel.

Jarek stepped closer and put his hand on the smooth wooden surface of Prisco's shoulder and looked down at him. Demetra watched from the doorway with her hand covering her mouth.

"Let's find the cook," Jarek said quietly.

He led her down the stairs as she pointed him towards the kitchen. Jarek entered without hesitation, fairly certain what he would find.

The kitchen was rather small for the house of one of the wealthiest men in the city. But jars and bottles of rare and expensive spices and ingredients filled crowded shelves on the stone walls. Next to an open window sat a large ceramic basin of water filled with porcelain plates.

A large puddle of water covered the floor in front of the basin. A soggy dress and an apron sat in the puddle. Jarek walked over and picked up the apron. Water trailed down and dribbled into the puddle.

"What's that?" Demetra asked.

"This is the cook."

"What do you mean?"

"I mean, that something turned all of them into whatever substance they were touching." He let the apron fall back to the floor with a wet *slop* before continuing. "Melina was walking barefoot on the cobblestones so she turned to stone. Orso was laying on silk sheets. Prisco sat shirtless in a wooden chair so he became wood."

"What about the cook?"

"She was washing the dishes," he replied.

He looked down at the pile of wet clothing and wondered if the process was as painful as Melina's silent scream suggested.

"The question is," Jarek continued, "why weren't you affected?"

He looked back at Demetra and saw she was sniffing a pot resting on the cold stove. Her face wrinkled with disgust when she looked up at him.

"It still smells awful," she said.

"What does?"

"This mushroom soup. Orso served it last night and insisted we all try it."

Jarek walked closer to look inside the pot. It was filled with a cold, brown soup that smelled like dirt and looked like something found in an open sewer.

"Did you try it?" he asked.

"No, I just pretended to so he would shut up about it." Demetra's eyes went wide. "But Melina did. She always did whatever Orso wanted. Do you think this is what killed her?"

Jarek shrugged slightly. "Maybe. Did he say anything about the soup?"

"Oh, he was making a big deal about the mushrooms. He said they were a gift from someone as a part of a business deal. He was always wanting to try some new food or spice from distant lands. That's why he has all this stuff." She waved her hand at the many bottles and jars around the kitchen.

"I'm starting to get an idea," Jarek said.

He was about to continue but closed his mouth quickly when the sound of the front door opening and closing interrupted him. They gave each other confused looks as they wondered who could have entered the house.

Through the closed kitchen door, Jarek heard footsteps cross the sitting area, walk up the stairs, and enter Orso's room. He didn't hear any reaction to the sight of a silken Orso lying in bed. Whoever it was, walked confidently as if they lived there. But according to Demetra, everyone who had a right to be in the house was already dead.

Unless she left something else out, he thought.

Jarek walked closer to Demetra to whisper, "Who is that?"

She whispered, "I don't know. No one else should be here."

As the footsteps came down the stairs again, Jarek moved closer to the kitchen door, hoping to open it just a crack to see who was roaming through the house. He jumped back when the door suddenly opened.

A man around Jarek's age stood in the doorway, and they quickly appraised each other. The man's hair was black and slicked back with perfumed oil. His red satin tunic was embroidered with gold thread. And his black leather shoes shone in the morning sun. Jarek noted the seal on the folded paper in his other hand.

Jarek asked, "Who are you?"

The man shot back with his own question, "Who are you?"

Jarek moved closer to Demetra as the two men refused to give any ground. The man was blocking their only means of escape through the kitchen door. Jarek noticed the man's eyes dart past Demetra for a moment.

"What are you doing here?" the man demanded.

"Wait, I know you," Demetra said. "You were at Orso's party a week ago. Your name is…Malco."

"Malco?" Jarek asked. "As in Malco Casassa the owner of the silver mine that has reportedly gone dry last month?"

Malco's eyes shifted back and forth between Demetra and Jarek as he slowly put the sealed paper into his tunic pocket.

Demetra said, "Yes, they were arguing about a deed or something. He wanted to make a trade but Orso wouldn't hear it."

The man's black eyebrows knitted closer together and his eyes shifted from her to Jarek to something behind her. Jarek knew the only thing behind her worth looking at was the pot of cold, brown mushroom soup.

Demetra looked to Jarek and asked, "What's a deed?"

While Demetra looked away, Malco used the opportunity to pull a long stiletto knife from behind his back. He lunged forward, aiming the sharp point at Demetra's gut.

The well-dressed man was fast, but Jarek saw the movement and he jumped between them. Rather than grab Malco, Jarek held his leather shoulder bag in both hands and used it as a shield. The tough leather caught the blade, deflecting it away, but the force pushed Jarek back against Demetra.

Jarek released his bag to grab Malco's arm, pushing the knife away from the both of them. They wrestled for control of the sharp blade, repeatedly bumping Demetra against the stove.

Demetra's Thandalussian nature kicked in, and rather than cower like any southern girl, she punched at Malco's face over Jarek's shoulder. The curses she threw at Malco in her native language echoed off the stone walls, and Jarek was certain that anyone on the street could hear them.

She scratched at the well-dressed man's eyes and he cried out. He clutched at his face with his free hand as he drew back away from the red-headed wildcat. Being unable to reach him, Demetra grabbed a frying pan hanging on the wall over her head and hurled it at Malco. The metal pan struck his face with a loud *clang*, breaking his nose.

As Malco cried out in pain, Jarek grabbed the pot of brown soup and threw it into his face. Malco gulped and sputtered out the foul-smelling liquid and froze. The rage on his face was replaced with shock and fear.

The transformation was so sudden even Demetra paused her assault.

Malco dropped the knife and ran out of the kitchen.

Demetra looked up at Jarek, clearly confused by the change of events. Jarek dropped the pot and grabbed her wrist, pulling her to follow him as he ran to keep up with Malco. When they exited Orso's house, Jarek spotted the escaping man's red tunic moving as fast as possible through the cobblestone streets.

"This way!" Jarek shouted.

"Go faster and you can catch him," Demetra huffed next to Jarek.

"I don't want to catch him yet."

"Why not?"

Jarek didn't answer so he could concentrate on Malco's shiny, red tunic and didn't lose him in the crowd. Malco never looked back at the pair as they pursued him through the narrow, twisting streets. He didn't try to hide, he ran with a determined purpose, which made it easy for Jarek and Demetra to keep up with him.

When Malco turned and ran towards a house, Jarek picked up his pace to catch up to him. He ran through a well-appointed sitting room and followed Malco's footsteps up the stairs. He was almost on top of him when the well-dressed man entered a bedroom. Once inside, Jarek tackled Malco to the wooden floor.

"Release me!" Malco demanded.

Jarek could smell the earthy-foulness of the soup soaked into Malco's satin tunic as he pinned him to the ground. Malco struggled to escape Jarek's grip with one hand but his other hand reached towards a writing table across the room.

"You must release me!" Malco pleaded as Jarek heard Demetra enter the room.

Jarek saw Malco's mouth open again to speak, but nothing more than a gurgling sound came out. It sounded like a wet cloth rubbing against itself. Jarek stood up when Malco stopped struggling and his face turned red. As he watched, Malco's flesh turned into red satin.

His cheeks became rosy like a northern girl's face on a cold day. But the red color became darker like crimson and his skin developed an unnatural shininess. Even Malco's wide-open eyes shifted from white to red until they were balls of satin cloth that perfectly matched his embroidered tunic.

Demetra stepped into the room to stand next to Jarek. She put a hand on his arm as she looked at Malco's corpse of exquisite cloth.

"What happened to him?" she asked.

"He poisoned the soup." Jarek continued when he saw her confused look. "I think when you saw Malco arguing with Orso, he came to make a deal for Orso's mine. Perhaps he thought he had some legitimate claim to it. When Orso refused, he sent the tainted mushrooms, knowing that Orso would want to try some new dish immediately. He probably bribed Orso's guards to keep them away from the house the following day. So, all Malco had to do was return after everyone was dead and steal the deed to the mine."

"But why did we chase him back here?" Demetra asked.

"There's only one reason for him to run back home."

Jarek stepped past the horrific satin bundle and towards the writing table. Resting on the far corner was an ornate box made of cherry wood carved with flowers on the lid. He opened the box and smiled at the contents. A small vial capped with leaded cork and filled with golden oil sat on a pillow of yellow satin. He held up the vial to show Demetra.

"An antidote," he said.

She looked down at the satiny remains of Malco and said, "Well I suppose it's too late for that."

"Let's try an experiment."

He led her out of the house and back to the streets, walking quickly away before the neighbors could call the city watch and ask them why they were chasing Malco through the streets.

As the sun continued to rise, the streets were starting to fill up with people starting their day. Eventually, it became more difficult for Jarek to push his way through the crowd, and he soon saw why. A large crowd had gathered in the middle of the street.

There were the usual on-lookers, some of which came from several streets over after hearing the rumor of the strange occurrence. But also, wagons stopped in the street as the horses refused to step over the fallen figure. Jarek ignored the dirty looks of the southern citizens as he pushed his way past them and into the small circle that had formed around Melina.

The girl's bright yellow dress still clung to her body, but someone had stolen the poor girl's broken sandals, a testament to the unscrupulous culture of the populace. Perhaps the only reason why her golden jewelry was firmly emplaced through the holes in her stone ears was that no one was brave enough to approach her unnatural form.

Jarek and Demetra knelt beside Melina, and he studied her face in the sunlight. Despite the twisted pain on her features, she was still quite beautiful. He peeled off the lead from the vial and uncorked it. Then he tipped the golden contents into her open mouth. The glass vial clinked on her stone teeth, and he tapped it to make sure she got all of it. Then he sat back on his heels.

"Do you think it will work?" Demetra asked quietly.

Jarek shrugged. "I don't know. It might be too late for her. But I thought she deserved an attempt at least."

The crowd around them murmured. A few asked questions and Jarek thought to try and answer them, but then he hushed the crowd. A soft, high-pitched whistle grew from Melina's throat. The sound grew from a thin whistle to the cry of a child until it became and scream of a full-grown woman.

The dark gray color of Melina's stony skin slowly grew pale until it became chalk white. Then the white grew pink and her flesh slowly became normal. Her fingers clutched at her belly and her bare feet rubbed against each other. When her scream finally subsided, she opened her eyes. Jarek smiled down at her and Demetra threw herself on top of her shivering friend.

"So cold," Melina whispered through chattering teeth.

The crowd grew even more agitated and talkative at the sight of the once-stone girl rising to her feet with her friend's help.

"We better get her home," Jarek said as he pushed through the crowd.

Jarek walked with the girls as they talked quietly and Demetra tried to explain the events of the night, but he could tell the girl was too disoriented to fully take it all in. Eventually, they arrived at the girls' modest room in a run-down apartment building, and Demetra helped Melina to bed. Then she spoke with Jarek at the door.

"I can't thank you enough for your help," she said.

"I'm just glad it worked. Otherwise, she would have become a permanent fixture in the middle of the street."

Demetra shivered at the thought.

Jarek said, "When she wakes up, show her this."

He took a sealed paper from his shoulder bag and handed it to Demetra who looked down at it.

"What's this?"

"The deed to Orso's mine. I took it off Malco while we were wrestling.

I figure after what the two of you went through, the least he can do is give you his mine. After all, neither Orso nor Malco have any use for it now."

Her green eyes were wide as she looked over the flowing script and large seal of the official document. When she didn't say anything, Jarek continued, "Come by my place tomorrow and I'll forge the necessary signatures."

Demetra asked in a small voice, "Why didn't you keep it?"

Jarek laughed, "Oh, I think I've had quite enough with mining towns."

An Unexpected Flight

O Sapphire, O Kambria

By J. Thomas Howard

Prelude

Under the ruby sun, a *ptero* was a terrible sight. The creature stood nearly the height of two men at the shoulders. Its toothy beak was almost large enough to swallow a man whole, and its wingspan dwarfed many trees. This morning, this dreaded creature exuded no terror, because it was caught in a monstrous gale. Clinging tightly to its back was a man, a rider in a saddle. Both struggled futilely against the storm.

I

Under the sapphire rays of light, a slender youth stood alone, amongst the fern-trees, with flint-tipped spear in hand. She was jet like a starless night. Her features were not particularly comely at first glance, but she had eagerness in her mien that burned slowly, like the coals of an old fire.

She saw a *nygal* glide overhead from one fern-tree to the next. They alone dared to swim through the air as the insects did. It would be a difficult hunt, but a satisfying meal. She was eager for the lizard's flesh.

She adjusted her *bone-fish* armor, to avoid giving off any sounds in her pursuit. The spear and buckler were the chosen weapons of her people, and she knew them well. She stalked her prey, and when she moved it was ethereal, like she was a piece of drift caught in the wind.

When at last the spear struck true, she feasted eagerly, for she was faint with hunger. She had forsaken every oath of fellowship in her tribe and broken the most sacred of taboos. Love had commanded her to do it. They had taken her sister, her dear Kambria, to sacrifice to the *dymetra-men*, as has always been done with the chief's eldest daughter before the coming of their eighteenth rainy season.

Doubt had told the warrior not to pursue her sister, but she could not forsake Kambria, no matter what the dream-women told of the need for the *dymetra-men's* favor.

So Jain sat alone by a simple fire, fearful of the beasts that stalked her world, but resolute against that dread all the same.

II

Many rainy seasons prior to Jain's anxious ponderings, a horrid scene had transpired, as it always had, in the land where *Per* the sun and *Mia* the shattered moon held court.

A slender woman of dark features and stubborn beauty lay strapped to an altar of stone. She screamed, wailed, and pleaded, as many had done before her. She would not stoically embrace her duty.

Surrounding her were men, though they were not as she was. Their frames were thicker. Their faces were longer; almost bearing snouts with many dagger-like teeth. They had no ears, only gaping holes to hear, and their noses were all but gone, leaving wide openings for the stealing of air. They did not have hair nor scale adorning their bodies, but what covered their exteriors was like the hide of the beasts that roamed the land where *Per* and *Mia* reigned.

For all their alien countenance, the *dymetra-men* used the same flint for blades, and the same exoskeletons of fish for armor. Yet, these cognates could not hide the horror for which they were named. From their spines erupted great sails of skin and bone. They were colored in various patterns, like arrogant banners. They mirrored the ferocious and lumbering *dymetra* for which the jet people had named them.

One amongst them did not have this protrusion, and she sat upon a throne of limestone. Perhaps, in the shadows of night she would have seemed beautiful, but here before the raging fires her true likeness was revealed. The inhuman features smirked as the girl writhed.

It had always been this way. The sorcery of old had made them separate and above the pitiful humans. It was their sacred task to preserve the order of *Per* and *Mia*. The dark people of the fern-forests were no different than the animals. Their feeble language meant nothing.

The sorceress stood. The taut hide of the *estem*, stretched over dried *puzzlegrass*, thundered their exhalations, for the drumming had come to its climax.

Fire caught the sapphire jewel embedded in the witch's head. It had been placed there when she was an infant, when the plates of her skull were soft and malleable. Just as it had been done for the ones who came before her, back to the beginning, when the sorcerers of old created the boundary that kept this land apart from all others.

The enchantress ambled forward, watching the sails of her harem in the firelight. Their patterns and colors enticed her. She wondered from whose seed the next sapphire lady would be born, but she stayed her lustful thoughts and attended the task at hand.

She held a dagger of obsidian tied to a bone handle. Holding the blade above the writhing girl, she plunged it into her stomach. The screaming resounded even above the hammering of the drums. The sapphire enchantress reached into the warm innards. She twisted and pulled forth a still beating heart. The gem in her forehead grew lambent just as the youth's life expired.

"The magic will endure!" the sapphire queen declared. The drums were as silent as the still warm corpse; the only sound in the hall was the dripping of blood.

III

Jain stalked through the fern-forest looking for the trail of the *dymetra-men*. They were arrogant and unchallenged in their rule, so she doubted they would cover their tracks as her people did, but she had not yet found their spoor. She did find the trail of an *esthem*, creatures of massive girth and squat bodies, which she followed, and found it resting in a pool too small to be called a lake. It was too large a beast for her to hunt on her own; and its meat would have gone to waste.

Hungry but undeterred, Jain continued her search, and upon a glade she found what she sought. She was too eager in her discovery, for unbeknownst to her a predator was in the bush. The warrior turned to see a charging *dymetra*, the creature that was a sobriquet for the men she pursued. The beast at the tip of its amber sail stood as tall as her. These exuding neural spines made up most of the height, but the squat body was beautifully muscled with singular intent. Its jaws were open.

Desperately, Jain rolled aside, just missing the crunch of hungry teeth. Her heart thundered. To slay the largest of the *dymetra* was a trial that only the bravest survived, initiating them into the rites of manhood. The victorious would take the sail and hang it by their hut, upon a shaft, as banner to their valor.

The creature turned and lunged once more, this time faster, expending all its energy. Jain feigned surprise, and just as the teeth came she slapped the *dymetra* across the face with her bony buckler. It was a dangerous gambit. A clawed limb could still skewer her, but the predator was stunned. It had not expected its prey to fight back so fiercely. Jain drove her flint spear into the neck.

The *dymetra* howled terribly and jerked away with Jain's spear still caught in its flesh. She felt her sweat pour. She was unarmed against this great killer. The furious beast charged once more, undeterred by the spear ensnared in its neck.

Jain slapped the protruding butt of her spear with her buckler. The creature yowled with pain, but the weapon stayed put. So began a dance where with each charge, Jain stuck the shaft, irritating the beast, and soon that frustration turned to fatigue, and that was a deadly state.

The *dymetra* took labored breaths; Jain ran and with all her strength yanked the spear from her enemy. She then drove the flint tip into the eye of her attacker and pushed until it found brain.

Jain wondered if the men of her tribe had witnessed her kill, would they let her fly a sail? Would she stand amongst the honored few? It did not matter now; she had forsaken them and the rites of her people.

The victorious warrior continued on her enemies' trail. There was still one predator she feared even more than the *dymetra*: the *titanoph*. They were far larger than a man, with two great daggers for teeth and little strands of hair on their skin, not unlike a man. That was where the similarities ended as these creatures had the same long snouts and earless faces of the *dymetra*.

As if Jain had called the beast into existence she saw one; but it was dead, the surrounding soil wet with its blood. It must have died recently, for she saw no scavengers about. Even the insects had barely come. Jain inspected the wounds. They did not come from tooth and claw.

She looked up from the beast. There, beneath a towering fern-tree rested a man. He was unlike any other she had seen. He was shorter than most, but his frame was far more muscular. His shoulders were wide. His skin was ruddy like ochre, and he did not bear a handsome face.

Jain feared him, for he was as unknown as what lingers in the shadows of night. He had seen her. He held a weapon unlike any she had seen; it shimmered in the light, like fish beneath water.

Strangely, he wore coverings over his feet, and his clothing wrapped all his legs. Two sashes crisscrossed his chest. In them she saw many more artifacts of the shimmering substance. The shapes reminded her of the sharpened flint her people threw.

"You killed this *titanoph*?" Jain foolishly asked, forgetting the danger all strangers possessed.

The man studied her and then replied. He could speak their language though it was muddied with alien sounds and a grating imperfection.

"Is that what this is? I have never seen its like before. Where am I? Why does the sun burn sapphire here and not ruby?"

"*Per* has never been ruby," the girl replied. "Who are you? I do not fear you. I have slain a *dymetra*. Know that I am a great warrior!"

The man smiled, belying his rugged features. "I do not know what that is, but I presume it is even more fearsome than this beast. I mean you no harm. I am called Raul."

"Jain was the name my mother sung at my birth," she answered.

"Hail, and well met. Have you seen my *ptero*?"

"What is a *ptero*?"

Raul looked puzzled then answered. "A great lizard, with the beginnings of *feathers*. Its wings are as wide as one of these fern-trees."

"You are either a liar," she responded, "or have eaten too much of what is only for the dream-women. No creature besides the insects have wings, save for the *wygal*, and they are far smaller than you and I."

"I do not lie," Raul replied. From his corded belt he pulled forth a strange object.

"What sorcerous bauble is that? Are you in league with the *dymetra-men*?"

"I do not know of whom you speak, and I practice no magic. I must find my steed. This is one of her *feathers*. They help her fly."

"How come you here?" Jain asked, trying to allow the man's conquering of the *titanoph* to not frighten her. His words were strange and she knew few of them.

"We were caught in a gale. When the winds died down, my mount and I flew over an endless jungle covered by a gleaming filament which we could not pass through, but eventually we found a puncture in this barrier and flew in to rest and recover. My mount, she went hunting, but never returned."

"Your story smells of the dream-food. I have my own errand, I will depart in peace," Jain said. She had lingered too long.

"Please, let me come with you, I know not where I am."

"You do not fear me?" she asked.

"I do, I am no fool. I know the emerald wastelands are death and danger. When I flew overhead, I saw no human redoubt. Do your people live amongst the trees? You must be mighty warriors to do such."

"I have no people," she bit back angrily.

"Nor I any in this place. It is safer to travel together."

"I tell you now, touch me and die."

"I have no such intention," Raul answered.

"All men have such intentions," Jain replied.

Raul smiled. "I suppose that is true in a way, but I wish above all things to find my *Amlia* and leave this place."

"I am on my own errand and cannot suffer the delay."

"If your errand is dangerous, and honest, I can lend you my *sword*. I am lost, and have naught else to do. I am in sore need of a companion."

"*Sword*, is that your weapon? I suppose if you can kill a *titanoph* you can kill a *dymetra-man*."

"I do not wish to kill a man."

"They took my sister and intend to sacrifice her. They deserve to die!"

"If what you say is true, I would wish to kill such a man."

"They are not men," Jain growled. "But you may accompany me. Better to keep an eye on you than have you hunt me as I hunt the *dymetra-men*."

IV

They traveled until nightfall, taking some of the *titanoph's* flesh with them. When dark came they built a fire and cooked the meat. There they sat and traded beliefs.

"The dream-women say our land, where *Per* the sun and *Mia* the shattered moon reign is sacred. They say the *dymetra-men* keep out the evils of greater worlds in exchange for the first-born daughter of each chief. Without their magic, they say the very air would change and all our land would die. I have always wondered if they spoke truth, or if our elders taught lies to enslave us and keep us fearful. Now I have met you, and I fear they speak the truth."

Raul's ruddy features matched the firelight. He spoke. "It is said the sorcerers of old pilfered beasts from eons past from the very palace of Death. They were arrogant, for these monsters conquered the men who had liberated them and took dominion of the world. I see none of the fauna of the jungles I know, but these animals here are also unlike you and I. They are not of milk and fur, as they say the world was before the sorcerers' great transgression. I wonder if these creatures too were stolen from Death, and this place set aside by some forgotten wizard."

"Maybe what your people believe is also a lie," Jain said. "Truthfully, we will never know. What passes is always forgotten."

"That is true, life is an awe beyond us. You called the moon shattered.

I wonder if it is a mere coincidence your people believe the moon was broken too. They say it was once a circle as is the sun."

"We have heard such. It is said that our people once defied the *dymetra-men*, and in so doing broke the moon."

Raul pondered this but did not speak for a time. "I would take first watch," he eventually said. Jain assented, though she slept with her spear in her hand.

V

Jain knew the day of her sister's demise, for it was written in the movements of the broken moon. When the largest shard, *Kambria*, for which her sister had been named (as all first-born daughters had been) crossed the sun she would be struck dead. Always before the coming of the rainy season did the long-dead limb of *Mia* cross the face of *Per*. They were running out of time to find the hidden lair of the *dymetra-men*.

They followed the trail at a brisk pace. It was clear in the devastating footpath the *dymetra-men* felt threatened by nothing, not even the saber-toothed *titanoph*.

This Raul was clearly a veteran of danger. He was sharp in his observations, when he would give them, and his signals were quick and deadly silent. She was glad of his seeming friendliness; she could discern he was a great hunter and a man one would not want as an enemy.

The pair came at last to a gulch so thick with fern-trees they cast shadows that created a false dusk. A babbling stream whispered its way into the dark. It beckoned, even if the dimness did not.

The *dymetra-men* had rummaged through the brook. Their refuse could be seen floating in it. Cast off effects lay scattered here and there. Pieces of flint littered the shore. The remnant of a fire was smoldering.

Jain saw her companion take two of the shimmering weapons from his sashes, as if readying to throw them. She had guessed correctly; they were like the sharpened flint her people hurled. She inspected the campsite and saw a piece of the cerulean beads from her sister's necklace. It had been carelessly trampled on, as if the substance had no meaning. Jain snatched it up and tied it quickly into a strand of her hair.

Then a stone caught her attention. It was unlike any other. It was porous gray, and running through it was what looked like a reddish-brown vein. She cautiously touched it.

Raul came to her so silently she almost missed the padding of his feet despite their strange coverings.

"It is from the old ones. This ravine is deep and this jungle is so thick. These ruins would be impossible to see from above."

Jain spun just as flint flew past her head. She saw her companion throw his own projectiles in retaliation. He let out a curse, they had missed, and he drew his shimmering blade.

Two *dymetra-men* charged from the gloom. Jain had only ever seen them from afar. Their terrible sails were bright with color, and their gray hide was inhuman, but nothing revolted her more than their faces, neither *dymetra* nor man, yet stealing from both. She wanted to recoil but instead deflected a spear strike with her buckler.

The force of the blow staggered her. Her enemy's spear came back fast, striking downward, after halting mid-air from the deflection. Jain sidestepped, barely dodging the spear-tip. The *dymetra-man's* strength was stunning.

The miscreated warrior pressed his advantage, his spear cutting through the air. Jain jumped back. She dashed left and then ran forward. Her spear struck fast before her enemy could recover from his overconfidence. Flint found flesh, but it was not a mortal wound. She pulled her spear free just before the retaliatory strike could disembowel her, but the blow cracked her *bone-fish* armor.

Jain feinted as her father had taught her. Then she stabbed with all the rage that welled within her. The *dymetra-man*, eager with arrogance, responded too slowly. The flint-tip of her spear disfigured his face, ruining his eyes. In his blind thrashing, he managed to knock Jain's spear free. She ducked under the wild motions and drew her flint dagger. Then she sprang up and ran the blade along the warrior's throat, just above where his *bone-fish* armor guarded. Blood spilled down the breastplate, and the terrible creature fell, its sail pointing skywards like a gravestone.

Jain turned to see how Raul had fared. To her shock he stood triumphant over his attacker as if it was nothing. His strange blade had seemingly cut through spear-shaft, *bone-fish* armor, and flesh in one fell swoop.

"What magic is that flint?" Jain asked.

"Not flint," he answered. He scoured their surroundings, when he seemed satisfied he came to her. "Hand me your spear."

"Why?"

"I would give you something."

Reluctantly, Jain obliged. She watched as the man carefully undid the wrappings of her spear-tip. He took one of his shimmering projectiles and tied it to where the flint had been with a grace she did not expect.

"It should cut through their armor and their flint."

"Thank you," Jain replied. "I will call this spear Raul, in honor of you."

"You name your spears?"

She nodded.

"It did not already have a name?"

"That name became unworthy of it," Jain answered.

VI

They traveled further into the hidden ravine for a full day and night, but the trail seemed endless. The shard *Kambria* had just begun to touch the Sun. The eclipse was nigh, which meant that this day Jain's sister died.

"We must hurry," Jain said.

Raul munched on the legs of a *trilo* that she had speared from the stream. Their exoskeleton was soft, unlike that of the *bone-fish*.

"Would that we had found my mount," the man mused.

Jain sensed the shared longing between them, both lost, both missing the familial. They continued, and she hastened their speed to a dangerous pace. As if by luck they found what they sought, folding out of the verdant mystery were half-submerged palisades of gray decay. Raul paused, as did Jain, and they surveyed the strange fortress. She could hardly fathom a hut of such magnitude.

"They keep no guards?"

From the yawning gateway the thundering of drums beat in rhythmic exaltations. The two warriors, weapons at the ready, made their way into the breach.

They followed the snaking hallways ever in the direction of the clamoring drums. They saw none of the *dymetra-men* but their effects littered the ill-lit chambers. Here and there braziers burned, but they could not wash away the shadow that entombed the *dymetra-men*'s great-hut.

The thundering came to a fevered pitch. Jain grew frantic, but at long last they emerged into an amphitheater lit by countless fires. In a dread circle around a stone altar were the drummers. They bore smaller sails than the warriors who were gathered in the center of the circle. At the end of the chamber was a decaying throne. Atop it sat a creature like the *dymetra-men* but different. The creature had no sail.

It stood, and Jain saw the analogues of the feminine of her own body. But the creature's form was perverse—like the beast was the sun and the woman in her was the eclipse.

Jain saw in the center of the chamber the naked body of her sister tied to a profane altar. They had smeared her with strange ochers and even above the smell of her enemy she could smell the reek of the mysterious oils poured onto her sister's skin.

They were hopelessly outnumbered, but Jain intended to charge. Her shimmering blade would cut through flint, *bone-fish* armor, and flesh. She would sell her life dearly. She could not let her beloved sister die like this!

She telegraphed her intent to Raul. The man nodded his assent. His willingness to fight in this hopeless endeavor revealed nobility in his character, and Jain was glad to have met him.

Like stinging insects his daggers flew. They slaughtered a handful of drummers before the *dymetra-men* could even react. The musicians scattered; their cruel countenances could know fear!

The warriors showed no such emotion. They charged, spears at the ready. Raul and Jain met their advance. Raul's terrible sword clove weapon, armor, and flesh alike.

Jain sidestepped the oncoming strike of a spear and drove quickly with her own weapon. It pierced through armor and her enemy fell, his dying features twisted into a cognate for human shock.

The next was not so foolish, seeing the magic of their blades. He deflected her strikes with his buckler, avoiding the tip of Jain's spear. A well-placed strike shattered her already cracked breastplate. She fell back gasping for breath. Her attacker loomed over her, driving his spear toward her exposed flesh. Jain deflected with her buckler, though the strike still pierced through the shield and grazed her abdomen.

Jain swung her spear up, and the shimmering tip sliced open the warrior's throat. She rolled aside, just dodging the falling body.

A force crashed into Jain's shoulder. She struggled mightily, but she felt the sting of claws. A *dymetra-man* was pinning her shoulder down with his gnarled foot.

The warrior stood over her triumphantly and brought his spear down. Shimmering violence erupted from his stomach. Jain saw her fighting companion pull forth his blade, but his gambit had cost him. A flint projectile slammed into Raul's face. Blood erupted from his cheek and he staggered. Jain rolled, snatching up her spear. She drove the weapon into her companion's advancing attacker.

They stood back to back now. The enchantress of the *dymetra-men* was advancing. In her hand was an obsidian dagger. She seemed perturbed by the disturbance, but the ritual would commence regardless.

There was no way through. Their weapons were a deadly magic against their enemies, but they were still surrounded and outnumbered. Though *dymetra-men* were now cautious in their approach, fearful of the magic weapons, it was only a matter of time before the pair was overwhelmed.

Jain wondered if she could make a desperate charge for her sister, but then a crazed idea came to her.

"Will you follow me?" she asked her companion. He nodded through his bloodied mien. Jain deflected a strike, brushing off an advancing *dymetra-man*. Then she crouched and with all the strength in her thews leapt onto the shoulders of her companion. He did not stagger. Jain pushed off him, flipping herself into the air. The tip of her spear caught the ground, breaking, and she vaulted over her enemies to land beside the altar. It was a sport she and her sister had watched the men of her tribe play, and was glad they had emulated it often in their own games.

Jain stood before the chieftess of the *dymetra-men*. She was without her spear, but she drew her flint dagger and attacked, sending out vicious strikes. The chieftess parried with her obsidian blade. The flint chipped against it. Jain's weapon was dangerously outmatched. Seeing this, her enemy pressed her advantage.

The chieftess of the *dymetra-men* was beyond Jain's skill to surmount. The enchantress knew the blade too well. Jain's heart tightened. All her struggles were futile. Either the chieftess would best her or one of her warriors would spear Jain from behind. Raul could only distract them for so long.

She was going to fail!

Then a desperate thought came to Jain. There might be a way she could defeat the enchantress after all, but it would cost her everything. Seeing her sister stir on the altar, Jain accepted the price.

Jain left an opening. She felt the horrible cool of the obsidian slide into her. The chieftess's features were incapable of smiling, but her face was exultant. Jain twisted her wounded abdomen against the stinging pain, and in so doing yanked the weapon from her enemy.

Immediate dizziness came to her, but before Jain staggered she slammed the tip of her flint dagger into the sapphire jewel that rested in her enemy's head. It punctured the jewel, shattering it, and bit deep into the brain case. The enchantress convulsed and fell backwards. A few spasms rolled across her frame and the mighty chieftess died.

Then Jain fell. She heard the cries of the *dymetra-men*. They were not the shouts of warriors but the laments of babes.

Raul stood over her.

"They fled the moment she died. Your sister is saved!"

Jain looked to her sister atop the stone slab. Kambria stirred. Jain crawled to her, feeling her lifeblood pouring from her stomach. She reached up and cut the bindings free; with each strike her knife felt heavier.

Her sister roused from the drugged sleep.

"Jain?"

The young woman looked around at the desolation.

"What have you done?"

"I have saved you from your fate."

"But…what will the *dymetra-men* do to our people?"

"Nothing," Jain said. "Their chieftess is dead by my hand."

Jain collapsed. Her last sight was of Raul standing beside her sister. She hoped her faith in him was well placed. She took solace knowing he would at least be a better companion to her than a sacrificial blade.

Epilogue

They laid Jain to rest under a cairn of stones. Kambria sung the songs of passing, though it was forbidden to do so for one who had broken taboo. Kambria then donned her sister's clothing and remaining armor, for she had none of her own, and it was all she had left of her sister.

The height of the eclipse had passed, and the sun was burning a little stronger in the sky. Kambria thought the sun was strange, as if its color was just adjacent to what it should be.

"My sister trusted you, stranger," Kambria said. "I cannot return to my people. We have broken the immemorial covenant with the *dymetra-men*."

"I am called Raul," the man replied. "If you come with me I will keep you as safe as I am able. I am searching for my mount. She is a great creature that can fly through the sky and carry us both far from here."

Kambria accepted his offer but not without a pang of guilt and a dark foreboding in her heart. In the end, she felt she had no other choice. She could not return home, and to wander the forest alone was certain death.

In time, they found the man's strange mount. She was frightened of it, but after much coaxing she sat behind him in the saddle. They took to the sky, and Kambria clung to the man. She was wary of the height, but fear gave way to wonder.

When they reached the tear in the sky that Raul and his flying mount had come through, Kambria looked back wistfully at the home she could never return to.

She wondered, was the pact truly broken? After all, a chief's daughter had died that night. Just not the one promised.

Whatever the truth, she had no choice now but to live, and in so doing try to honor the sacrifice her sister had made.

Welgar the Cursed

Welgar the Cursed

By David A. Riley

Welgar the Northerner was always proud of his looks, but the rites of a sorcerer-priest ended that. In exchange for unequalled strength and stamina bestowed on him by an Agryptian god, his skin was ravaged into the likeness of a revived corpse. His pallor became that of the living dead. Even his thick, blond, braided hair and the golden beard that adorned his face were reduced to wisps of faded grey.

Apart from the cheapest, drink-sodden whores, women shy from him, while children recoil in horror on seeing him.

In a bid to restore his body to what it was, Welgar has visited every apothecary, healer, and sorcerer in the city, but no one in the opulent metropolis of Oriaska can offer help. Granted he is stronger, quicker, and more resilient than his old self - which for a mercenary could be regarded as a boon - these are qualities he would gladly forsake to be the man he once was.

As his friend I have often told how he heroically, if unintentionally, came to be like he is, but that has not made life easier for him, especially the looks of pity he sometimes glimpses. Pity is something no Northerner seeks nor wants.

As we sat over our cups one night, he said to me, "I have lingered in this city too long. It is time I left."

"Where will you go?" I asked, disliking the look of sadness in his colourless eyes.

"To war, maybe. I've heard there are skirmishes to the east with a tribe of horse warriors intent on pillage. Prince Hadron has raised an army to push them back."

"You don't need the wages of a mercenary," I said. "The king rewarded us well for rescuing his daughter. You must still be a wealthy man."

Welgar shrugged. "Truth is I am sick of the stares." He glanced around the tavern where too many of its customers averted their eyes when he turned their way. "Maybe I'll find a cure for this curse that damned Agryptian placed on me."

Though we both knew it had not been intended as a curse, but rather a means to enable him to overcome his enemies in that dark sorcery-ridden city.

I understood. Despite the extra strength he has been given, the shrivelling of his flesh has been a hard burden to bear.

"I could come with you…" I began.

But Welgar interrupted me. "My path is not yours, my friend. You are a city dweller, suited to telling tall tales and enjoying the luxury of a soft bed and fine food. You would hate where I intend to go. You may like to talk about adventures, but you do not *want to live them. Our time in Agrypt was more than enough for you."*

I could not disagree.

Nadrain the Storyteller
The Saga of Welgar the Northerner

~*~

The following day, saddlebags filled, Welgar rode from Oriaska heading east, a shield strapped across his shoulders. As soon as he was out on the open road with no one to see his mutilated face he pulled back the cowl of his red silk cloak. The sun shone off the chainmail that showed through gaps in his leather jerkin. It would be a hot day's ride, and he clicked his tongue to urge his mount forward, eager to be on his way before the sun rose too high.

He knew Prince Hadron's mercenary army lay somewhere ahead and was confident he would be able to follow its passage. An army on the move was easy to trail.

Even so his meagre provisions were almost exhausted when several days later he saw its baggage train in the distance on the lower slopes of a broad valley that meandered between a range of ragged, tree-clad mountains. It was a sunny day, and though it was still some distance away the details he could see were spectacularly clear. As was the dense black smoke that rose into a cloudless sky.

Warily, Welgar studied it. That wasn't smoke from campfires, of that he was sure. It was as if the wagons themselves had been set ablaze.

Checking that his sword was loose in its scabbard, slung from a baldrick at his side, he urged his horse forward at a brisk canter. His bluish-grey lips drew back into a savage snarl when he saw the destruction. His suspicion it was the wagons that had been set afire was affirmed. Vultures were already squabbling over the bodies scattered between the wreckage.

As he drew nearer through the thick smoke that blew across the carnage, it was clear an attack had happened only a short while ago. Pools of blood were still spreading from the bodies, most of which had been mutilated. Some, perhaps those foolish enough to surrender, had been nailed to the sides of the wagons. Their charred skeletons were all that remained after the wagons had been set alight.

He hoped they were killed before that happened, but he doubted it.

He recognised the sigils of Prince Hadron on many of the tunics. Most died with weapons in their hands. As he took in the carnage, he realised there were so many bodies stretched across the landscape this must have been most, if not all of Prince Hadron's army.

Of the enemy dead he saw no sign as his horse meandered through the destruction. The bay snorted uneasily at the acrid smells that assailed its nostrils.

"Easy," he murmured.

Whoever did this had not lingered, not even to loot the slain.

Perhaps they had been in a hurry to pursue what remained of the broken army.

Feeling exposed on the valley floor, Welgar headed for the nearest hill. The dense pine forest that covered it would give him shelter for the night, and he could watch the valley without being seen.

As he headed uphill, he wondered if Prince Hadron had underestimated the size of the horse warriors' forces. If so, that boded ill for the towns, villages, and scattered farmsteads between here and Oriaska. It didn't bode well for the city either…

After feeding his horse, Welgar settled down for the night, nibbling at the last of his supplies. As dusk darkened, and there was still no sign of troops along the valley floor, he lay down to sleep. Tomorrow he would search for what might remain of the prince's army… if any had survived.

Despite his tiredness he slept fitfully, which was probably why he was instantly awakened by the noise of something moving through the woods. Though he suspected it was nothing more than a nocturnal animal hunting for prey, it could also be sniffing out his horse. Or even him. With his demonically enhanced abilities, he felt little concern for himself. Nevertheless, he drew his sword. If anything intended to attack his horse he would be damned if he'd be stranded here on foot for want of doing something to protect it.

As he crept towards it, his gelding grunted, perhaps disturbed by his movements. Welgar narrowed his eyes, certain he could smell something strange, a musky odour.

"You have keen senses, warrior. Keener than you were born with."

It was a man's voice, thickly accented.

"Show yourself, stranger," Welgar responded. "There's a patch over there between the trees where the moon shines through."

Close enough as well he could easily reach them with his sword if they appeared to be a threat.

"If you can restrain your natural inclination to slaughter me on the spot,

I'll do that."

"As long as you are unarmed there'll be no bloodshed," Welgar said.

"So I must place more trust in you than you place in me."

"I'm not the one skulking around at night. Show yourself or I'll use my 'keen senses' to hunt you down. You can trust me on that. If you have any weapons leave them behind."

The man sighed, though there was a hint of amusement which galled Welgar. And warned him the man felt safe enough despite the presence of his sword, which made him suspect sorcery, of which he had already seen too much in recent years. Though experience had taught him no sorcerer was immune to a determined thrust from a sword or a dagger.

Less secretive now, the man strode out onto the moonlit patch of grass. He was a small man with a wrinkled, sallow face, with thick, oily, black hair streaked with grey. Dressed in cured animal skins: jerkin, leggings, and boots, with a fur hat on which a protective layer of copper scales had been sewn, his bowlegs indicated a life spent on horseback since infancy, and Welgar wondered if he was one of the horse warriors for which Prince Hadron had been searching.

"Are you alone or are there more of you?" Welgar asked, approaching him with caution.

"I am alone," the man said, though Welgar knew he would say that however many of his fellow horse warriors were stalking through the woods.

"You speak our language well," Welgar said. "Is it your language too?"

"I spent years amongst your kind. As a slave," the man added. He looked too relaxed for Welgar's taste, noticing with distaste numerous odious-looking charms hung from cords around his neck, reawakening his suspicions the man was some kind of sorcerer - or a shaman, as those who lived outside civilised lands called them.

"Some sorcerers would have used a glamor to make themselves unnoticeable," Welgar said.

"Which only works if you can avoid making sounds to draw attention to yourself. Hard to do in a wood where, as a horseman, I find it difficult to walk in silence."

"How did you know I was here?"

"You have a strong aura, swordsman. What is inside you is plain to see for such as me. You have an unmistakable glow, even from a distance."

"So much for Agryptian gods."

The man nodded. "I wondered from whence it came. It is strange to me." He studied Welgar's death-mask face in the moonlight. "I see you paid heavily for whatever you were given by it."

Welgar bridled at the reminder of his disfigured looks.

"What should I do with you?" he asked gruffly.

The stranger laughed. "I have not surrendered. I am still a free man and intend to remain so. You have recognised me as a shaman. You would do well to keep that in mind."

Welgar tightened his grip on the hilt of his sword. "You can be sure of that." He forced himself to relax. "What have you come for?"

"To tell you that you waste your time if you are looking for the army sent to attack my people. It is destroyed. What remains is scattered to the winds."

"And its commander, Prince Hadron?"

"He flees. Though we will find him soon enough."

"Then what?"

"That is up to our king."

"Why have your people come here?"

The shaman laughed again. "Is it not obvious? You have pleasant lands. Too pleasant for you. Now it is time we tasted this pleasantness. We are a warrior race and what we want we take. If you are not strong enough we take what you have. It is what our gods command. And our king, *glorious and feared be his name*, is a servant of our gods."

Welgar snarled. "You'll not find us easy to conquer, shaman."

"Defeat of Prince Hadron proves otherwise." The man showed him a gap-toothed grin. "Strung from my horse's saddle are the heads of five cavalrymen I killed myself. I would have strung more, but I ran out of room and had to leave the rest to rot with their bodies." His laugh was like the baying of a demented jackal.

Welgar studied him carefully as anger rose inside him. Though apparently not armed, he suspected the shaman had less obvious weapons. He would not have stepped out so easily if he hadn't. Yet Welgar knew he had two advantages over the shaman: the enhanced speed with which he was able to react and his increased strength. Just how aware the horse warrior was of these he wasn't sure, though he was certain the man had grasped a little of his abilities.

But perhaps not all.

"Are you here for me to surrender?" Welgar asked.

"To *join* us. You are not of the people who live hereabouts. You are a stranger from the north. Like mine your people are horsemen. Nomads. Your settlements are always on the move, not decadent cities. You should ride with, not against us."

"My people don't nail prisoners to wagons then burn them alive."

"Do your gods not rejoice in the sufferings of your enemies when sacrificed to them?"

"The only sacrifices my gods rejoice in are from those who offer themselves freely."

The shaman shrugged dismissively, a look of contempt twisting his overripe lips. "Perhaps your gods are weak. Perhaps it is time you gave them up for ours."

Which was when Welgar decided he was done with words and was about to close in on the man when the shaman dropped a small object onto the grass as he muttered words in his native tongue. Sensing danger, Welgar instinctively backed away as a cloud of dust erupted into the air and swept towards him. Just in time, thanks to his demonically enhanced reflexes, Welgar wheeled away and threw himself between the trees. Emerging from the forest seconds later he came to an abrupt halt.

Facing him across the hillside in the bright moonlight stood a long line of horse warriors, bows raised and pointing towards him. One, more grandiosely dressed than the others with a burnished bronze breastplate and a spiked helmet edged in fur, shouted an order and one arrow was loosed. It thudded deep into the turf only inches from Welgar's feet.

Stepping out from between the pines behind him, the shaman called, "You cannot escape, swordsman. Accept our hospitality or die."

~*~

With his hands bound behind his back it was an uncomfortable ride as Welgar and his captors cantered along the valley floor. By midday they finally caught up with the rest of the army. Welgar was shocked to see how large it was, so vast he could barely see the head of it through the dense clouds of dust stirred up by the horses.

Taken to the back of the baggage train, his horse was tethered to one of the ox-drawn wagons heaped with provisions. Two wounded horse warriors sat on the back of the wagon, laughing and chattering, though their dark eyes never stopped watching him, nor did their hands relax on their bows. Not that he would get very far if he tried to escape, with his hands bound and hundreds of warriors riding all around him, guarding the rear of the baggage train.

"Hey, corpse man!" One of the horse warriors rode up alongside Welgar, a broad grin on his thinly bearded, pock-marked face.

Welgar turned towards him, not surprised when the horseman made finger movements as if to ward off the evil eye as he looked at his face. It was a reaction he had seen all too often from people startled by the ravaged skin stretched tight across his fleshless features.

"Had a good look, you bow-legged bastard?" Welgar asked.

The horse warrior grunted and spat on the ground before riding off to a chorus of jeers from the two guards sat on the wagon.

No one else bothered him till they encamped at dusk, when a bewildering array of animal skin tents were erected, and campfires lit to heat up cauldrons of overpoweringly spicy stew. While all this was going on he was left on his horse, until the shaman appeared. Ordering his guards to help Welgar down, the shaman led him to a large campfire around which the senior commanders of the host had already gathered, sitting cross-legged on the ground.

"Tonight you must decide if you are to join us," the man said as one of the guards cut the bonds on Welgar's wrists.

"If I don't?"

The shaman grimaced. "Not good for you," he said, laughing. "But entertaining for the rest of us. Choice is yours. Sit and eat before you decide."

The shaman lowered himself beside Welgar as they were handed wooden bowls filled with stew. Less self-conscious of their behaviour than city dwellers, Welgar was discomfited that most of the warriors sat around the fire were staring at his face, though they seemed more curious than hostile or even shocked. No doubt they had seen worse mutilations, and his mind strayed back to those tortured at the baggage train.

Finishing the stew, Welgar was handed a beaker of fermented mare's milk. He recognised it from his homeland and drank it with relish. It had been many a year since he'd last tasted anything like it.

When he finished, the shaman prodded his arm. "Time for you to tell our king if you will accept his offer to join us."

They rose and walked around the fire, stopping on the far side where for the first time he saw the horse warriors' leader. He was unmistakable, sat on a raised thronelike chair covered in animal skins. The king was taller than most of his people, which Welgar reckoned would put the man at shoulder height if they stood side by side. He was broad, with powerful shoulders and a deep chest, hidden beneath a magnificent tunic of scale armour decorated with precious stones and edged in gold. His sallow face boasted a heavy beard intricately plaited down his chest. He watched Welgar with deep-set eyes that glittered in the firelight.

"King Aggron, this is the captive I told you about," the shaman said, bowing deeply.

The king leaned forward for a better view. "Never have I seen a living man with a face like yours, Northerner. Was what you gained worth it?"

Welgar shrugged. "I was given no choice. It was thrust upon me."

Laughing mirthlessly, the king turned to the shaman. "Seybell, we need to see if this man is truly as exceptional as you think before we offer him the chance to join our great army."

The king clicked his fingers and those sitting nearest parted to let through a group of heavily armed guards. Shuffling between them, ankles chained, appeared a dozen men. Though bedraggled and blood-stained, Welgar recognised the two-headed hawk sigil on their jerkins; they had been part of Prince Hadron's army.

More guards formed a barrier between the prisoners and the king, the curved blades of their scimitars bared as they set their shields on the ground like a wall.

Some of the guards unlocked the chains from the prisoners' ankles, then handed each a sword. Welgar heard bows creak and at least forty arrows were aimed at the men.

"You have one chance of freedom," Seybell announced to the prisoners. "You fight one man. If you kill him freedom is yours. If you refuse, archers will kill you now." He turned to Welgar. "That choice is yours too, Northerner. Kill them first or they will kill you. If you and they refuse, for you there will be a night of torture."

Handed back his longsword, Welgar was pushed towards the prisoners, some of whom grimaced when they saw his face.

"How do we kill a dead man?" one called out.

Welgar stepped towards him. "I'm no more dead than you are. Yet."

"A warning, Northerner," the king called out. "If you decide to let them kill you, all of them will be tortured to death. This must be a real fight. I will know if it is not."

Before Welgar could decide what to do one of the prisoners launched his own attack. Without thought, Welgar parried the blow, then found his blade sinking deep into the man's chest as if of its own volition. With a grunt, Welgar tugged it free.

"*Leave it to me!*" A voice rasped like the grinding of something immensely large deep inside his head, as an uncontrollable shudder passed through his body. It was like nothing he had ever experienced before. His limbs moved but not at his bidding. It was as if he were nothing more than a marionette, and he suddenly knew, with a feeling of despair deep in his stomach, that whatever had entered into his body all those months ago in Agrypt when the sorcerer-priests linked him to their god was asserting its control. "*Do not worry,*" the voice added gratingly. "*I am here for your good. Your body will be yours again when I have finished.*"

In that instant he found himself rushing forwards, his sword moving so fast it was nothing more than a shimmering blur that took heads and limbs from its victims even swifter than Welgar could see what was happening. Blood splashed in crimson fountains from sliced flesh. Again and again Welgar cut and thrust and swung his sword in an irresistible maelstrom of death. Those pitted against him stood no chance, even those who threw down their swords, though most were skewered by arrows from the watching archers even before Welgar's sword touched them.

It was over so fast some of those looking on rubbed their eyes in disbelief. Seybell, sensing more of what he had witnessed than the rest, stepped back warily. As a shaman his sight had been all but blinded by the intensity of the light that glowed from within the swordsman's body. Never had he been so close to such a powerful entity as that which had infused the northerner with its godlike vigour. For the first time the shaman felt afraid.

"What have I done?" he whispered to himself, then gasped as Welgar stood before him, immense and radiant. The shaman's head spun through the air with a look of astonishment etched on his face to land at the feet of his king, whose disembowelled corpse had already toppled to the ground before his throne.

The terror that seized the horse warriors' camp was unstoppable. Onwards and outwards the carnage spread so that even those furthest from its centre fled in panic, not even knowing what it was they were trying to escape...

In the days that followed many managed to find refuge in the hills and forests, a broken force that would never be able to wage war again. Some became brigands, but most died whimpering from fear, haunted by shadows.

~*~

The next morning Welgar picked himself up from the ground where he had finally collapsed when the carnage had ended and the demon or god relinquished its control of him. All around lay the butchered remains of a once ferocious army, now nothing more than a feeding ground for vultures. There were so many bodies not even the jackals that prowled around the field of destruction fought each other over what was there.

Still stunned and unsure what really happened, Welgar wiped the blood from his sword and sheathed it. He called for his horse, and was surprised and relieved when the gelding came into view. Gathering provisions from the abandoned wagons, he gazed once more at the slaughter, unable to believe he had been the cause of it.

In a moment of anguish, he looked at his reflection in a pool of water, horrified at what he had become. He stared at the ravaged visage of death that gazed back at him. Was this what he now was, a vile contagion, a curse?

As he mounted his horse, Welgar wondered what it was that lurked inside him. Was it truly a god as the Agryptian priests had claimed, or a blood-lusting demon as he often suspected? The deaths his sword had caused shocked him, there were just so many. Already the stench was becoming unbearable as the sun scorched down on them.

Perhaps his looks really mirrored the horror of the thing that was deep inside him - as he wondered how long he would be able to bear its presence.

Only time, he knew, would tell.

Ride the Fire Steed

A Crimson Warrior Tale by Adrian Cole

Dark fogs curdled along the stretch of bleak coastline, their sour smell permeating the air, drawing coughs and curses from the rowers. A dozen of them, scrawny men in ragged clothing, poled the long, flat barge parallel to the shore.

This was a jumble of quaysides that had slumped into the estuary like so many cracked tongues of stone, interspersed with long tendrils of vegetation, bloated roots, and with brutally twisted knots of metal, relics of days long past when this place had been a thriving hive of human endeavor. These days the men plied their trade monotonously, eking out a bare living from it, bending their backs as they worked their slow way, mile after mile towards the trading post. It had once been part of a luxurious port, but its history was all but forgotten, tangled in a past that no longer had relevance for this world.

Unusually there were two passengers. The traders had been content to take their money, rare coins from another moldering city that still held value, and didn't ask questions, though their curiosity might have been aroused, at least by the nature of the two travelers. They'd come aboard much further north, stepping out of shadows like ghosts from another age, bringing with them two sturdy ponies that looked like the mountain breed beyond the city, about which little was known. Side by side, the two ponies stood calmly, almost as though their energy had been switched off. They appeared to be content, relaxed. Of the two travelers, the first was the most remarkable, clearly from its partly concealed crimson armor a warrior, a rarity in these times. Its companion was a man of medium build, dressed in simple but tidy habiliment, trousers, thick shirt and a jerkin. That he was armed, with both a sword and a knife, which hung from his leather belt, was not common. Those who ruled this realm, the Kaizen, looked upon humans carrying weapons as insolence.

While the man was both bare-headed and without any face covering, revealing himself to be of middle age and of good health, the other was tightly wrapped in armor, mostly hidden beneath a long cloak of some very thin material, with a mask of light mail covering the face so that only the eyes were visible. They had the sharpness of an eagle's stare and on the few occasions when the figure spoke, the voice was low and a little harsh, challenging, possibly authoritative, which gave the traders to believe this person had at least once been someone of standing in human circles. Humanity, though, had lost its place in the mastery of the world, and only the remotest wild places had not been ground under the heels of the invading Kaizen.

Presently the barge was eased towards the shore, where buildings loomed up out of the swirling fog. They may once have been proud towers and spires, linked by high walls, but now they were shattered and broken, leaning their spoil into each other, doors punched through stone like tunnels, where pipes and wires spilled out like the innards of gutted beasts. All Humanity's cities here in the north were like this, remnants of something grander, at best ruptured memories of endeavor and enterprise. Almost all were empty shells, reclaimed by the forests. The traders poled the barge alongside a flat stretch of quay from which tussocks of matted brown grass sprouted at intervals, weeds that threatened to prize open the slabs and lever them into the river.

"Go through there," said the man who had the role of master of the barge, a stooped, thin-haired fellow, whose expression showed little interest in anything other than getting the barge tied off as he watched his companions working the ropes. His two passengers disembarked with their ponies and the man thanked him. The other figure was already studying the mangled remains of the port, the journey along the river already forgotten.

The streets leading off from the quay were uneven, in many places victims of more weeds and grasping plants, though none of these appeared to be vigorous, just consistent in their recolonization of the area. In time they would blot out all evidence that Man had been here at all. Up in the stones, countless razorgulls watched. These were bloated scavengers of the skies, fat gulls with long bills, serrated for tearing at flesh, their commonest food since the ravages of the wars, and their bright red eyes gave warning of their lack of fear of humans, potential victims. At any moment a host of them might wing down and attack like a pack of huge winged rats. Something about these two travelers deterred such an attack, however.

Slowly the two travelers walked their ponies down the street as indicated. It was midafternoon, though the sun was a pale orb somewhere behind the ever shifting clouds of fog. These billowed far inland, a shroud over the rotting urban landscape. The two had gone perhaps a quarter of a mile, when they came to the place the traders had told them of: it was an inn, or what passed for one. Silent now, though its doors were open, it was wedged between two former warehouses, whose roofs had long since fallen in, and whose rotting rafters had become the roosting places of flocks of other birds, black-winged and raucous. Their eyes studied the two travelers eagerly, though like the razorgulls, none of the aerial creatures moved from their place. They preferred to do their killing at night.

Inside the inn it was barely furnished, a few tables and chairs scattered about. It was gloomy, partially derelict, typical of the neglected buildings found all along the coast, remnants of the past, a vision that showed no will to build a better future, a resignation of effort. Man had become a beaten animal, gradually succumbing to oblivion as the Kaizen bloomed and spread.

A man emerged from the shadows and stared in surprise at his visitors. "Who sent you?" From his tone and nervous manner it was evident to them that he assumed they were from a higher authority, which could only mean the Kaizen.

"I am Skarrack. I serve as squire to this knight. Otherwise we serve no one."

The man looked bewildered. "I had no idea such as you existed. Certainly there are none in Borrabund, this city. Men have become its rats."

"Are there Kaizen here?"

"Rarely. They are mostly to the far southeast, a long way from us, or across the sea in the islands. They visit occasionally, our warders. There's a small company in the southern suburbs of the city, but we rarely see them. We're nothing to them."

Skarrack nodded, understanding well enough. Men knew their place. They did not rebel. His own spirit had come close to being broken, but these days he bore himself with a little more grit. The Kaizen were powerful, not immortal. They could be killed. "We need a place to rest for the night. Food for us and our two ponies. At dawn we move on." He pushed a few coins over the counter. "Will these suffice?"

The man gaped at them, then gently picked them up. "Indeed! You are too generous."

"Keep them. Feed us well."

The innkeeper lifted glasses and a jug of fresh water from below the counter. "Why are you here? What can our dead city offer such as you?"

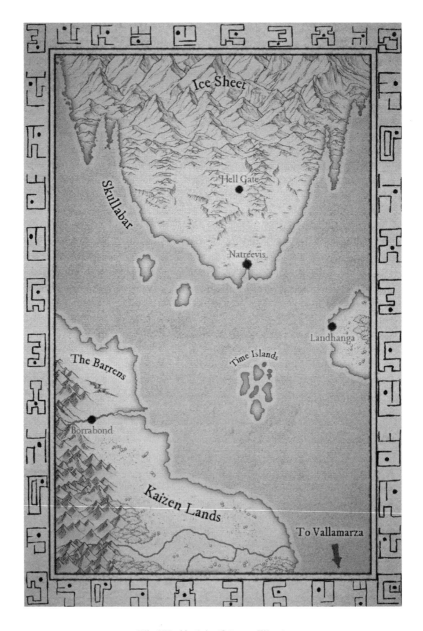

The World of the Crimson Warrior

Skarrack poured two glasses and handed one to his silent companion, who turned away, lifting the thin mask and drinking. "Nothing," said Skarrack. "We travel north."

"Beyond the city?"

"Yes. To the mountains."

The man looked aghast. "Do you not know of their dangers? Even the Kaizen would not go there. It is an evil place. There are many legends, stories to ward off those who would trespass, but they are there for a reason."

"We know the legends," said Skarrack.

"You're not afraid?"

"Let's just say we're careful."

~*~

Dawn was a dull orange glow in the east, only partially opening the fog curtain as Skarrack and his companion mounted their ponies and moved slowly out of the city limits and on into the higher ground along what had once been a well-used road. Its surface had become badly pitted, the slabs that had formed its base split and in places so seriously ruptured they had to be circumnavigated. No wagons had passed through here for years. Gradually the surrounding buildings, no more than mangled hovels now, fell away to be replaced by knotted banks of vegetation, briars and thorns, and Skarrack used a blade to hack them aside.

By mid-morning they were up in the first low foothills of the mountain range that soared up to the north and west of them, the road crumbling away to an even more rutted path, turning towards the huge black mass of rock and natural stone buttresses. Skarrack's companion held up a gloved hand and they paused, the ponies becoming statuesque.

"What do you hear?" he said.

"Among the rocks," came the sharp, low voice. "An ambush."

"Kaizen?" He felt his blood running cold. Exposed as they were, they'd be a poor match for a company of the monstrous invaders.

"No. Humans. A score, no more." Their blades gleamed in the brightening sunlight. "All around us. Are you ready, Skarrack?"

He nodded. His companion had exceptional skills and not a little sorcery, so he knew he would enjoy a degree of protection in any skirmish, but even so, his hackles rose at the thought of fending off a score of assailants. He didn't have to wait long for their attack. They broke from cover, men on foot, but well-armed, though their swords, knives, and staves had not been made by craftsmen. As they rushed in, tightening their circle, both Skarrack and his companion swung their own blades, cutting brutally and ramming home sword points to deadly effect. In moments seven of the attackers were spread on the ground, torn apart, bloody corpses. They had not been fighting men, neither trained nor experienced. Desperation had goaded them into this futile attack.

The two defenders were skilled horsemen and they twisted and turned the ponies, which had been bred for this sort of tight action, chopping this way and that in a blaze of movement that the human assailants could not hope to break down. Almost all of the men were cut to pieces, weapons snapped, heads opened up, limbs hacked off in showers of bright crimson. The speed of the killings was frightful, and the surviving three assailants gaped at the horror around them. Swiftly they leapt back up into the low rocks beyond the clearing and were swallowed by the forest.

"Let them go," said Skarrack's companion, dismounting and wiping the blade that had wrought so much havoc on a dead man's shirt.

"Will they bring others?"

"I hope so." The green eyes met Skarrack's stare, and in them he read something dark and forbidding, a promise of more death to come.

"We should leave, and quickly," he said. He took no joy in the death he had meted out to these wretches.

Mounted once more, they moved swiftly along the path towards the ever-nearing mountains. As he watched the surrounding landscape, a mass of tangled trees, overhung with lichen and creepers, weeds that seemed to be bringing the forest down in the same way that the buildings were being dragged into the earth, his mind slipped back to earlier conflicts involving his companion. She had been a Fire Witch, one of the coven of sorceresses serving the last kingdom of Man on the island of Vallamarza. When the Kaizen swept in, the king had used the Fire Witches to summon demons, the Crimson Warriors, believed to be from another realm beyond this world. Even their terrible powers had not been enough to better the Kaizen, and as a last desperate resort to win favor with the invaders, the king had betrayed the Fire Witches and the Crimson Warriors. It had been a terribly misguided act and it had backfired. The Kaizen swarmed, destroyed almost all of humanity and now ruled, unchallenged and omnipotent.

Skarrack's companion had escaped and now rode on her own private trail of vengeance against the Kaizen, using the powers of the Crimson Warriors invested in the blade she carried and the armor of the demons she wore. Skarrack had served her once, and seen many men die to help her win back some of humanity's lost ground and pride. He had a simple choice: go back to being a pitiful member of a downtrodden, defeated slave nation, or break free and go with the Crimson Warrior as her squire. His spirit had not been altogether broken and he chose the latter.

The mountains suddenly reared up out of fading mist, like a huge wall, sheer and forbidding. There appeared to be no way through them, but a long, black gash soared skyward, a narrow chasm into the heart of the range. The path wound down through more twisted vegetation and disappeared into the darkness at the foot of the gash like a choked drain. Skarrack's companion pointed to it. "That's our way through."

"Do you know what they call that place?" he asked.

The masked face turned to him, the green eyes narrowing. "Are you getting cold feet, Skarrack? You needn't come with me. I free you from service to me, if you wish."

"Yonder lies the Death Walk. Whatever is beyond the mountains is protected by that pathway." He did not want to name the things he had heard tell of.

"The Burning Blade will protect me – and you, if you chose to come. I need to get through. What I seek is in the valley locked in the heart of these mountains."

He shrugged. "I'll come. There's nothing for me back here. Let's ride on."

"Not yet. Feed the horses. There's a stream nearby. Let them drink. Then we'll wait."

"For what?"

"The men who escaped us will run to their masters. The Kaizen. We are wanted by them. For questioning. Word of a Crimson Warrior will bring them running like slavering dogs."

"The Kaizen are coming for us! Then we should waste no time in fleeing."

"I've a mind to kill a few before we go."

Skarrack gasped. With anyone else, he knew it would have been suicide. A hundred of Humanity's best fighters could not hope to defeat or beat off a small pack of the Kaizen warriors. His companion, however, was no ordinary warrior. With the Burning Blade, she could distribute an awesome killing power. And yet, to stand alone would be tempting death.

He would have argued, but he understood that there must be a purpose to her actions.

"You meant for those men to betray our whereabouts," he said.

"I did. I want the Kaizen to find us. I'm going to kill them."

"But there could be too many!"

"No, not at first. A dozen at most. They are arrogant enough to think they can take us with no more than that. We are merely humans," she added ironically, and gave a soft laugh, but Skarrack's blood ran no less cold.

~*~

Later, when they had fed and watered the ponies and eaten a little food themselves, Skarrack realized his companion was tasting the air, sensing something, distant vibrations perhaps. She turned to him. "Take the ponies down the trail and go into the first shadows of the mountain path. You'll be safe enough there." She had pulled a second sword, not the one she had used so effectively against their human assailants. This was the Burning Blade. It shone brilliantly, like burnished gold. Skarrack had once seen its terrible powers unleashed, still utterly amazed at the furious energies locked inside it and what they had achieved. He looked at it, that power dormant now, staring only for a moment, then mounted his pony and nudged it the other away down the path.

Behind him, the Crimson Warrior waited. She could feel the ground beneath her trembling to the hooves of the Kaizen mounts. They came closer, the forest echoing to their shouts, the pounding of hooves. As she had expected, there were a dozen pursuers. They burst through the trees and as one, pulled up sharp, their huge, vaguely reptilian mounts screaming like wild beasts hungry for the kill. She studied them, their black armor embossed with golden sigils, its segments fitted to their massive forms like those of large insects. Their grotesque steel helmets scattered reflected sunlight and their long, curved weapons swept to and fro in preparation for action like the weaving heads of serpents. She knew the Kaizen were fast, too fast for a normal human, but she put her faith in her training and her own blade. It was not as long as theirs, cast from a pale metal, and as she waited it emitted wisps of curling, white mist.

Two of the Kaizen unfurled a long net and they dragged it between them. As she had expected, they did not want her dead, but captured. It would give her an advantage. There was to be no discussion, no foreplay. The Kaizen charged forward, supremely confident. Her speed caught them unawares as she ducked below the first sweep of a blade and cut through the forelegs of the leading mount, swung round lithely and did the same for another. Amid screams of agony and the obscene snarls of the falling riders, two of the Kaizen were flung earthwards, briefly blocking the attack of their fellows. It was enough. The Crimson Warrior used the Burning Blade to deadly effect and two Kaizen heads were sheared clean from their necks, spinning through the air, a trail of bubbling blood like pennants in their wake.

One of the net-men tried to lift the net up and over his intended victim as he rode in, but the Crimson Warrior lifted her weapon like a staff and its blade severed the thick netting as easily as if it were parting the soft strands of a spider's web. Part of the net dropped, coiling around the legs of the rider's mount, bringing it down in a jumble of limbs, the Kaizen smashing into the ground, his sword flung from his reach. The Crimson Warrior stepped in and ran the point of her blade under the chin of its helm and it tore through flesh and sinew, killing the warrior at a stroke.

The assailants grew wary, but some of them tried to ring the Crimson Warrior, though each time one of them attempted to race in, she was ready, the Burning Blade, ablaze now like a torch, cut through armor and bone as easily as it would have done a block of soft wood. One by one the Kaizen were unhorsed and slaughtered, their bloody corpses hacked apart and scattered across the clearing. Those of their steeds that did not suffer the same fate turned aside and galloped off into the forest, the sound of their screams diminishing as they fled the scene of horror. When it was over, the Crimson Warrior stepped out of the misty red haze that surrounded her killing ground and faced the last Kaizen rider. Cautiously it eased its steed back.

"Go to your masters," said the Crimson Warrior. "Bring as many of your vermin as you like. I will be waiting for you."

"Your arrogance is misplaced; nothing stands in the way of the Kaizen. Not for long. You'll pay for this day's work with agonies beyond your imagining." With that the Kaizen wheeled his steed and rode at breakneck speed back through the forest. The Crimson Warrior briefly examined her victims. None had lived, nor had their steeds. She left the glade and trotted down the path towards the towering mountain wall.

~*~

Skarrack and the Crimson warrior stood at the entrance to the tall gash in the rock wall. Light stopped at the entrance, unable to filter inwards, as if the air within was part of a black pool. It was silent, the weight of it intense. The two ponies shied away from the place, eyes filled with evident terror, and although the Crimson Warrior calmed them, their terror was a barrier to forcing them in. She turned from the dark entrance and led them to a small, grassy clearing where there was a pool, fed by a white fall of water from the rock face directly above. There she tethered the ponies and it seemed to content them.

"We go forward on foot," she told Skarrack. "We'll recover the ponies and our supplies when we return."

He stared at the black path into the mountain, less reassured than the ponies. "This is not good," he said.

"No. It is not. Alone, you would be dead within an hour." She unsheathed the Burning Blade and it hummed with a life of its own, and gave off a pale light. Sorcery was its blood, that much had always been clear to Skarrack. Power from another age, another world perhaps. Enough to swathe them both. She entered the darkness, pushing it back a short distance, enough to show the broken floor. He stayed at her back, his ears alert for the slightest sound. In the silence he tried to recall the old legends he had heard about this place, the Death Walk.

It was said to be the only access to a once sacred valley, where a goddess from long before the old wars of man had hidden herself away from the chaos and destruction of the nightmare times. She had protected herself by using dark magic to render the Death Walk, a jagged passage that snared and crushed all those who tried to use it as a means of entry into her haven. In so doing, she had weakened her powers and it was said that she had ever since been degenerating, the price she had had to pay for her refuge. Local myths said she was long since dead, her spirit sometimes seen high on the mountain ridges, blown by the high winds, a mournful figure, redolent with sorrow. Man had tried to block up the opening to the Dead Walk, but each time the mountain had reacted like a living entity and cast the blockage aside, so that the way was always open, though no one dared travel it.

Skarrack had no idea how long they had been going forward, treading over rocks and flattened stones that might once, in antiquity, have been steps. The walls closed in above, making the great gash resemble a tunnel, and in places cold water dripped down, or ran in shining trickles down the bare rock, forming small, inky pools. The air was chilling, but the pale light of the blade set an aura around the two travelers. Beyond its halo, things moved, their sounds of slithering and sliding growing more pronounced and disturbing. Skarrack caught glimpses of shapes hanging high up in the vault, globular and slick, like elongated gourds, live things that threatened to drop. His skull crawled at the thought of their touch. And always things were shifting away from their advance, retreating but not dismissed.

There were other strange shapes, twisted metal pipes that had split open to reveal clotted bunches of flesh-like growths which hung down, slick with oily fluids. Serpentine creatures writhed within the fattest of these, like elongated cannibal maggots feasting on the superstructure of a biological structure, its purpose unfathomable, lost in ages gone by when machines had fought machines in the ultimate insanity of conflict. Some of the roots that dangled like lianas in a forest were more wire-like than vegetable, tangled and integrated in patterns that defied the imagination.

"Madness is our greatest foe in this place," whispered the Crimson Warrior. "These beings hover between this world and some charnel realm, dredged up by the kind of sorcery that brought humanity to its knees in the chronic wars. The Burning Blade offers clean magic, cauterizing the wounds the old powers inflicted. Trust it in, Skarrack."

After that, as if the horrors festering around them had heard the words, things did strike at them—long, black tendrils, or fat, worm-like creatures, bloated toad-things and shambling quasi-spiders, but the Burning Blade's light was like acid to them all, crackling as it blazed. Skarrack closed his mind to the madness threatened by the sight of these revolting outpourings of darkness, and he knew that had it not been for the Burning Blade, he would have rushed back out into daylight, shrieking and babbling for the rest of his days. Eventually the horrors must have sensed their ineffectiveness, and withdrew. Another deep silence fell, and as the two travelers climbed a long, shattered path of disintegrating steps, they saw light in the distance.

It proved to be the way out into clear, clean daylight. Verdant trees and thick underbrush smothered the path beyond, but Skarrack and his companion used their normal blades to clear a way through. Though the work was strenuous, it was a relief to be doing something, out of that cloying darkness. At the edge of the pressing trees, they came to the edge of a wide valley, set here like a jewel in the heart of the mountain range, its thick grasses and rolling plain lit by the midday sun, high above the encircling rim of ragged mountain peaks. Birds soared above, but these were not the horrific razorgulls, instead brightly plumed and fair of song, and Skarrack drew in lungfuls of the fresh air, hugely relieved to be in such a restful atmosphere.

"The land of the goddess," said his companion. "A world apart."

"Is she alive?"

"Look around you. Everything here has been fed by her power. Of course she's alive!" The Crimson Warrior removed her grim mask, for once revealing her head and long, trailing hair. Black as a raven's wing, it gleamed in the sunlight. It was the first time he had ever seen her face. He would never have expected her to be so young, barely twenty summers. Her green eyes regarded him and he felt himself color with embarrassment. She saw this and laughed, the sound rising in the still air, a natural joy in this extraordinary haven.

Her candid stare had disarmed him. "What is your name?" he asked, haltingly.

"I am Estarziel, daughter of King Attras. I suppose I am queen of Vallamarza, though that island is nothing more than a graveyard now."

He repeated her name softly, then looked away, stirred by the disquiet it caused him. "I see fruit on those trees," he said stiffly. "I wonder if it's safe to eat."

She laughed again. "The sword will warn me, if not. But here, in the land of the goddess, I am sure we will be protected. She will know I have come to serve her."

"Why are we here?" he asked.

"To claim a gift from her." But Estarziel said no more, walking through the long grass as if she had always belonged here. He followed, feeling a wave of calmness now, the dire oppressiveness of the Death Walk removed. This place was like a garden, its walls holding back the worst that the damaged world could conjure. They did eat the fruit, enjoying its richness, and Skarrack felt almost intoxicated by it, as if he had taken a long draught of wine. He became more aware of his surroundings, noticing clouds of butterflies and more soaring birds. There was no threat here, no promise of menace such as permeated the nightmare outer world.

"The world we know was more like this once," said his companion. "Humanity almost destroyed it long before the Kaizen came."

He was about to question her more, but she clapped her hands and pointed. Further down the valley, grouped together, were a dozen horses. They were splendid animals, with flowing manes and vivid of color, some grays, others all shades of roan. As one their heads came up, bright eyes fixed on the girl.

"They serve the goddess," she said. "And will take us to her."

The horses whinnied and swung round, galloping up one of the valley slopes towards a copse where they waited in front of it, as if summoned there. Skarrack and the girl went quickly after them and the steeds parted, deliberately creating an entrance into the low trees. There was a glade beyond, a natural, large bower and at its heart rested a wide block of stone. Its sides had been majestically carved with horse images.

"The goddess lies within it," said the girl. "She sleeps, but in her dreams she hears us. She has waited years without number for our coming. In her glory days she was among the greatest of the gods and goddesses who ruled humanity, before people became arrogant and thought they could manage their affairs without the gods, thus diminishing their powers. You have seen the result of their folly."

"You said she has a gift for us."

"If we are worthy. Help me to move the lid."

Skarrack did so and after a concentrated effort they pulled the heavy slab free and set it down in the grass. Inside the stone sarcophagus there was a deep bed of leaves and flowers that had somehow defied the darkness they had been in and which dazzled the eye with their lustrous colors, fresh and vivid, burgeoning. Skarrack drew back as he saw the bed of leaves heaving, tumbling gently aside as a figure sat up and looked around in wonder at the glade. She was a woman who had known many years, though she had aged uniquely, her features unblemished, her skin soft and clear, her eyes bright. She stood, a little dazed, but climbed effortlessly out of the sarcophagus. Skarrack felt a glow, a suffusion of distinct power.

He and the girl bowed as if to a monarch.

"I heard you coming, from a great distance," she said, her voice clear and musical, and she smiled, vivid white teeth flashing in the sunlight. "You have come for my gift."

"We have, majesty," said the girl.

"Such power is dangerous. Humanity has sought its like down all the ages, and often it has been the instrument its own destruction."

"The world is dying," said the girl. "The Kaizen invaders are choking the life from the last remnants of humanity, and unless something rises to defy them, they will obliterate us and all that has gone before."

"Yes, I have sensed that in many troubled dreams," said the goddess, her voice welling with sorrow. "Then it is time for the passing on. My time will soon be over. Such powers that I have, I will give to you. Use them wisely."

"What must I do?"

The goddess walked around the glade slowly, taking in its every detail, as if recalling the beauty of its plants and trees, remembering, perhaps, days of wonder from long ago. She called out once and immediately the horses that were waiting outside entered the glade and she stroked the noses of each of them as they dropped their heads to her.

"My children," she said. "Your work begins now." She turned to the girl. "Estarziel, you carry the Burning Blade? Unsheathe it."

The girl did as bidden and light sparkled and danced on the metal. Her eyes fixed on it, the goddess walked forward. "My power must be linked to the power of the sword, strengthened by the powers of the clean earth. I am ready." She opened her arms.

Skarrack's face clouded. She was asking to be slain? Estarziel stepped forward as if she had known this would happen.

"Do not flinch," said the goddess. "It is time."

Only for a moment did the girl pause, then she slowly pushed the point of the Burning Blade into the flesh of the goddess. Light flooded the glade and Skarrack was forced to turn away. Estarziel pulled the blade, now slick with the blood of the goddess, out of her flesh. But she showed no pain, only smiling as if in private triumph. "Drive it into the earth!" she cried. "My blood will feed it. The gift will be yours."

Estarziel thrust the blade into the soft loam beneath the grass and at once the ground heaved, pulsing with light and energy. The goddess began to fade, her body slipping downwards, absorbed by the earth, taken back into it, adding to the dazzling light that flowed like waves from both her and blade. Startled, the horses bolted back out of the glade. Skarrack's eyes were closed, but he felt the swirling of power, seething within the light like a physical force, though it held no fear for him, only a strange elation.

In a while silence dropped over everything. It was broken by the sound of hooves; this time a single horse entered the glade. It was a stallion, fully grown, a magnificent gray, with a mane like billowing snow. Its eyes blazed, possibly with fury at the passing of its mistress.

"The Fire Steed," said Estarziel. "This was the gift, as promised." The astonishing beast came to her and its brilliant eyes looked down at her so that for a moment it seemed as though it must surely trample her into the ground for her act. But instead it bowed its head and nuzzled her, almost knocking her from her feet. She pulled the Burning Blade free and resheathed it, then with a quick leap and twist, swung up on to the back of the stallion. It reared up, snorting and giving a challenge to the world, as though reveling in powers that had been dormant within it.

"There will be a steed for you," the girl told Skarrack. "It will chose you, so be patient." She nudged the Fire Steed out into the valley where the other horses were waiting. Skarrack followed. For long moments nothing happened, then each of the horses cantered slowly up and circled him, until one of them, a strawberry roan came very close. Amazed, he stroked it and whispered to it before gently mounting it. From that moment on, he knew his life had been changed.

~*~

At the mouth of the Death Walk, Estarziel again donned her mask and helm, and led the Fire Steed into the darkness. There was no need to unsheathe the Burning Blade: light from the stallion flung back the shadows, and it did more, for the walls shuddered as if not made of stone but were instead thick curtains, drawing back. Deep within the mountain something heaved and strained, as though long-lost machines ground into sluggish life. The Death Walk opened wider and whatever horrors resided within it scuttled and shrank back, poisoned by the light.

The riders came to daylight and rode out into the warmth of the afternoon. Behind them they heard the final protestations of the stone, a distant roar, and then, with a great belch of dust, the Death Walk closed in on itself, sealing its passage a final time. Skarrack studied the clearing where Estarziel had earlier fought the Kaizen. Their bodies were gone, nothing of them remaining. Floating high above on the air thermals, a dozen razorgulls drifted. Somehow Skarrack did not think they had removed the dead.

"Protect the ponies and our supplies," Estarziel told him.

"You can't fight them alone. There will be far more of them. I'm better prepared this time."

But she waved him back. In the sunlight, with her cloak flung back, her crimson armor shone fiercely, as if lit from within, and as she again drew the Burning Blade, its own light speared outwards in all directions. Overhead, the razorgulls glided swiftly away. Skarrack watched unhappily, but slowly urged his steed to the place where he had tethered the two ponies. They lifted their heads at his arrival, unconcerned.

The girl heard the drumming of hooves and again prepared herself to face the Kaizen. By the sound she knew there were at least thirty of them. They appeared along the edge of the clearing, a long row of them, spread out and eager to launch a unified attack that should have swept her off her mount and crushed her to a pulp. Their leader, a massive warrior, half as wide again as any man, kitted in glittering mail and with a helm cast in the snarling visage of some demon from the Kaizen pantheon, edged forward and raised a curved blade. It hissed like a dozen serpents as the Kaizen made passes with it in the still air.

"Throw down your weapon!" the warrior roared in a voice that would have reduced many a human warrior to frozen inactivity.

The girl raised her blade. Wisps of smoke-like tendrils drifted upwards from it. "Come and take it," she called.

For answer the warrior kicked his steed forward and his company held their ground, no doubt confidant that their leader would quickly settle this. The Kaizen raced across the grass, his steed's hooves tearing up great sods as it rushed upon the girl. The Fire Steed, like the Burning Blade, began to glow, as if drawing up from the earth around it new powers, natural forces of nature which imbued it with light and strength. It need no guidance from its rider to determine its strategy with the Kaizen, ducking and swerving to one side as the huge horse rushed in upon it. The Kaizen blade hummed as it swept through the air in a devastating blow that would have smashed the girl from her mount. Instead she dropped under the blade and thrust her own weapon upward. In a blaze of fire it ripped into the thick chest plates of the Kaizen's armor and he let out a tortured shriek of agony.

Somehow he clung to his mount, wheeling it in readiness for another pass. He was not as swift as the Fire Steed, which turned in a blur. Estarziel rode in without hesitation, the Burning Blade leaving a trail of tiny embers in the air behind it as it hissed through the armor and neck of the Kaizen, severing the head as easily as if shearing a fat gourd in two. Blood pumped from the neck as the warrior's body catapulted backwards, ripped from its stirrups. The riderless horse galloped off in sheer terror as the Kaizen crashed into the ground in a final explosion of blood.

The girl wheeled the Fire Steed and studied the long row of Kaizen, each warrior as still as a statue, their emotions masked by their helms. Eventually another of them edged his steed forward.

"You have killed Ul-Ranaaz, a mighty commander, but you cannot possibly defeat us all," the Kaizen said. "Give yourself up and we will promise you fair treatment from our Overlord. A warrior such as you could do well in the service of the Kaizen."

"I have come to drive your kind out of these lands," she replied. "Tell your Overlord I am not alone. The days of the Kaizen in this world are numbered."

Skarrack, watching and listening from the far edge of the clearing, shook his head in disbelief. *She's gone too far. She has great power, but against so many, it will not be enough.*

The conversation was over. The Kaizen had had their reply, and evidently their orders from elsewhere. At a signal from their spokesman, they closed in, though more cautiously than their former commander. At a word, a group of them surged, no more than six of the huge warriors able to fight the Crimson Warrior at any one time at close quarters, and as her sword whirled in a blazing arc of flame, her steed abruptly flared with light of its own, the rays spearing outwards around it like an immense halo. As the Kaizen rode into this light, their own steeds were seared by the sudden terrible heat, and four of them reared up, so stunned that their riders lost control of them and they swung away, losing their footing and crumpling to the ground. The second wave of riders behind them were caught up in the confusion and Estarziel turned her own steed this way and that with dazzling effectiveness, light as the wind, and dealt out blows that killed or maimed several of the Kaizen. The hooves of the Fire Steed burned with molten heat, smashing into the assailants and burning a path through them.

Those of their number yet to join the affray raised spears and as one, hurled them at the Crimson Warrior, but all of the thrown weapons either burst into flames, or skidded off the radiance around the fantastic figure as if they had struck glass. One of the spears flew close to where Skarrack hung back, digging into the earth a few yards from his feet. He snatched it up and held it before him, though as yet none of the Kaizen had paid him any heed.

Leaping clear of the tangled horses and bodies, Estarziel met the next wave of attackers, searing the Kaizen. Her steed was now ablaze with supernatural energy; the Kaizen tried to close with it, but they burst into flames, living torches. Their steeds shrieked in agony and flung their riders from them, bolting out into the forest. Estarziel rode among the blazing figures and cut them to pieces, her war cry a chilling shriek that had the remaining Kaizen wheeling and reconsidering their next wave of attack. They used their spears as lances and drove at her, but as they came in for the killing blows, the spears simply snapped in half like rotten branches, as if they had exploded on rock. Again Estarziel rode around them at a speed that almost defied the eye. As she passed them, she cut them down.

There were now seven Kaizen remaining alive, the best of their horsemen, who had danced their steeds to and fro and avoided the murderous Burning Blade. In desperation they circled the Crimson Warrior, determined not to flee, but to bring her down. Skarrack watched nervously. The others had died through their arrogance and over-confidence, expecting to triumph as all Kaizen did when faced with human opposition, no matter how powerful the subordinate species. These last seven applied cunning and patience, and the odds swung back in their favor, Skarrack could see.

Six of them circled her again, jabbing cautiously, tempting her to lunge at them, or close in for a kill. The seventh was even more wily and kept his distance, weighing his spear carefully. Skarrack understood its intention: it would pick the one unguarded moment when Estarziel was engaged and then unleash the spear. It would probably do enough damage to render her defense weakened, enough for the others to take the killing advantage. Skarrack ducked down and moved forward, holding his own spear at the ready. He waited until he was sure the Kaizen would try for a throw, and when the warrior's arm drew back, out of the line of sight of the Crimson Warrior, Skarrack flung his weapon.

He watched it arrow to its target and strike the Kaizen's breast. The armor deflected the point of the spear, but it shore upwards and rammed under the lower hinge of the helm, flinging back the Kaizen's head. It was enough to alert Estarziel, who ducked aside from two spears being rammed at her and swung the Burning Blade in an arc of fire. The head of the Kaizen spear-thrower flew through the spark-filled air and the rider collapsed. After that, Estarziel made short work of the remaining warriors, ramming her blade into the breastplates of each of them, splitting their hearts and sending their charred remains to join the scattered dead across the clearing. The horses had fled back down the pathway through the forest.

"Their empty saddles will be word enough for other Kaizen," said Estarziel, watching them go and loosening her mask. "I owe you my life," she added, looking down at Skarrack, a rare smile on her lips. "They almost had me with that trick." Her steed quickly relaxed, its fiery coat no longer a-glow. It gave a soft snort and tossed its great mane imperiously.

Skarrack wiped sweat from his brow and gazed in amazement at the piled dead. One warrior had done this! Of course, he had seen her powers before, but this destruction was beyond belief. The goddess had passed unimaginable power on to her.

As if Estarziel read his mind, she said, "I'm not immortal." She laughed softly, and he was surprised at the transformation in her, from burning, murderous demi-goddess to young girl "And you didn't dream this." She patted the neck of her steed. "It was real. The power of the goddess lives on."

~*~

A short while later, as the sun fell behind the mountains, Skarrack finished checking the fallen Kaizen, heaping them up, preparing a pyre. None had survived. Estarziel kicked one of the corpses to one side and pulled off its helm, tossing it away. She gazed dispassionately at the fixed grimace of the dead warrior. Skarrack watched in fresh horror as she ripped aside the breastplate as easily as parting wet leaves, to expose the mottled flesh beneath. Taking the Burning Blade, she uttered the words of an incantation, and the hue of the blade changed, turning from white, through flame to cold, cold purple. Then, as Skarrack gasped, she pushed the blade deep into the warrior's chest, holding the hilt firmly with both hands.

Amazingly, the eyes of the fallen opened. They held a look of acute agony.

"How many Kaizen are in and around the city of Borrabund?" said Estarziel.

"In the company of Ul-Ranaaz, there were sixty of us," said the hollow voice from what should have been dead lips. "Only six are left alive."

"Where are they?"

"We have barracks to the south of the city. They are there."

"How far to the next Kaizen hold?"

"A hundred miles to the south, with the Overlord."

Estarziel pulled the blade free and the Kaizen's eyes closed, his head lolling to one side in the final slide into oblivion. She rose, wiping the blade on thick sheaths of grass.

"We'll take a few pieces of armor back to the city," she said. "Evidence of our victory."

Skarrack heard movements behind him and swung round, expecting to see more of the huge warriors, intent on vengeance. But from around the clearing, the herd from the valley of the goddess observed him, snorting at the blood of the fallen, though evidencing no fear.

"They will all need riders," said Estarziel. "Just as you were chosen. In Borrabund, we will gather support and clear away the remainder of the invaders. We will become a new army. This part of the north will belong once more to Humanity." She slid the Burning Sword into its scabbard and swung up on to the Fire Steed.

Skarrack heard the weapon moan in approval. *Sorcery*. The word made his head spin. So much havoc had been unleashed in this world through it. Was it to be the only way back for his people?

"Once these lands are ours, they'll not be surrendered to the Kaizen again." Her smile was chilling, her eyes studying the heaped dead. "It will be bloody work. If you don't have the stomach for it, Skarrack, then take the ponies and ride up into the wild mountains of the north. Live among the goats. What do you say?"

The road ahead he saw was all darkness. Fire and steel. He tossed a lit brand on to the pyre and immediately flames roared, beginning the inundation. Fire and steel. And wild sorcery. So be it.

Afterword & Acknowledgments

I hope you've enjoyed these twelve tales—all quite nicely told, don't you think? If I may be so bold, I believe we've experienced some excellent adventures together. Because a project like this is a collaboration, of sorts. It takes the authors, of course, but also readers like you and an editor (or 'project manager') like me to bring us all together. Bottom line, I had a blast compiling and creating this anthology. Thanks for reading!

And thank you, Kickstarter Backers! Without your interest and support this anthology would not have gotten off the ground. I want to especially recognize the following 'super backers' who provided a bulk of the funding to pay our authors and illustrators for their works of creativity.

Michael Ehart
David Bakke
Gerald P. McDaniel
GhostCat
Indigo Pohlman
Michael T. Burke
Tommy Maguire
Ayube Amiruddin
Brian Rossell
Bruce Harpham
Candice R. Lisle
Charles Gramlich
Christopher L. Corbett
David A. Riley
Donovan Marc Phillips
Duncan Wilcox
Frank Lewis
Grant Odom
Howard Blakeslee
Jason Ray Carney
Kai Nikulainen
Mark E. Hall
Matthew Carpenter
Michael Nusbaum
Mike Combs
Richard Novak
Riju Ganguly
Roel Torres
Roy Riggs

Fans like you keep the world of Contemporary S&S spinning!

This community is quite large, but we're all fairly well connected, it seems. And we support one another despite our differences as to just what defines today's expression of this fantastic genre. In a few pages you'll read a discussion about that very topic. Quite enlightening and entertaining!

And because there are so many interesting creative endeavors popping up nowadays, I wanted to keep up with all the latest news. So I started a weekly round-up. It's my humble attempt to help connect us. You can sign up for free at: tulefogpress.substack.com. And send in your links!

I also want to acknowledge our advertisers. At the back of this volume are some other sword and sorcery and genre-adjacent projects that I think are worth looking into — yes, including one of my own short novels. (grin)

Another project of mine is a spec-fic zine, *Residential Aliens* (*ResAliens* for short). I have open submissions and try to feature an S&S tale in each issue. The pay is horrible, but contributors do get a paperback that usually runs about 80 pages, which is pretty cool. Ask for submission guidelines at TuleFogPress@gmail.com. Here's the cover of Issue #6 (available from Amazon). You might recognize a few of the names in the ToC!

Thanks again to all involved in this project! – Lyndon Perry

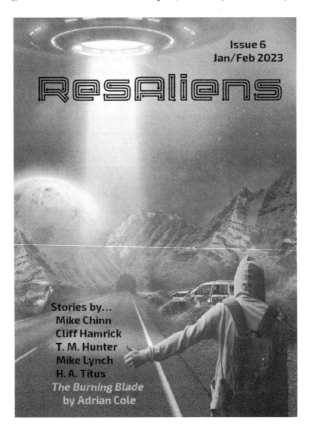

Swords & Heroes Contributors

Thanks to all who contributed to *Swords & Heroes*. Your check's in the mail.

Adrian Cole has been writing fantasy since the 1970s, when his *Dream Lords* Sword & Planet trilogy was released by Zebra Books. He has subsequently written numerous short stories and some two dozen novels, and won the prestigious British Fantasy Award for best collection in 2015, with *Nick Nightmare Investigates*. His most recent work is the epic *War on Rome* series, the first volume of which, *Arminius, Bane of Eagles*, has been published by DMR Books.

Charles Gramlich grew up on an Arkansas farm but moved to New Orleans in 1986 to teach psychology at Xavier University. He has written in many genres, including westerns, science fiction, fantasy, and horror, as well as nonfiction. His most recently published works are six books under the pen name A. W. Hart in the *Concho Texas Ranger* series. He is happy to connect on Facebook and blogs at charlesgramlich.blogspot.com.

Cliff Hamrick is an author of fiction and non-fiction. His storytelling journey began when he was nine years old and started playing Dungeons and Dragons with his friends. He writes fantasy, science-fiction, and mysteries. When he is not writing, he works as a counselor in private practice in Austin, TX. He loves being in the outdoors and hiking in one of the greenest cities in the state and visiting the gun range to shoot small bits of lead through pieces of paper. Visit his website at cliffhamrickwrites.com.

David A. Riley writes horror, fantasy and SF stories. A professional writer since 1970, his stories have appeared in a variety of publications, including those published by Doubleday and DAW and in magazines such as *Aboriginal Science Fiction*, *Dark Discoveries*, and *Fantasy Tales*. He has five collections of stories in print as well as four novels: *Goblin Mire*, *The Return*, *Moloch's Children*, and *Into the Dark*. He also runs Parallel Universe Publications which has published over 50 titles, including *Swords & Sorceries: Tales of Heroic Fantasy*, with Volume 6 coming later this year.

Frank Sawielijew is a Russo-German author with Bulgarian roots whose stories are heavily inspired by the pulp classics and often mix elements of fantasy and science fiction into a flavorful blend. He writes in both English and German, and his short stories have appeared in various anthologies and magazines since 2015. With a background in ancient and medieval history, he regularly draws inspiration from mankind's most ancient tales and cultures, from Bronze Age Mesopotamia to early modern Europe. He has also contributed his writing and level design to computer games developed by small independent companies. When he's not working on commercial projects, he likes to design fan missions for the classic Thief games.

Gustavo Bondoni is a novelist and short story writer with over three hundred stories published in fifteen countries, in seven languages. He is a member of Codex and an Active Member of SFWA. His latest novel is a dark historic fantasy entitled *The Swords of Rasna* (2022). He has also published five science fiction novels, four monster books, and a thriller entitled *Timeless*. His short fiction is collected in *Pale Reflection* (2020), *Off the Beaten Path* (2019), *Tenth Orbit and Other Faraway Places* (2010) and *Virtuoso and Other Stories* (2011). In 2019, Gustavo was awarded second place in the Jim Baen Memorial Contest and in 2018 he received a Judges Commendation (and second place) in The James White Award. He was also a 2019 finalist in the Writers of the Future Contest. You can find out more at his website gustavobondoni.com.

J. Thomas Howard is a fantasist from the receding woodlands of Southeastern Pennsylvania. His stories are inspired by the traditions of Sword and Sorcery and Sword and Planet with a desire to revitalize and refresh these classic genres. These stories have been featured in a variety of small press publications from *Broadswords and Blasters* to *Whetstone: Magazine of Amateur Sword and Sorcery* and many in between. If you would like to know more about his fiction visit jthowardpulp.wordpress.com.

Jason M Waltz is a lot of things, most often not the exact one needed at any given moment. He does believe in heroes, though, and strives to bring the heroic through presentation and publication. Heroes: They're what Jason—and Rogue Blades (rogue-blades.com)—does, whether through writing, publishing, teaching, or reading.

Lyndon Perry is a writer, editor, coffee drinker, and cat wrangler. He and his wife just moved to Puerto Rico with their 19-year-old orange and white tabby, who seems to be adjusting to beach life. He releases his projects, and those of a few others, through his indie publishing venture, Tule Fog Press.

Michael Burke is a lifelong fan of fantasy, science fiction, and horror, propelled into these realms at a tender age when he discovered his father's cache of pulp novels. A passion for comic books soon followed. These flights of fancy lurked in the recesses of his brain while he decided what he wanted to be when he grew up. In 2000, Michael co-founded the award-winning comic and collectible store, Comicazi, in Somerville, MA. When not found among the comic stacks at the shop, he can be found at home, releasing the hobgoblins of his mind into story form. Michael has been published in print and online in *Whetstone: Amateur Magazine of Sword and Sorcery*, *The Horror Zine*, *Northern Frights*, *Witch House*, and the 80s-themed anthology, *Totally Tubular Terrors*. His debut novella, *Last Sunset of a Dying Age*, is included in *West of Hell: Weird Western Horror Stories* in Book 2 of Crystal Lake's Dark Tide series. *Fragments of a Greater Darkness*, a collection of his sword and sorcery tales featuring Ahanu Foxcloud, has just been released by Tule Fog Press.

Nancy Hansen is an avid reader and has been a prolific writer of speculative fiction and action/adventure stories for over 30 years. She's authored numerous novels, as well as short stories that appear in various anthologies for a growing number of publishers. Her works are available on Amazon, Barnes & Noble, Smashwords, and elsewhere. Nancy currently resides on an old farm in beautiful, rural eastern Connecticut with an eclectic cast of family members and one very spoiled dog. Her author page at Amazon is here: tinyurl.com/yrtvssjk

Teel James Glenn's stories have been appeared in over 200 magazines including *Weird Tales, Mystery, Pulp Adventures, Cirsova, Silverblade*, and *Sherlock Holmes Mystery*. His novel, *A Cowboy in Carpathia: A Bob Howard Adventure* won Best Novel 2021 in the Pulp Factory Awards. He is a member of Horror Writers Association, Private Eye Writers of America, and other professional writers groups. You can find him on Facebook and Twitter as @TeelJamesGlenn. Visit his website at TheUrbanSwashbuckler.com.

Tim Hanlon has been a history teacher since the dawn of time. He tries to follow the tenets of Stoic philosophy but generally fails. Since he began submitting stories during the great lockdown of 2020 he has had some success with tales selected for anthologies by Specul8 Publishing, Sundial Magazine, 18th Wall Productions, DMR Books and Wicked Shadow Press. When not writing or reading, Tim enjoys banging on about craft beer with friends, boxing, and getting caught in the rain.

Tom Doolan was born in California but lived most of his youth as a military dependent in many different states as well as Germany and Okinawa. Tom is a former US Army paratrooper and a Desert Storm veteran. He is an avid D&D player, and this led to his mother allowing him to watch the 1982 classic Conan the Barbarian at the age of thirteen. Tom soon discovered the writings of Robert E. Howard and has been a dedicated fan ever since. He currently lives in Madison, WI, with his wife, kids, and cats.

Copyrights and Illustrations

Swords & Heroes: An Anthology of Sword and Sorcery © 2023 by Tule Fog Press.
All rights reserved. Lyndon Perry, Editor and Publisher, Vega Baja, Puerto Rico

The Color and the Dash © 2023 by Jason M Waltz (Foreword)
Keeper of Souls Copyright © 2023 by Charles Allen Gramlich
The Path One Doesn't Choose Copyright © 2023 by Gustavo Bondoni
Lord of the Blood Copyright © 2023 by Michael T. Burke
The Price of Rescue Copyright © 2023 by Teel James Glenn
The Vault of Bezalel Copyright © 2023 by Tom Doolan
On Neutral Ground Copyright © 2023 by Nancy Hansen
The Swordsman and the Sea Witch Copyright © 2023 by Tim Hanlon
The Necromancer and the Long-Dead King Copyright © 2023 by Frank Sawielijew
Lady in Stone Copyright © 2023 by Cliff Hamrick
O Sapphire, O Kambria Copyright © 2023 by J. Thomas Howard
Welgar the Cursed Copyright © 2023 by David A. Riley
Ride the Fire Steed Copyright © 2023 by Adrian Cole

The individual stories in this collection are copyrighted by their respective authors. These stories are fictitious; any resemblance to actual events, locales, or persons, living or dead, is entirely coincidental. All illustrations in this anthology are used by permission. The copyright of each image belongs to its respective creator. The artwork portrays fictitious scenes; any resemblance to actual events, locales, or persons, living or dead, is entirely coincidental.

Swords & Heroes cover image (Shieldmaiden) by WarmTail, design by Cliff Hamrick
Swords & Heroes cover image and design (Horse and Rider) by Cathleen Swart
page 8 - *Keeper of Souls* by Jacob Aybara
page 22 - *Swordswoman* by Cathleen Swart
page 36 - *At the Mouth of Shezmu's Temple* by Sumit Roy
page 50 - *Rescued* by David Bartell
page 64 - *In the Vault of Bezalel* David Bartell
page 80 - *On Neutral Ground* by Sumit Roy
page 94 - *The Sea Witch Attacks* by David Bartell
page 108 - *She Seeks an Audience with the King* by David Bartell
page 122 - *Lady in Stone* by Sumit Roy
page 136 - *An Unexpected Flight* by David Bartell
page 150 - *Welgar the Cursed* by Rizky Nugraha
page 164 - *World of the Crimson Warrior*, map by Adrian Cole
page 188 - *The Knight and the Dragon* by Sumit Roy

No part of this publication may be reproduced, stored in a retrieval system, or transmitted in any form or by any means without prior written permission from the publisher, except in brief quotations in printed or online reviews. Email TuleFogPress@gmail.com for information.

The Knight and the Dragon

Round Table Discussion

A Conversation about Sword & Sorcery, edited by Lyndon Perry

Recently, via a Q&A email exchange with some knowledgeable folks in the Sword & Sorcery community, I hosted a virtual round table discussion about the current state of S&S. Here's a list of our eight participants and a scandalously short description of their current connection to the genre:

AC = **Adrian Cole**, author of the *War on Rome* saga (DMR Books)
CB = **Cora Buhlert**, 2022 Hugo Award Winner for Best Fan Writer
CE = **Curtis Ellett**, publisher of *Swords and Sorcery Magazine*
DMR = **D. M. Ritzlin**, author and publisher of DMR Books
MH = **Morgan Holmes**, reviewer at Castalia House Blog
PA = **P. Alexander**, owner/editor of Cirsova Publishing
RF = **Richard Fisher**, acquisitions editor at *Savage Realms*
WM = **William Miller**, author and publisher of *Savage Realms*

Let's pretend we're live and listening in on the panel as they share their thoughts…

There's been a resurgence of interest in heroic fantasy – specifically Sword & Sorcery – in recent years. What do you attribute this to?

CE: I think it's been building for a while. I know more than a few fantasy fans who never lost interest in Sword & Sorcery after having discovered it during its last boom in the '70s and '80s. When the internet and electronic publishing made it possible to publish relatively cheaply and reach a far-flung audience markets naturally developed to fill an existing, if initially small, demand. These markets were driven by fans. They didn't depend on mass-market sales; writers didn't have to be locked into the tropes publishers thought would sell. This allowed the genre to expand a bit, diversify, and become more inclusive, reaching some audiences that might have rejected earlier S&S.

MH: It might be the convergence of several factors. First, the big publishers dropped it. There was a noticeable change in 1985. The trend was for Tolkien imitations and ever larger and more expensive paperbacks. The 1990s was the era of the big, fat, fantasy novel. There has probably always been a certain level of interest for S&S. Remember that Tor Books kept the Conan pastiche novels going through most of the 1990s. There is a desire for some action oriented fantasy with a hard-boiled edge to it. Technology now allows for the [print on demand] publication of books or magazines. Fans turned editors/publishers can create what the Big 5 won't do. It is sort of like the punk rock attitude of the late '70s and early '80s of D.I.Y. (Do It Yourself).

AC: These things seem to me to go in waves, and undoubtedly the ongoing impact of the Lord of the Rings/Hobbit movies, combined with the Game of Thrones TV series has created a demand for more of the same. (Interestingly when LOTR became a massive seller in the '70s, fantasy got a real boost in the aftermath.) As fans develop an appetite for fantastic fiction, the waves spread out and even the less popular sub-genres get a shot in the arm. S&S originally centered around REH, Leiber, Moorcock, and Vance (i.e., they were at its forefront when it first became 'recognized' as Sword & Sorcery) and in the main it was Howard's Conan that spawned the most clones. I think that movie technology and advances in CGI have contributed to the popularity of fantasy, so that new generations of readers enjoy the more fantastical creations found in fantasy writing. Heroic fantasy has become a major genre in its own right over the last forty years or so, and the demand for it isn't slacking!

CE: It doesn't hurt that epic fantasy has been alive and well over the years, reaching huge audiences with best-sellers and blockbuster movies and shows. S&S has found an audience from people who were encouraged to explore more widely in fantasy literature after being attracted by the heavily hyped (but often excellent) big fantasy productions.

PA: Sword & Sorcery has always been popular, as has heroic fantasy. I think the big shift is that while the mainstream media and publishing have moved away from them, democratization of publishing has opened new outlets that allow for writers and readers to connect with the action fantasy that they love.

CB: A large part of the reason is that epic fantasy with a cast of thousands, each with their own POV, has been dominant for so long now that many people are looking for something different. Sword & Sorcery with its limited cast of characters, personal stakes, and wild and dangerous magic offers the perfect counterpoint. Furthermore, S&S also meshes well with the grittier worlds and protagonists of grimdark fantasy. Another reason is that there is a great interest in stories from the perspective of marginalized people who did not traditionally get to be fantasy protagonists. Sword & Sorcery protagonists tend to be outsiders, which makes it the ideal genre for telling stories about marginalized people kicking butt.

RF: Print to order publishing is a primary factor in this resurgence. You see, the fandom never went away. Indie authors and publishers now have the ability to circumvent the major publishers and publish the things a big publisher would not. This platform allows an author to put his/her work into the hands of a reader half the world away. It gives the indie publisher a worldwide market at a fraction of the cost it would take to go it alone. This grassroots movement hasn't gone unnoticed. As everyone is aware, Baen has recently shown an interest in publishing S&S, with numerous books in the works.

DMR: At the risk of sounding arrogant, DMR Books has a lot to do with it. Over the past several years I've released 8-9 titles a year (including reprints of classic out-of-print material as well as stories by current authors). Additionally, we regularly update the blog with articles about classic authors of fantasy and speculative fiction, many of whom are unjustly forgotten in this day and age. One author even told me I singlehandedly brought back sword & sorcery. I appreciated the compliment, but I wouldn't go that far!

WM: For the last several decades the traditional publishing industry has acted as gate keepers, deciding what the masses would be allowed to consume so far as popular fiction, and Sword & Sorcery was not on the list of approved literature. Oh sure, a few pieces slipped through here and there, but largely trad publishers ignored S&S claiming there was no market for it. But self-publishing has opened the doors for all of us knuckle dragging Neanderthals to finally get our fix of axe wielding barbarians in loin cloths and pretty maidens.

How would you describe the difference between heroic fantasy and Sword & Sorcery? How else would you describe the S&S genre?

DMR: Michael Moorcock once described S&S as 'Captain Blood meets

Cthulhu.' In other words, it's a combination of swashbuckling adventure fiction and cosmic horror. That definition, succinct as it is, seems pretty accurate to me. The horror part is important in keeping S&S distinct from heroic fantasy. Also, Sword & Sorcery pushes the envelope in a lot of ways, primarily in its depictions of brutal violence, but other areas as well, such as sex. You could say S&S is the 'lunatic fringe' of fantasy. It's not safe, and it's not supposed to be!

RF: This question can lead to trouble. No two people are going to agree on this and often the two names have been used interchangeably to label the genre. To me, heroic fantasy lacks the supernatural horror of a good S&S story. The protagonist in an S&S story isn't intrinsically heroic, but often is thrust into the role by circumstances. The protagonist is often just trying to survive. In my mind heroic fantasy is just scaled down epic fantasy.

CE: Sword & Sorcery is one branch of heroic fantasy. Heroic fantasy in general focuses on a protagonist(s) who has to confront some evil and has some heroic attribute that contributes to their success, be it uncommon strength, skill, possession of a magical artifact, or simply the fortitude to persevere in the worst of circumstances. In Sword & Sorcery, the evil they confront is usually local and personal. In contrast, epic fantasy usually involves confronting world-destroying threats. Hallmarks of sword & sorcery are dark corrupting magic, violent action, and outsider heroes.

MH: I would place Sword & Sorcery as a distinct type of heroic fantasy. Heroic fantasy has been around longer. For example, *The Saga of Jarl the Neatherd* by H. Escott-Inman from 1903 is a heroic fantasy with dwarves, magic swords, etc. Sword & Sorcery is a product of post-World War One attitudes. You saw prose get shorter, more precise, leaner, and hard in delivery with genre fiction. Compare an issue of *All-Story* magazine from 1914 to an issue of *Argosy* in 1937. The writing is overall better. Sword & Sorcery is a product of the pulp magazines. It is the convergence of the historical adventure with elements of the supernatural. Sir Walter Scott meets Edgar Allan Poe. The genre started out in *Weird Tales* with historical settings and gothic atmosphere. Within a few years, the settings were fantastic forgotten ages with dollops of H. P. Lovecraft's cosmic horror. The characters changed from D'artganan swashbucklers to brawling, drinking, wenching barbarians.

PA: I think that the difference is largely over nitpicks, wallpapering, and such, because there is a lot of overlap. However not all heroic fantasy is Sword & Sorcery and not all Sword & Sorcery is heroic fantasy. S&S largely grew out of taking mythic adventure and placing it in a gothic form. For instance, if you took adventures of Greek mythic heroes but dip them in gothic language and presentation, you'd get Sword & Sorcery. There's also the inclusion of the picaresque fiction tradition in a lot of fantasy.

Sword & Sorcery didn't spring forth in a vacuum and many constituent parts were percolating in the '20s and '30s that form the most recognizable elements of the genre today. Sword & Sorcery does not necessarily have to be 'heroic,' however, and this is part of where the picaresque traditions come in. In terms of Frye's anatomy of literature, Sword & Sorcery would also encompass the Ironic forms, as well as high and low mimetic, while Heroic Fantasy would necessarily avoid the Ironic mode.

WM: I could probably write a 500 page treatise on that subject, but I'll try to keep this brief. Heroic fantasy tends to deal with more lofty ideals and heroes who subscribe to higher standards, realms of black and white. Whereas sword and sorcery deals in shades of grey. Howard's Conan never set out to be a hero nor was he interested in 'saving the day'. He was usually focused on material gain and lusty wenches. Conan was only interested in saving the kingdom from a dragon if it meant saving his own hide and, in a very human way, I think it's far easier to relate to Conan than Frodo. Sure, we would all like to be the selfless Frodo, but we're probably a lot closer to Conan.

CB: I consider sword and sorcery a specific subgenre of heroic fantasy. As for how to define sword and sorcery, I really like Brian Murphy's definition from *Flame and Crimson: A History of Sword and Sorcery* (which is a must-read for every S&S fan, BTW). Murphy identifies seven key elements of Sword & Sorcery, namely men and women of action, dark and dangerous magic, personal and/or mercenary motivations, horror and Lovecraftian influences, shorter episodic stories, inspired by history and outsider heroes and heroines. Not all seven elements will appear in every single S&S story, but several of them should be present or the story is something other than Sword & Sorcery.

AC: Personally I think S&S has mutated since it first appeared (or was recognized as S&S). Generally, people have continued to think of Sword & Sorcery as beefy barbarians giving hell to a standard array of monsters, sorcerers, evil kings, while slinging a brazen hussy or two over their shoulders. That particular model got almost totally played out by the '80s and very few writers have been able to keep it alive in fresh and original ways today. (S&S got a pretty bad press after that.) However, my view is that other, equally as fabulous S&S writers, produced fiction that stretched well beyond the confines of what you might call the heroic fantasy model (such as in the countless LOTR clones, as in the works of David Eddings, Raymond Feist, Robert Jordan et al). Ironically I think it is these other, breakaway writers who have pushed the boundaries beyond the aforementioned two basic blueprints who have created the quality S&S and Heroic Fantasy genre, rather than the legion of copyists who have unfortunately tended to define them. Wonderful writers such as Michael Shea, Phyllis Eisenstein, and Roger Zelazny, to name but three. Things have become more blurred in terms of definitions, but I see that as healthy. What both genres need is originality, and not slavish devotion to a formula.

Who are some influencers creating an interest in heroic adventure?

MH: I think Rogue Blades Entertainment primed the pump starting back in 2008. *Return of the Sword* is in my view an important book. The writers were mostly unknown, the prose could be rough around the edges but it has sincerity. DMR Books has had an impressive run and really holds the torch for old fashioned Sword & Sorcery.

DMR: *Tales From the Magician's Skull* and its editor, Howard Andrew Jones.

WM: If I say *Savage Realm Monthly*, is that self-aggrandizing? In all seriousness, guys like Steve Dilks and girls like Morgan Kane are putting out some seriously hard-hitting fantasy fiction, stuff that takes you in its teeth and shakes you. I'm proud to say SRM featured a Steve Dilks story in our premier issue. Authors like David Riley with his *Swords and Sorceries* publication spring instantly to mind as well. I'd also like to turn people's attention to the very talented Moose Matson who produces SRM's audio versions. Moose is a fantastic guy and he narrates a fantasy tale like no one else. It is a special treat to hear Moose narrate a story. He's awesome.

CE: While I've been part of the S&S community for a while, I haven't been very involved with it until recently, so I can't name too many movers and shakers. Oliver Brackenbury's *New Edge S&S* comes to mind. I'm looking forward to seeing what comes out of it in the future.

PA: There are a lot of people, right now. I wish I could name them all, and I feel like any omission would be a slight, so I'll name just a couple rather than try to encompass an entire scene. Dave Ritzlin is one of the biggest names as far as publishing goes, and he's doing a lot to not only bring out new S&S works but also collect and restore a lot of older works as well. Robert Zoltan has his hands in a number of things, including some comics and zine work, but I think his most important contribution has been his *Rogues of Merth* series, which shows what an S&S duo like *Fafhrd and the Gray Mouser* could look like if they were loveable rogues and not just scumbags. His Dream Tower Media podcast had a highly irregular release schedule, and I don't know if he's still doing them, but they were always fantastic.

Adrian Cole is an unsung hero of Sword & Sorcery and Heroic Fantasy. He's a journeyman author in the best possible sense, who has been working since the '70s as part of that generation's Sword & Sorcery revival, and he has continued to this day. Both Dave Ritzlin and I have been publishing his newer works, including a sequel series to 1970s *Dream Lords* saga that Cirsova Publishing has been running in its magazine since 2016.

AC: There are a good many magazines devoted to promoting S&S around, and most of them clearly encourage new approaches. It's also heartening to see that some of the old 'isms' are being outlawed (sexism, racism, etc.). Leading the way in the resurgence of interest is the excellent magazine, *Tales From the Magician's Skull* (Goodman Games) which encourages a divergent approach. Among the new wave of publishers, I'd single out DMR Books (and not just because they publish me!). Dave Ritzlin is doing an excellent job catering to a variety of tastes across the board.

CB: There are a lot of great magazines focusing on Sword & Sorcery such as *Tales From the Magician's Skull, Heroic Fantasy Quarterly, Whetstone, Old Moon Quarterly, Swords and Sorcery Magazine, New Edge Sword and Sorcery Magazine, Savage Realms* and of course the latest revival of *Weird Tales*. Small presses include DMR Books, MV Media, Parallel Universe Publications and Tule

Fog Press, who recently joined the eco-system with this anthology, *Swords & Heroes*. There are also a lot of great S&S and heroic fantasy authors currently writing such as Howard Andrew Jones, Scott Oden, Adrian Cole, Jen Williams, A.K. Larkwood, Milton J. Davis, Remco van Straten and Angeline B. Adams, Dariel Quiogue, Kirk A. Johnson, J.T.T. Ryder, Peter Newman and many others.

We also have a lively online culture of discussion of old and new sword and sorcery with podcasts such as *The Cromcast, Rogues in the House, the Appendix N Book Club, So I'm Writing a Novel*, or the *Dark Crusade* leading the way. Blog and websites like *Black Gate, Dark Worlds Quarterly* or the *Goodman Games* offer a lot of reviews and discussions of classic and new Sword & Sorcery. The recent *Thews You Can Use* newsletter and the weekly link round-up at the DMR Books blog compile all the genre news in one or rather two handy locations. Finally, the *Whetstone Tavern Discord* server and several Facebook groups and subreddits offer a place for virtual watercooler discussions. Apologies to everybody I have forgotten.

RF: A few others that haven't been mentioned yet include:

- Jason Ray Carney – academic, author, editor. Jason's involvement within the community is myriad. Responsible for the magazines Whetstone and Witch House. Instrumental in the Whetstone Discord channel.

- Jason Waltz – author, editor and owner of Rogue Blades Entertainment and Rogue Blades Foundation. Jason's RBE and RBF publishing companies typically print collections which put the hero back in heroics.

- Seth Lindberg – author. He's moderated S&S group on Goodreads for many years and taken roles with *Tales From the Magicians Skull* magazine and Gencon.

- Howard Andrew Jones – author, editor. For years now he has been on a grassroots campaign to give S&S better curb appeal. He's gained a multi book deal with Baen and has been instrumental in getting Harold Lamb collected and reprinted. He is also the house editor at *Tales From the Magicians Skull*.

- David Riley – author, editor. David's Parallel Universe Publications is the publisher of the four *Swords and Sorceries* anthologies. Volume Five came out this past November.

- William Miller – author, editor. William's Literary Rebel publishes *Savage Realms Monthly*, a magazine devoted to sword & sorcery and dark fantasy.

What's refreshing about today's S&S stories/publications? How is it different than the classic era of REH, Carter, Lieber, Moore, etc.?

AC: Personally I think the only real difference is in the style of writing. That's not to say the writers today are better, far from it. But what they have in common with the best of the classic writers is their enthusiasm, their flair, and their dedication to their subject material. When the 'golden age' of S&S began to pall, it was mainly due to the lack of these vital ingredients – publishers were tossing out stuff that was little better than hack work. Many of today's writers are refreshing because they take pains and set the bar as high as they can.

DMR: There are so many writers today it's impossible to make generalizations about the current state of the genre. One thing I've noticed is a trend of stories with extremely low magic. Maybe there will be a magical light source, or a monster that isn't supernatural (so it's basically no different from a regular animal), and that'll be it. I don't consider this a good thing.

RF: Much of the new stuff out there lacks the same flavor, though there are a few authors that emulate that old style well. Schuyler Herstrom, Willard Black, Steve Dilks, Byron Roberts. People are more conscious of being insensitive. I feel like there are two camps here. On one hand you have the traditional stuff touted by purists and general fans. On the other you have authors attempting to expand boundaries and gain a more diverse readership.

CE: S&S is becoming more inclusive. It is becoming less Eurocentric, more accepting of LGBTQ+ themes and characters, and less male-dominated. I think this is a reflection of our society in general and is a very good thing. For the record, I am white, straight, and male. I haven't done much market research, but based on the Facebook followers of *Swords & Sorcery Magazine*, the same is mostly true of my audience.

MH: We will see what shakes out with the current crop of Sword & Sorcery writers. Most are fans just entering the field. Hopefully, many will stick with it and improve in skill and scope. Maybe a few will make the jump to the big publishers in time. What is refreshing is just seeing the D.I.Y. attitude.

WM: For me personally, I'm most interested in those authors who can take the spirit of S&S and tell a story with the kind of stripped down, bare knuckle prose of modern fiction. Don't get me wrong, I love the poetic works of the late great REH and Lovecraft, but that kind of reading requires more work. Guys like Riley and Victor Rodriguez can tell a story where the pages practically turn themselves.

PA: I think that there are a lot of publications whose editors are familiar with classic works, rather than simply know them by reputation. Many writers and editors are looking to use them as a baseline for creating a new wave of Sword & Sorcery rather than undermine it. Of course, there are still the anklebiters, the denigraters, and the skinsuits, but there's so much energy behind the earnest writers and purveyors of fiction in the classic tradition that it's easy to laugh them off.

CB: Sword & Sorcery was always a remarkably diverse subgenre, set in worlds with many different cultures and languages and featuring women warriors and characters of color (Gray Mouser, one of the foundational characters of the genre, is not white) from the very beginning in the 1930s. During the second S&S boom of the 1960s and 1970s, this trend continued and gave us more women warriors like Joanna Russ' Alyx and Pat McIntosh's Thula, black heroes like Charles Saunders' Imaro, an anti-hero on the cusp of outright villainy with Karl Edward Wagner's Kane and of course a drug-addicted albino elf in Elric of Melniboné. If Sword & Sorcery had continued in these directions, it might have held on, but instead the genre collapsed under the weight of too many bad 'Clonans' in the 1980s.

Today's S&S is continuing on the path the genre was heading before it took a wrong turn into Clonan territory in the 1980s. We are seeing settings based on African, Asian or Native American cultures and we are also seeing a greater diversity of heroes and heroines with plenty of female warriors, LGBTQ characters, characters of color, disabled protagonists, anti-heroes, characters who manage to combine adventuring and parenthood, etc. And of course we still get the sword-swinging barbarians of yore, too.

Finally, classic Sword & Sorcery from the 1930s to the 1970s occasionally contains attitudes, stereotypes and terms that are considered offensive today. Now anybody who claims that all vintage sword and sorcery was racist, sexist, homophobic, etc., has obviously read very little of it, because the vast majority of vintage sword and sorcery was none of those things. On the contrary, it was often quite progressive for its time. However, today's S&S largely ditched the less enlightened attitudes of the past, while keeping the action and adventure that we all love.

What are you currently reading and/or recommending?

DMR: I've been swamped with so many manuscripts for work I don't spend enough time reading for pleasure these days. However, I recently found a copy of Brian Lumley's *Khai of Ancient Khem*, and I'm enjoying it.

CE: I really enjoyed *New Edge Sword & Sorcery, No. 0*. I am really looking forward to future issues. I'm currently working my way through the back issues of *Whetstone*. I'll be adding *Tales From the Magician's Skull* to the list when I've caught up there. There are also all the submissions to *Swords & Sorcery*, which take some effort to get through. These days I read mostly short stories within the S&S genre. Outside of it, I read history, non-fiction generally, and shorter non-S&S fantasy or space opera novels. I've particularly enjoyed reading Rebecca Roanhorse and Tasha Suri lately. Both are writing epic fantasy in non-European settings. I'm not interested in 1000-page novels that are only parts of five- or six-book series anymore. Keep books to 500 pages or so and series length to four or less. Unless it is a true serial where each book stands on its own. Then you can write as many as you like.

MH: I try to keep up with what is new: Tales *From the Magician's Skull, Savage Realms, Swords & Sorceries* etc. Just getting ready to order the new S&S issue from the current incarnation of *Weird Tales*. I generally recommend DMR Books anthologies both new and reprint.

WM: Currently I'm wading through a whole crop of submissions (apologies to all the authors patiently waiting) and enjoying *Theft of Swords* by Michael J. Sullivan.

PA: I'm on the home stretch of Paul Knaplund's *The British Empire: 1815-1939*. The part they don't teach you in school about the Indian/Hindu Nationalist movement is that the Brits kicked it off by raising the age of consent in India to 12. On the fiction side of things, I recently finished *The Mote in God's Eye* by Niven and Pournelle, and I've just started Donald J. Uitvlugt's *Tiao Ju's Endeavor*.

CB: I'm currently reading *Arminius: Bane of Eagles* by Adrian Cole, which is alternate history with a strong sword and sorcery/heroic fantasy feel. The actual Battle of the Teutoburg Forest (which did not take place in the Teutoburg Forest) happened about 120 kilometers south of where I live and the battlefield was discovered in my lifetime, so I had to read the novel.

I also want to give a shout-out to British author Jen Williams whose work doesn't get the attention it deserves in the Sword & Sorcery community. Her *Copper Cat* series (three novels plus a couple of novellas) is absolutely S&S, while her *Winnowing Flame* trilogy is a mix of S&S and epic fantasy. Her latest work is a historical horror novella called *Seven Dead Sisters*, which would have felt right at home in the 1930s issue of *Weird Tales* and is therefore at Sword & Sorcery adjacent. Finally, every S&S fan should read *Flame and Crimson: A History of Sword and Sorcery* by Brian Murphy.

AC: I tend to go back and read a lot of fiction from the '60s to '80s, which will probably horrify a lot of folks. If I were going to read fantasy today, I'd go back and re-read *The Dying Earth* or *The Broken Sword*. There is one exception, for me, and that's historical fiction. Some great new works are still appearing, such as Manda Scott's magnificent *Boudica* quartet. And Bernard Cornwell's *Uthric the Saxon* saga is priceless.

RF: Currently reading:
Sinbad and the Great Old Ones by Gavin Chappell
Jiao Tu's Endeavor Episode One: The Kidnapped Mouseling by Donald Jacob Uitvlugt

Recommend:
Arminius, Bane of Eagles by Adrian Cole
Mask of the Sorcerer by Darrell Schweitzer
Samhain Sorceries edited by Dave Ritzlin
Track of the Snow Leopard by Dariel R A Quiogue
Gunthar Warrior of the Lost World by Steve Dilks
And many others.

DMR: It's great to see such a surge of interest in S&S compared to just a few years ago, but all things considered, we're still small time. The genre needs more readers, and I know there are tons of people out there that would like S&S, but they just don't know about it. That's why it's so important when you read a great book to tell your friends about it, leave reviews on Amazon and Goodreads, etc. That's the only way things will get bigger and better.

Thanks, everyone, for a great discussion.
– Lyndon Perry

SWORDS & SORCERIES
TALES OF HEROIC FANTASY

Featuring some of the best writers in the fantasy genre today.

PARALLEL UNIVERSE PUBLICATIONS

SWORDS CLASH WITH ANCIENT SORCERY IN THIS EPIC ALTERNATIVE WORLD TRILOGY!

In an alternative Romano-Celtic Europe, Arminius, the Germanic tribal leader and destroyer of three entire Roman legions in the Teutoburger forest, and Germanicus, ambitious Roman conqueror and potential heir to the Empire, avoid assassination attempts and set out on a course that will eventually see them clash in a war that will shake the foundations of their world.

Set in the forbidding landscape of the Germanic forests, across the northern seas, in the far reaches of Caledonia and mysterious regions of Britannia, to the heart of Rome itself, WAR ON ROME races to a dramatic climax that will determine the history of European generations to come.

Fabulous fantasy action and intrigue from Award winning author, **ADRIAN COLE**, whose works include *The Omaran Saga*, *Elak, King of Atlantis*, and *The Voidal Saga*. Available on Amazon and from DMRBooks.com.

ALSO AVAILABLE FROM DMR BOOKS:

Necromancy in Nilztiria by D.M. Ritzlin
The world of Nilztiria is an ancient one. Beneath its brilliant crimson sun and demon-haunted moons wondrous treasures lay buried, waiting to be uncovered by intrepid adventurers. If you crave stories of adventure and wonder with a touch of gallows humor, look no further than these thirteen tales of Nilztiria!

Terra Incognita: Lost Worlds of Fantasy and Adventure
David C. Smith, Adrian Cole, Howard Andrew Jones and four more of today's top fantasists weave tales of undiscovered lands beyond your imagination.

LYNDON PERRY

THE SWORD OF OTRIM

AN EPIC FANTASY

CRUSH YOUR ENEMIES
SEE THEM DRIVEN BEFORE YOU

READ
SAVAGE REALMS

From RBF: Coming HOWARD DAYS 2023!

HITHER CAME CONAN

"A Must for Those Who Argue Which Conan Tale is Best!"

edited by
Bob Byrne,
Bill Ward,
Howard Andrew Jones, &
Jason M Waltz

The book you shelve next to your Del Rey Conan Trilogy!

Made in the USA
Columbia, SC
13 May 2023

6d96ca6f-544c-4022-bcdd-5e037878e33aR01